She entered the Provost Dungeon

The subterranean chamber felt even clammier than Dani recalled, its dark cavities even less inviting. Even if she had not been eager to conclude the night's work, the dungeon offered plenty of incentive to make short order of her cleanup.

Before she had even reached the Redcoat mannequin, a shuffling sound stopped her cold.

For a second, she could only listen to the throbbing of her heart as it futilely cast itself against the rib cage that held it imprisoned. Her shaking knees threatened to lock as she slowly turned. Dani could see the door, but what stood between her and it? She could scream, but would anyone hear her? These terrifying questions fastened her with an ice-cold grip.

Dani hugged the brick column, pressing herself into its shadow. Suddenly, hands seized her from behind, but her scream was cut short by the cord wrapped around her throat....

ABOUT THE AUTHOR

A native of Little Rock, Arkansas,
Laurel Pace attended New York University
and the School of Visual Arts in New York
City. She worked for several years as a
producer of radio and television
commercials. Her transition to professional
writer came when she was asked to write
copy, in an emergency, for the advertising
agency where she was employed. While living
in West Germany, where her husband was
directing a student exchange program, Laurel
started writing fiction. She now lives in
Atlanta with her husband and their five very
loving cats.

Books by Laurel Pace

HARLEQUIN INTRIGUE
112–DECEPTION BY DESIGN

HARLEQUIN AMERICAN ROMANCE
192–ON WINGS OF LOVE
220–WHEN HEARTS DREAM
312–ISLAND MAGIC
370–MAY WINE, SEPTEMBER MOON

Ghostwalk
Laurel Pace

Harlequin Books

TORONTO • NEW YORK • LONDON
AMSTERDAM • PARIS • SYDNEY • HAMBURG
STOCKHOLM • ATHENS • TOKYO • MILAN

For my wonderful Low-Country friends,
Jackie and Dee,
who introduced me to old Charleston
and her many charming ghosts

Harlequin Intrigue edition published November 1991

ISBN 0-373-22174-6

GHOSTWALK

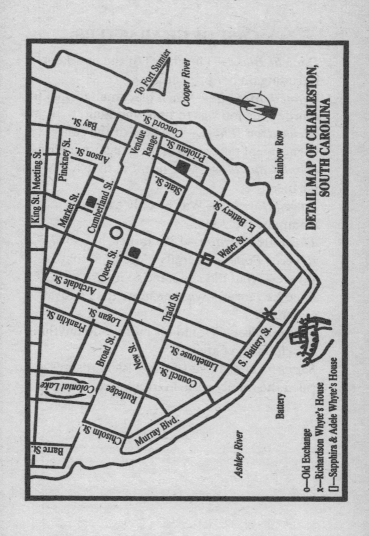

DETAIL MAP OF CHARLESTON,
SOUTH CAROLINA

To Fort Sumter

Cooper River

Rainbow Row

Bay St.
Pinckney St.
Anson St.
King St. Meeting St.
Vendue Range
Concord St.
Prioleau St.
State St.
Cumberland St.
Market St.
E. Battery St.
Queen St.
Water St.
Archdale St.
Logan St.
Tradd St.
Franklin St.
Broad St.
New St.
Limehouse St.
S. Battery St.
Council St.
Rutledge
Colonial Lake
Chisolm St.
Murray Blvd.
Barre St.

Ashley River

Battery

o—Old Exchange
x—Richardson Whyte's House
[ ]—Sapphira & Adele Whyte's House

CAST OF CHARACTERS

Danielle Blake—The ghosts of the past kept intruding on her present.

Kenneth McCabe—When blackmail turned to murder, his job was to find whodunit.

Richardson Whyte—The host of the gala engagement party was in for a nasty surprise.

Derek Cannaday—Was he more than a business partner?

Powell Boynton—Was he only a sailing teammate?

Theodore Boynton—Like father, like son?

Rebecca Pope—The only niece of Richardson Whyte—what did she stand to inherit?

Beatrice Lawes—Was she more than a loyal secretary?

Steven Lawes—Would his mother do anything to help him get ahead?

Sapphira and Adele Whyte—Richardson's aunts ruled the family with an iron hand.

Chapter One

From Battery Park, the house could be seen clearly. Even among its illustrious neighbors, it stood out—a great white-porticoed monument to Richardson Whyte's affluence and his heirs' good fortune. Tonight, every window lining the ground-floor piazza blazed with light. Figures darted behind the sheer curtains like shadow puppets. Everyone in the household would be in a frenzy now, making last-minute preparations for tonight's gala. No one would have time to pause, to part one of the curtains, to glance out at the darkening park. No one would know that they were being watched.

The person began to walk toward East Battery, slowly, with the placid gait of someone with nothing more to do than relish the refreshing salt air blowing in off Charleston's harbor. Who would guess that the leisurely stroller had a mission? Tonight, it would be just as simple. The house would be swarming with guests, its bright chambers overflowing with the orchestrated chaos of the celebration. The person would pass easily among the revelers, welcomed as one sharing their common purpose. Not one of them would suspect.

Elation and fear flooded the person's mouth with a sour taste. Inside the coat pocket, the cold hand flexed, fighting its own trembling. Then it closed over the hard steel. The fingers traced the short barrel, lingered on the blunt silencer and were still.

Tonight, a ghost would walk among them, leaving only death in its wake.

DANIELLE BLAKE OPENED the oven door a crack and frowned at the rows of herbed cheese tarts arranged on the baking sheet. She cautiously poked one golden brown surface, testing the custard's firmness.

"No fingerprints on the finger food!" a teasing voice reminded her, right over her shoulder.

In spite of herself, Dani jumped and let the oven door abruptly spring shut. When she turned, she found her assistant, Elaine Brewster, grinning sheepishly.

"I'm sorry. I didn't mean to scare you," Elaine apologized.

"That's all right. I just didn't hear you come into the kitchen." Dani adjusted the bib of her blue-and-white-striped apron in an attempt to recover her dignity. "I suppose with Halloween only two weeks away, I should expect a few spooks. How's the party going?"

Elaine playfully elbowed Dani's arm before lifting a tray of canapés from the marble-topped kitchen island. "Great! Thanks in large part, I might add, to the sumptuous buffet provided by the Moveable Feast Catering Company. You should hear Mr. Whyte raving about you to his friends."

Dani smiled modestly. "Richardson is such a generous-hearted person. I'm sure he would sing our praises if we served up peanut butter and jelly on white bread." In response to Elaine's skeptical chuckle, she conceded, "But it's a relief to know things are running smoothly—for now, anyway." She rushed to hold the swinging door open. Before her assistant could scoot through with the hors d'oeuvre tray, however, Dani caught her. "By the way, is that new bartender doing okay?"

"Well, he's kind of slow," Elaine hedged, trying to squeeze through the door. "But he seems like a decent guy."

Dani blocked the opening with her outstretched arm. "Be honest, Elaine," she warned. "Is there a problem I need to see about?"

"I don't think Ken's ever handled a crowd this large, that's all. Where did Mr. Whyte find him anyway?"

"I don't know. All Richardson told me was that he was new in town and looking for work as a bartender. Apparently, he had some sort of hard-luck story and Richardson felt sorry for him." Dani shrugged, giving Elaine the chance to maneuver the tray through her barricade.

"I'll give him a hand as soon as I restock the buffet," Elaine offered. "Don't forget the cheese tarts!" she called over her shoulder as she hurried down the hall.

Elaine's reminder sent Dani rushing back into the kitchen. But as she pulled the baking sheet from the oven and arranged the tarts on a silver tray, visions of a crisis developing at the bar filled her mind. If only she could have used one of her tried-and-true bartenders! But Richardson was always trying to help people down on their luck. Perhaps too often for his own good, Dani reflected.

As a child, she had heard her mother utter that good-natured lament many times. Now Dani suspected that the generosity her mother had in mind had frequently been directed toward their own family. After all, Richardson Whyte and Dani's father had been close friends. In the years following Dan Blake's tragic death, Richardson had probably felt responsible for his longtime sailing partner's widow and child. He had certainly always remembered them at Christmas and on birthdays, even during the many years when he was living in Brazil.

Dani took a last anxious glance around the kitchen before gathering up the tray. No, she simply was not going to let anything spoil Richardson Whyte's party—even if she had to roll up her sleeves and mix drinks herself. The catering service was *her* business; it was *her* responsibility to anticipate glitches and to smooth them out. Pausing only to reanchor a barrette in her thick, auburn hair, she shoved through the door and headed for the banquet room.

Despite the grand scale of the ballroom, Dani had to pick her way to the buffet tables, taking care not to nudge any of the elegantly dressed guests. Richardson had told her he was planning a party for two hundred people to celebrate his niece's engagement. To judge the throng assembled in the vaulted Federal Period ballroom, very few of them had declined the invitation.

While she rearranged serving dishes and made mental note of those that needed replenishing, Dani kept an eye on the bar. No, it was not her imagination; a bottleneck was definitely in the making. She could make out the tawny head of Richardson's bartender, frantically ducking and turning behind the wall of guests he was attempting to serve.

Reminding herself to be tactful, Dani was moving toward the bar as fast as she gracefully could when Richardson Whyte intercepted her.

"Dani! I'm so glad you've decided not to hide in the kitchen all night." The craggy lines of his face softened as he greeted her.

"You know what they say. A good caterer stays in the background." Dani smiled, redirecting her attention for the moment to the tall, aristocratic-looking man.

"Well, now, I've never put much stock in anything 'they' say. Come, let me introduce you to some more of the guests. Powell! Theodore!" Richardson hailed two men dressed in dinner jackets.

Dani smiled and nodded graciously as Richardson introduced her to Theo Boynton, his niece Rebecca's fiancé, and to Theo's father, Powell. Every time Dani had emerged from the kitchen that evening, Richardson had seized the opportunity to bring her into contact with as many of his guests as possible. In truth, the gathering was a fledgling caterer's gold mine, peopled as it was with the cream of Charleston's wealthy and influential society. Richardson, bless his heart, seemed bent on making the most of the occasion to introduce her to potential clients.

"Everything is superb, Miss Blake," Powell Boynton was saying. "I'm certainly grateful to Rich for recommending you to the Hospital Auxiliary. I know you'll put together a splendid spread for our Halloween benefit."

"Thank you. I'm really looking forward to catering a costume ball." Dani smiled again, but as her gaze drifted back to Richardson, she sobered. Despite his jovial conversation, the spare patrician features looked drawn, the hazel eyes distant and preoccupied. Something was troubling Richardson. When she noticed him glance nervously toward the bar, her anxiety surged anew.

Dani was waiting for the chance to excuse herself and make a break for the bar when a syrupy drawl intruded on the conversation. "Theo! I've been looking all *over* for you!" Rebecca Pope, Richardson's niece, feigned a little-girl pout as she descended on the gathering. But the crystal blue eyes that met Dani's carried a calculating glint. "How marvelous to see you again, Dani. I've been dying to tell you, your little snacks are quite nice."

Dani clenched her hands inside the apron's copious pockets and ignored the "little snacks" snub. Although she and Rebecca had attended the same college, they had never been good friends. They had moved in different circles, and what little contact Dani had had with Rebecca had only confirmed her impression of a snobbish and spoiled girl. The blond debutante now appeared intent on monopolizing the conversation as well as Theo's attention.

"Congratulations, Rebecca." Dani forced out the words. "I hope you'll all excuse me for a moment." Giving Richardson her most genuine smile, she nodded cordially and then headed for the bar.

To her relief, the crowd had dispersed somewhat, save for a few latecomers just collecting their drinks.

"How's it going?" Dani surveyed the chaotic assortment of bottles, shakers, jiggers and garnishes strewed across the wet tablecloth.

"Just fine," the bartender told her through clenched teeth. The corded sinews tensed beneath the tanned skin of his neck, and he did not look up from the row of glasses he was filling.

Dani glimpsed an open copy of a paperback bartender's guide peeking from beneath the table's edge, but she pretended not to notice as she slipped behind the bar. In response to a guest's impatient request, she reached for a bottle of Zinfandel and began to dispense two glasses.

"Thanks." The bartender shot her a glance. He looked as if he were uncertain whether to smile or not.

For some reason, Dani hastened to give him a smile of her own. Her eyes lingered on Ken McCabe's strong profile for a moment, the straight nose cut in an uninterrupted plane from the broad brow to the wide, firm mouth.

"Hey, I said vodka, straight up." A young man, no doubt one of Theo's old law school cronies, thrust his glass across the bar.

Dani caught the twitch in McCabe's lean neck just as she grabbed the glass. "Sorry about that," she apologized. Dumping the iced drink into the basin beneath the bar, she poured a portion of vodka into a fresh glass and handed it back to the man.

"Thanks. Again," McCabe murmured under his breath as soon as the man was out of earshot. This time, he paused long enough to give her a full-blown grin.

"Anytime." Dani eased from behind the bar. She started when he suddenly reached out and caught her elbow.

Just as quickly, he released his hold. "Say, have you seen Mr. Whyte?" he asked. Grabbing a towel, he began to blot the bar, but his dark blue eyes traveled the room with the intensity of a minesweeper.

"Just a few minutes ago. Why? Do you need to talk with him?"

The bartender hesitated, his cobalt blue eyes narrowing as if he were considering her question. "No, not really." He folded the towel into a neat, deliberate rectangle and then stuffed it beneath the bar.

Dani regarded him quizzically, but he was already arranging a row of glasses on the bar, preparing to fill the next order. "You should be able to take a break soon. When the Ghostwalk stops here, everyone will head for the piazza to watch." She frowned, searching the crowd for a glimpse of Richardson's iron gray head.

"The Ghostwalk?" McCabe's gently arching eyebrows rose in interest.

"It's an old Charleston tradition," Dani explained, still scanning the room for Richardson. "Every year around Halloween, a drama group stops at various houses in the historic district—houses that have a ghost in their history, that is. They reenact the ghostly legend at each place. It's a lot of fun."

"I bet. And this house has a ghost?"

Something in the bartender's tone caused Dani to turn to face him. "I suppose it must, if it's part of the walk this year."

McCabe only nodded, but when he smiled, Dani sensed he was doing it for her benefit. Feeling strangely ruffled, she excused herself and followed the stream of guests moving toward the piazza. When she spotted Richardson standing alone to one side of the crowd, she waved.

"Are you going to watch the Ghostwalk?" Dani asked as she joined him.

Richardson's weary smile made him look much older than his sixty-three years. "Only if you'll join me."

"Of course, I will! It's the caterer's job to see that everyone has a good time—and that includes the host!" Dani took the arm that Richardson offered her in his courtly fashion. But as they walked onto the torchlit piazza, she was struck by the melancholy cast of her companion's face, its deeply lined contours heightened by the fuzzy yellow light.

The drama troupe, dressed in elaborate eighteenth-century costumes, had already assembled on the steps of the piazza and in the courtyard. The crowd's collective voice sank to a murmur as the narrator stepped forward and began to relate the legend associated with the house. It was a complicated tale, harking back to a murder that occurred in the house's earliest days. As she listened, Dani tried to pick out the soon-to-be murdered husband, his faithless wife and her blackhearted lover from among the costumed actors.

"I suppose the fellow with the sword is the villain," Dani whispered, leaning toward Richardson. When she glanced up at him, however, he was staring blankly across the piazza, his thoughts focused elsewhere. Even when the players began their performance, he scarcely seemed to notice; his eyes remained fixed on the dark harbor just visible through the palmettoes. Something was definitely preying on the man's mind, Dani thought, something far more burdensome than a novice bartender.

"Mr. Whyte? Excuse me, sir."

Dani felt Richardson start. They wheeled in unison to face the uniformed housekeeper leaning through the doorway. "I'm sorry to interrupt, Mr. Whyte, but you have a telephone call."

"Who is it?" Richardson sounded as tense as he looked.

"He wouldn't say, sir, and I didn't recognize his voice. But he claims it's urgent." The housekeeper took a couple of steps backward, beckoning toward the house.

"Will you please excuse me, Dani?" Richardson's face had taken on a pallor not unlike that of the drama troupe's ghost.

"Of course." Dani watched as he pushed his way through the guests, almost rudely, and then hurried into the house.

Maybe he had been expecting this important call all night. Maybe that was what had been bothering him, some complicated business deal or a chancy investment. But as Dani tried to refocus her attention on the drama that was now in full swing, she could not shake the memory of his worry-clouded face. In the limited time she had spent around her old family friend, she had never seen him this preoccupied or depressed.

Except for his sister, his niece and his two aging aunts, Richardson had few living relatives; his sojourn in Brazil had probably weakened ties with friends in Charleston. Perhaps he needed someone to share his troubles with. Dani glanced back into the now-deserted hall. Of course, he might interpret her concern as an invasion of his privacy. On the other hand, hadn't he been extraordinarily supportive when an unexpected stroke had claimed her own mother's life five years ago? Richardson had flown all the way from São Paulo to offer his condolences. The memory of his heartfelt sympathy was enough to decide the issue. Turning her back on the Ghostwalk performance, Dani walked back into the house.

In the hall, she paused. When she and Elaine had unloaded the Moveable Feast van that afternoon, Dani had noticed a telephone in the library. Not wanting to butt in on Richardson's conversation, she waited a few seconds. When she heard nothing, she carefully opened the library door a crack. Finding the book-lined room empty, Dani retreated into the hall.

She was on her way back to the ballroom when she spotted Ken McCabe. The bartender was loitering in the alcove beneath the free-flying staircase; unlike the helpers she had employed in the past, he made no effort to look busy as she approached.

"I took that break you suggested." McCabe clasped his hands behind his neck and stretched wearily. For the first time, Dani noticed the well-developed musculature of his chest and shoulders, now outlined clearly beneath his white shirt.

"Good. Have you seen Richardson Whyte?"

McCabe nodded. As he joined her in the hall, Dani was suddenly aware of his powerful build, of the energy housed inside his deceptively compact frame. "I saw him go upstairs just a few minutes ago. Why?"

It was only a casual question, but for some reason Dani felt that McCabe was prying into her business. "I need to talk with him," she said, a little curtly.

Dani turned on her heel and headed up the stairs. Prompted by a sixth sense, she glanced over her shoulder and found Ken McCabe watching her. His movements were studied, almost calculated, as he smiled and then sauntered toward the piazza. Something about this bartender had gotten to her—and when she tried to put her finger on it, she felt even more at a loss. Although he was far from a pro, he wasn't completely incompetent, either. No, it wasn't his performance behind the bar that bothered her. It was more the enigmatic looks he gave her, the way he made her feel. Trying to think *that* through was something she didn't have time for right now.

On the landing, Dani hesitated. From the courtyard below, she could hear the Ghostwalk's performance building to a climax, the sounds of staged threats and feigned swordplay. A strange apprehension suddenly gripped her, a vague uneasiness that sent a shiver rippling down her spine.

"Silly! You're like a kid watching a stupid horror movie!" Dani muttered to herself.

At the far end of the hall, a thread of light outlined a partially closed door. As Dani made her way down the corridor, her shadow loomed and then receded between the dim wall sconces.

Without warning, a piercing cry rose from the pit of the stairwell. Dani froze, motionless save for her heart pounding furiously against her rib cage. Only when a swell of applause followed did she release the breath she had been holding. The audience's clapping had just subsided when another shriek shattered the silence of the deserted hall.

Dani's throat went dry and for a split second, she could only listen to the blood thrumming through her ears. For this last horrendous cry had come not from the Ghostwalk players below, but from behind the lighted door at the end of the hall. Urgency suddenly goaded her into action. Dani raced down the hall and threw open the door.

At first, she could only see a pair of feet extending from behind the big desk. A hideous, numbing dread mounting within her, Dani dashed across the room to find Richardson Whyte sprawled on his back against the balcony doors. One hand was pressed to the front of his shirt in a vain attempt to stanch the blood trickling between his fingers.

"Oh, my God! Richardson!" Dani's head throbbed from the scream wrenched from her throat.

Richardson's glazed eyes stared up at her. His mouth opened, releasing a rivulet of blood from each corner.

"Dani!" His voice was so weak, she could barely discern her name.

"I'm here, Richardson. You're going to be all right." The words tumbled out as Dani knelt beside her friend. Her hands were shaking, but she willed them to be steady as she tried to comfort the wounded man. "Just lie still. I'll get help."

Richardson's clammy hand grappled for hers as she attempted to rise. He choked and gasped, and Dani could tell he was struggling to speak. She instinctively grasped the cold hand and felt something hard pressed into her palm.

Richardson's eyes widened with strain. His crimson-stained mouth gaped. Then the hand holding hers relaxed, and Dani knew he was dead.

Chapter Two

No! No! Richardson, please. My God, say something. Please! Dani's mind reeled as she knelt over the lifeless man, her hand still clutching his unresponsive fingers. But she knew her efforts were futile.

Dani struggled to her feet. A murder had been committed. The chilling awareness penetrated her shock, put her numbed senses on alert. The killer could still be around, on the balcony or somewhere in the courtyard below—even hiding in that very room. Her legs felt unstable, her muscles as if they had turned to jelly, as she lunged through the door.

A scream broke from her tight throat as strong hands seized her from behind. Dani struck out with her fist, but the assailant nimbly pinned her arms to her sides and spun her around.

"What the devil's going on?" Ken McCabe demanded, glaring down into her ashen face. "I thought I heard a woman scream...."

Dani shook her arm free and pointed into the room. "It was me. Richardson has been murdered," she gasped out.

She felt a tremor pass through the steely hands clasping her arms. Then McCabe released her and pushed the door wide open. His lean face contorted into a grimace when he spotted the victim, but he quickly took action. Rushing to the supine body, he dropped onto one knee and passed a hand closely over Richardson's colorless face. Dani's heart sank anew when he only shook his head and stood up again.

"Was he like this when you found him?"

"He was still alive." Dani's voice threatened to break, and she hastily swallowed. "I was in the corridor when I heard him cry out."

McCabe walked to the balcony. Ripping off his bartender's apron, he edged the French doors apart with the folded cloth. "Did you see anyone?"

"No." Dani waited in the doorway. She kept her eyes riveted on McCabe's back, avoiding the hideous sight of Richardson's outstretched corpse. Only when the bartender disappeared onto the balcony did she force herself across the threshold. "We have to call the police." When McCabe didn't answer, she added in a tone that said she wouldn't compromise, "Right now."

McCabe backed into the room with noticeable reluctance. "You're right," he conceded. "But let's try to keep things quiet. The last thing we need is for that crowd to get wind of this and panic."

Dani nodded numbly. "I'll use the phone in the kitchen."

Still covering his hand with the folded apron, McCabe closed the door behind them. "Good. In the meantime, I'm going to enlist someone reliable to help keep tabs on the doors. We don't want anyone—guests, servants, those actors, *anyone*—to leave until the police get here."

Dani gave him an uncertain look. "You think someone connected with the party is the murderer?"

At the bottom of the stairs, McCabe paused for a second and then looked up at her, standing behind him on the stairs. In the dim light, his blue eyes had darkened to the shade of a starless midnight sky. "At this point, I just don't want to take any chances."

As McCabe turned toward the piazza, Dani headed for the kitchen. The big marble-and-gray-tile room now looked surreal, the crystal and polished trays a bizarre contrast to the dark tragedy that had occurred upstairs. She rushed to the wall phone and dialed 911. Only after she had talked with the police clerk and hung up did she notice her red handprint smeared on the receiver. Recoiling in disgust, Dani plunged her hands into the pockets of her apron, rubbing them furiously against the smooth linen. When her fingers scraped a small, hard object, they paused and then closed around it.

In the aftermath of the horrendous murder, Dani had almost forgotten the tiny nugget that Richardson had pressed into her hand. She must have dropped it into her pocket without even thinking about it. Now as she lifted it up to the light, she could see that it was a miniature replica of a yacht, the head of a stick pin worked in fourteen-karat gold. A short chain, apparently broken, dangled from the stern of the boat.

Dani started and looked up as the door swung open.

"Well, it's just about time to pack it in—" Elaine broke off, halting stock-still in her tracks when she caught sight of Dani. Her round, brown eyes widened and she sucked in her breath. "What's happened to you? Oh, no! You've cut yourself!" With each dire conjecture, Elaine's voice grew more shrill.

"Calm down, Elaine! I'm not hurt." Dani was surprised by the sharpness of her tone as she seized her assistant's wrists and gave them a settling squeeze.

The young woman continued to shake her head, her eyes still glued to the front of Dani's apron. "For heaven's sake, Dani, that's *blood!*"

Dani pulled her companion to the kitchen island and gently eased her onto one of the stools. "The police are on their way."

"Police!" Elaine's voice soared to a terrified shriek.

Just then Ken McCabe charged into the kitchen, followed by a man in the unmistakable dark suit of a plainclothes detective. Another man, whom Dani vaguely remembered as one of the guests Richardson had introduced her to, someone named Kennedy or Cannaday, posted himself in front of the door.

"This is Detective Butler, Miss Blake—" McCabe began, but the man in the nondescript suit cut him short.

"You discovered the body, Miss Blake?"

"The *body?*" Elaine wailed. "What on earth is going on?"

Dani laid a reassuring hand on her assistant's shoulder for a moment and then turned to the detective. "I had gone upstairs to talk with Mr. Whyte when I heard a cry somewhere down the hall," she told him. "There was only one room with a light on in it, and that was where I found Mr. Whyte lying on the floor behind the desk."

Detective Butler's eyes narrowed, two black specks of bird shot embedded in a doughy, pink face. "Mr. McCabe, you don't recall hearing this cry, do you?" he asked, his beady eyes still trained on Dani.

"I had been standing in the door to the piazza, watching the play for, oh, about five minutes. When I walked back into the hall, I heard a woman yell. That was when I hurried upstairs to see what was wrong," McCabe explained.

"Then the person you heard scream was Miss Blake?" Detective Butler paused long enough for McCabe to nod. "But you didn't hear this cry that alerted Miss Blake to the murder taking place?"

"The Ghostwalk troupe was in the middle of its performance," Dani interjected before McCabe could answer. Much as she resented the detective's calling her testimony into question, she kept her tone deliberately even. "The ac tors were shouting. I'm sure Mr. Whyte's cry blended in with the noise."

"Miss Blake is right. There was so much commotion on the piazza, it was impossible to distinguish a single scream," McCabe put in. Over the stocky detective's shoulder, he telegraphed Dani a supportive glance. "I'm sure Mr. Cannaday can vouch for that, too."

The man stationed in front of the kitchen door nodded emphatically. "I was watching the Ghostwalk act. None of us in the audience could have suspected that something was amiss upstairs."

Detective Butler stroked the tip of his bulbous chin. He cast a skeptical eye around the kitchen before turning toward the door. "I'd like for you to show me exactly what you saw and heard in the room upstairs, Miss Blake."

Dani felt as if her feet were anchored in cement, so great was the effort required to follow the police detective upstairs. Her emotions had taken such a battering that evening; the last thing she wanted to do was walk into that room again and relive the ghastly experience. In the doorway, she hesitated long enough to comfort Elaine, buying herself some time in the process.

"Is Mike home with the kids tonight?" When Elaine nodded, she went on. "Good, then call him and have him come pick you up."

"What about you?" Elaine's voice quavered. "And we still haven't packed up yet."

"Don't worry about the stuff—or me. I'll be all right," Dani assured her. But as she turned to the men waiting at the foot of the stairs, a renewed wave of uneasiness roiled within her.

"Where were you when you heard the cry from Mr. Whyte's study?" Detective Butler demanded from the top of the stairs.

Dani forced herself to resist the detective's high-pressure technique. She thought carefully, trying to reconstruct events accurately in her mind before answering his questions. Still, when she reached the study door, she felt the blood drain from her face. A chalked outline marked the place where Richardson had lain. Dark stains splotched a crude Rorschach on the pale blue Aubusson carpet.

Two police officers were completing their inspection of the room. Detective Butler stopped to talk with them briefly before resuming his questioning. Fighting to suppress her emotions, Dani did her best to reconstruct the sequence of events.

"Mr. Whyte managed to say my name." She paused, clamping her trembling lips together. "Then he took my hand and pressed this into it." Dani fumbled in her pocket and produced the gold pin.

Detective Butler's small dark eyes squinted at the trinket. "Any idea where he got it?"

Dani shook her head. "I don't know. Mr. Whyte and my father sailed together. Maybe it has something to do with that." She hesitated. "Actually, I got the feeling that Mr. Whyte was trying to tell me something."

"What do you mean?"

Dani hesitated, trying to give form to her inchoate instinct. "He was struggling to speak, but couldn't. I'll never forget the look on his face, so desperate and yet so helpless. It was as if the pin was all he had to communicate with." She stared at the tiny pin cupped in her palm.

Butler's pudgy fingers plucked the miniature yacht from Dani's hand with surprising dexterity. "I don't know if buy this 'feeling' of yours, but there's no question that the pin is evidence. The chain's broken. Whyte could have ripped this stick pin off his assailant's lapel during a struggle." He jiggled the pin inside his closed hand for a mo ment. "I'll have to keep it, Miss Blake, at least until the case is closed."

Reluctant as she was to surrender Richardson's parting gift, Dani saw the hopelessness of arguing with Butler about anything. Then, too, she longed to conclude the wearying interrogation, to get away from that oppressive room and its hideous memories. Unfortunately, Detective Butler seemed bent on prolonging the interview.

"And you're certain you didn't see or hear anyone—except Mr. Whyte, of course—before or after you entered the room?" he repeated, stalking back to the desk.

"No." Dani's voice was heavy with fatigue. Butler had asked her that question at least three times already. With each repetition, she felt less like a witness and more like a suspect.

Ken McCabe had been hovering in the door, talking in a low voice with Richardson's friend, Mr. Cannaday. Now, however, he interrupted before Butler could launch another battery of questions. "You've already surmised that the murderer used a gun equipped with a silencer, Detective Butler. And it seems likely that he escaped from the balcony right after he shot Richardson Whyte. The drop isn't more than twelve feet or so, and the courtyard walls would have offered a lot of cover. It's very unlikely that Miss Blake would have heard or seen anything."

Butler looked up from the chalk outline and gave McCabe a sarcastic smile. "You seem to have thought this through real carefully, Mr. McCabe."

If the bartender was fazed by the detective's implication, his impassive expression kept his feelings secret. "I'd like to see the murderer brought to justice," he said evenly.

Detective Butler's heavy shoulders rose and fell as he sighed. "Wouldn't we all? Okay," he conceded. "We know where to reach you people if we need to. We'll be questioning everyone who was on the premises tonight in depth."

With the brusque gesture of a veteran homicide investigator, he ushered them out of the room and down the stairs.

Mr. Cannaday and McCabe followed the detective to the piazza, leaving Dani alone in the hall. When the well-muscled V of the bartender's back disappeared through the door, a fleeting pang of regret nipped at her, as if she had lost her only ally in the night's disastrous turn of events. Of course, she and Ken McCabe had only the most fleeting acquaintance. He had defended her testimony to Detective Butler, but that was insufficient reason to imagine any sort of bond between them. The fact that she found him very attractive had probably clouded her judgment.

Through the arched entrance to the ballroom, Dani could see the sad remains of the celebration. Another plainclothes detective was questioning guests, while the members of the five-piece dance band packed up their equipment in the background. *Just as if it were a normal party. Just as if nothing had happened,* Dani thought. It seemed so callous, and yet she realized that nothing remained for her to do but pack her things and go home.

When Dani pushed open the kitchen door, she was startled to find a costumed man seated at the marble-topped island, chatting with one of the maids. To judge from the man's frock coat and fake, mutton-chop whiskers, he was one of the Ghostwalk players, but his heavy makeup, under the bright kitchen light, gave him a garish, almost sinister look. As Dani hurried around the kitchen, assembling warming trays and leftover supplies, she caught snatches of his conversation.

"So they found the old boy stretched out upstairs?" The actor lowered his voice, but not enough to escape Dani's attention.

The maid nodded. "In his study. Someone shot him." Her clenched hand flew up to the starched white bib of her apron. "Right through the heart."

The actor whistled under his breath. "No kidding. What a way to go! Any idea who did him in?"

Dani felt herself bristling at the actor's flippant tone. Distressed as she was from the whole dreadful ordeal, she had to bite her tongue to keep from ordering him out of the kitchen. She was relieved when a policeman wandered into the kitchen, putting an abrupt end to the gossip session.

"I'm sorry, ma'am, but we'll have to ask you to leave everything here, just as it is, until the investigation is completed," the policeman informed her.

Dani glanced around the kitchen and then nodded. Feeling heavy, as if she had been drugged, she gathered up her jacket and handbag and then followed the policeman out the back door. A row of police cars lined East Battery, forming a barrier of revolving red lights between the house and the park. The grounds had been staked off from the rest of the world with yellow plastic ribbon. As she skirted the ribbon and made her way to the van, the fragmented static of radio messages followed her on the damp night air.

"Going home now?"

Dani lurched and then pivoted around on the brick walk. Her heart was racing so furiously, she waited a few minutes before trusting herself to speak.

"I didn't mean to frighten you," Ken McCabe apologized as he stepped into the yellow funnel of streetlight. "I guess they made you leave the catering stuff for now."

Dani nodded, but as McCabe took another step closer to her, her heart rate stubbornly refused to subside. He had abandoned the starched white bartender's apron and black tie for a light wool turtleneck and jeans. If anything, the formfitting casual clothes delineated his lithe frame even more frankly. Although he must have been as exhausted as she, his strongly-defined features gave his face a look of constant awareness. There was not much that escaped Ken McCabe's blue-black eyes, Dani guessed. She could almost feel their path as they moved from her face down her body and back again, taking her in, reading her mood.

"C'mon. I'll drive you home," he announced. The firm hand she remembered from an earlier encounter settled on her shoulder, albeit more lightly.

"I have my van." Dani pointed toward the metallic blue Aerostar pulled up at the curb, but she made no effort to shake herself free from his hold. Although she knew little more about Ken McCabe than his name and his questionable bartending skills, she welcomed the warm, reliable feel of his touch.

"If you give me the keys, I bet I can drive it." McCabe smiled, and for the first time in what seemed like an eternity, Dani felt her own drawn lips quiver in response. Then his face sobered again and he tugged her gently toward the van. "You've been through one hell of an ordeal. I don't think anyone in your position would want to go home to an empty house alone. And I can just walk to my apartment from your condo. It isn't very far."

"How do you know where my house is? Or that I live alone?" Dani ventured, handing him the keys.

McCabe fiddled with the lock and then held the passenger door open for her. "Mr. Whyte told me," he said simply, and then hurried around to the driver's side.

As she adjusted the shoulder harness, Dani wondered what else Richardson might have told McCabe about her. Right now, however, fatigue took priority over curiosity. Taking a deliberately deep breath, she forced herself to settle back against the seat, trying to ease some of the stiffness from her neck. From the corner of her eye, she watched McCabe maneuver the van through the narrow streets and then turn onto the waterfront drive.

"I'm sorry you ended up in the middle of this," Ken said after they had ridden for several minutes in silence. The keen blue eyes did not stray from the curving thoroughfare, but the lean jaw twitched slightly, suggesting that his own emotions had not gone unscathed. "You and Richardson were pretty close, weren't you?"

Dani stared at the windshield, watching a frown furrow her own shady reflection. "It's hard to describe our friendship. He and my dad were pals. After Dad's death, Richardson sort of took it upon himself to watch over Mother and me. He had a business in Brazil and spent most of his time down there, so we never actually saw him much. In fact, I suppose I could count the times in my life when I've talked with him personally. But he always remembered us, on holidays, when something important happened, like graduation. I'll always be grateful to him for flying back to South Carolina for Mother's funeral." Dani broke off abruptly.

She felt Ken's hand pat her knee, tentatively, as if the experience of showing tenderness were a new one for him. Then he quickly recovered his tight grip on the wheel. "Where should I park?" he asked, his voice once more crisp and matter-of-fact.

Dani directed Ken into the single-lane drive bordered by thick, dormant azalea bushes. Flipping down the visor, she pressed the button on the remote control for the automatic garage-door opener. As soon as he had turned off the engine, she unsnapped the shoulder harness.

"I appreciate your driving me home, but you really don't have to..." He was already out of the van and on his way to the basement door. Ken McCabe was obviously not going to be satisfied with anything less than personally escorting her into her home.

Inside the hall, he flicked on the light and led the way upstairs. Then he turned, took her jacket and draped it on the coat rack. "You need to get rid of this thing, too," he said quietly.

Following his gaze, Dani glanced down at the blood-stained apron she still wore. A shudder quavered through her.

"Try not to think about it," Ken admonished her in a voice as soft as the diffused overhead light. With a touch surprisingly delicate for a man of his strength, he turned her around by the shoulders and loosened the apron strings. She stood still, unresisting, as he slipped the apron over her head and then wadded it into a tight bundle.

Dani had lived alone ever since she had graduated from college, and she was accustomed to doing things for herself. Even as a child, she had developed a strong independent streak, had learned early to be a person others could depend on. The experience of having someone minister to her—especially a man as magnetically attractive as Ken McCabe—was a novel experience, and one that made her feel a little awkward.

If Ken noticed any self-consciousness on her part, he did not show it. He seemed at ease with his surroundings when he guided her to the couch, almost as if he were as familiar with the neat, simply furnished condo as she. Crisp October moonlight flooded through the large windows. From her seat, Dani watched him adjust the drapes without bothering to turn on a lamp.

"Have you got any tranquilizers?" Ken asked.

Shaking her head, Dani looked up at him, suddenly aware of his height, his tangible, masculine warmth as he leaned over the back of the couch. "I've never taken anything stronger than aspirin."

"Well, you need something stronger tonight. Surely you have something to drink."

"There's some Courvoisier cognac in the kitchen."

Dani pointed toward the bifold door, but Ken was already on his way. Apparently, his uncanny ability to familiarize himself with a new environment extended to her well-stocked kitchen cabinets, for within minutes, he returned with a generously filled glass.

"This'll help you relax." His big hands felt warm as they curved over hers, cupping them around the glass.

Dani took a sip of the fragrant brandy and swallowed slowly. "You seem to know what to do in a crisis." Her eyes followed Ken's well-proportioned form as it moved among the shadows.

He hesitated, bent over the overstuffed chair facing the windows. "Bartenders see everything. You learn to think on your feet and keep a cool head." When he turned, she noticed he was carrying her hand-crocheted afghan.

"I appreciate your speaking up when that detective put me on the spot."

Ken stooped and slid an arm under Dani's legs. Before she could protest, he lifted her feet onto the sofa. Then he shook out the afghan and gently tucked it over her. "Those guys give everyone a hard time. I wouldn't worry too much about what Butler thinks of you."

Dani stiffened, in part at the unexpected sensations Ken's touch had awakened, in part at his ambiguous comment. "You can't mean that he considers me a suspect? Richardson Whyte was my *friend!* If you could only have seen the look on his face when he gave me that pin! I feel certain he was trying to tell me something with the pin because he trusted me."

Ken straightened himself slowly, taking care to smooth a wrinkle from the afghan's border. "I believe you, Dani." It was the first time he had called her by name. In the shadowy darkness, it sounded oddly intimate. "Don't think about any of this right now. Just try to get some sleep." His hand covered hers again, but only for a moment. Then he took the glass and placed it on the cocktail table. "I'll leave my number by the phone in the kitchen. You can call me if you need anything. Okay?"

That she would call someone who was practically a rank stranger would have seemed ridiculous under ordinary circumstances. But tonight had been anything but ordinary. Not lifting her head from the couch cushion, Dani nodded. "Okay."

Ken lingered for a moment, looking down at her, a puzzling expression hovering on his face. She was grateful for the darkness, glad for the privacy it afforded her own suddenly warm face. When he turned toward the kitchen, she closed her eyes, letting her ears follow his movements. She heard the hall lightswitch's faint snap, followed by Ken's muted footsteps on the carpeted stairs. When the door closed, she knew he was gone.

But as Dani drifted off into a fitful sleep, her mind was filled with a violent montage of images: scenes from the party intercut with Richardson's horror-struck face; Detective Butler's drawling voice bombarding her with accusations; Ken McCabe's hands pulling her back from a gaping abyss; and above it all, the tiny pin, a phantom ship drifting through her dream, piloted by ghosts.

"DID YOU GET ANY SLEEP last night?" The dark circles under Derek Cannaday's eyes suggested that he had not.

Ken frowned as he closed the door to Cannaday's office behind him. "Not much. When I got back to my place, I was too keyed up to even think about sleep. I was an idiot to have used that bartender cover! If I'd been more mobile, I could have kept better tabs on Whyte."

Derek rounded his desk to tap Ken lightly on the shoulder. "Don't start blaming yourself. The bartender thing was Richardson's idea, remember? And we both did all we could to keep an eye on him. You've been in the security business long enough to know that the best plans sometimes fail."

"A man is dead because this one didn't work," Ken said grimly.

Derek fixed him with bloodshot eyes. "A man who was my good friend, Ken. Believe me, I know what you're feeling. Richardson Whyte was your client, but he was my friend and business partner for almost thirty years."

Ken shook his head apologetically. "I'm sorry, Derek. It's just that when I took this assignment, I fully expected to blow the whistle on whoever was trying to blackmail Richardson Whyte. Now, it looks as if the blackmailer has carried out his threat, and we haven't a clue as to who he might be."

Derek heaved a sigh laden with fatigue. "I had to give Butler the blackmail note, but I kept a copy for us." He slid open one of the desk drawers, pulled out a photocopy and handed it to Ken.

Ken frowned over the copy. It looked so crude, so childish, the clumsy letters cut from magazine ads and pasted to a single sheet of lined notebook paper. When his boss in Washington had told him that Derek Cannaday, an old client from Brazil, had a friend in Charleston who was being blackmailed, Ken had fully expected a sophisticated extortion plot. The first time he had seen the note Richardson had received, it had reminded him of a B-film gimmick, the sort of hoax that even a gullible movie audience wouldn't swallow.

I want $500,000 in unmarked bills. Put the money in a Piggly-Wiggly shopping bag and leave it under the second pew on the right in St. Michael's Cathedral at 10:00 a.m. on October 16. You are a rich man and I know you have the money. Do not be foolish. What is money compared to your life? I mean business.

He had almost laughed at the note's melodramatic tenor, but not now. On his and Derek Cannaday's advice, Richardson Whyte had not paid, and now he was dead.

"What do the police make of it?" Ken handed the photocopy back to Derek.

"They wanted to know everything about everyone present at the party. Butler kept asking me about greedy relatives and resentful servants. He was especially interested in that caterer who discovered Richardson."

Ken's throat tightened involuntarily. "Dani Blake? Surely they don't suspect her!" His voice rose, and he hastily dampened his outraged tone. He needed to maintain credibility with Derek Cannaday, something that a too-vigorous defense of a beautiful woman might damage at this point. "I mean, anyone could see that she was really torn up over what had happened. Richardson was an old friend of her family's."

"As far as the police are concerned, Richardson didn't invite any *known* enemies into his home. Miss Blake was the last person to see Richardson alive. Her fingerprints were all over his office. I'll agree with you that she seems an unlikely candidate, but..." Derek shrugged. "Where money is concerned, people will do almost anything."

Ken swallowed hard, choking down the same angry reaction he had felt when the detective had badgered Dani Blake the previous evening. "So Butler thinks this is going to be a sordid wolf-in-sheep's-clothing case?"

A jaded smile, devoid of amusement, drifted across Derek's lips. "Whatever Butler really thinks, you can be sure he's not going to share it with us."

"What did you tell him about our operation anyway?"

"Enough to keep us clear of any 'withholding evidence' charges." Derek retreated behind his desk and dejectedly tossed the photocopy back into the drawer. "Basically, Butler got the whole story. Associated Security used to provide bodyguards for my company in Brazil. When Richardson received the blackmail note, I contacted the Associated

Security office in Washington, and they put you on the case. I hope you were honest with Butler."

The headache that Ken had been battling all night released a sudden freshet of pain through his skull. "When he questioned me last night, I gave him the basic name-rank-and-serial-number business, told him I was working for Richardson, but I hated blowing my cover. You never know whose hands those police reports pass through."

"Your cover doesn't matter anymore. The case is now officially in the hands of the police."

Ken kneaded the back of his neck with one hand. "Are you comfortable with that arrangement?"

Derek looked surprised. "Why do you ask?"

"Because I'm not." Planting both hands on Derek's desk, Ken leaned toward him. "Derek, I want to keep this operation open."

Shaking his head, Cannaday stared emptily at the leather desk blotter. "There is no operation now. Richardson is dead."

Ken jabbed his fist against the desk's polished surface. "Precisely why I want to continue my investigation. If you don't want to keep me on the job, that's fine. I can't remember the last time I've taken a vacation—the company must owe me months, and I'll do this on my own time. But I'd like your cooperation."

Derek slowly looked up at Ken. "It's that important to you?"

Ken nodded and then drew a deep breath. "I've never had this happen to me before, have someone I was supposed to protect murdered right under my nose. I can't bring Richardson Whyte back, but maybe I can find his murderer. I owe him that much at least."

"You sound as if you're taking this personally, Ken." Derek regarded him with an appraising eye, his voice suddenly cool. "I can understand your motivation. You're a professional—you've lost a hand, and you want to set the record straight.''

Ken straightened himself. If Derek Cannaday thought him an unfeeling automaton driven only by the desire to check-mate his murderous opponent, so be it. "Will you work with me?"

"I'm in this with you, Ken," Derek said after a long second. "But I'm going to warn you. Keep a clear head. Don't let your need for revenge get in the way." His eyes drifted to the closed desk drawer. When they settled on Ken again, their unblinking focus was startling. "This murderer is a lot smarter than that note led us to believe. Be careful."

Chapter Three

The chapel was filled to capacity. As Dani followed the usher to one of the few available seats, she recognized a number of the solemn faces in the crowd. That many of Richardson's party guests were now his mourners seemed a cruel irony.

At the front of the chapel, the Whyte family was clustered to the left of the bier. Leaning to one side, Dani could see the dark outlines of two heavy, old-fashioned veils, rising just above the backs of the maroon velvet chairs. That would be Sapphira and Adele Whyte, no doubt, dressed in the black crepe of a bygone era. Dani knew from her mother that the two spinsters had raised Richardson and his sister after the children's parents were killed in a plane crash. The Whyte sisters were legendary in Charleston not only for their considerable wealth, but also for their eccentricity, and Dani's mother had often speculated on the trials young Richardson and his sister must have endured in their aunts' Meeting Street mansion.

Next to Sapphira and Adele was seated a woman who so strongly resembled Rebecca Pope, she could only be her mother. When Dani spotted Rebecca leaning on the arm of her fiancé, she rose. Dropping her gloves onto her seat to reserve it, she began her way down the aisle to pay her respects.

As Dani joined the line of people offering their condolences, she glanced over her shoulder and caught sight of a pudgy pink face. Detective Butler had stationed himself near the chapel door and was surveying the assembly with undisguised interest. When the beadlike eyes met hers across the distance, Dani's irritation flared. She stared at him, unflinching, for a long second before looking away. The man seemed to thrive on trying to intimidate people, just as he had relished badgering her during his interrogation. Butler had been more interested in tripping up her testimony than in rooting out worthwhile clues. Every time she thought about the high-handed way he had dismissed her feelings about the pin, she felt a fresh wave of resentment. And then he had had the gall to confiscate the pin!

Much as she disliked Detective Butler, she shouldn't have been surprised to find him at the service, Dani reflected. Hadn't she always heard that a murderer often attends his victim's funeral, as a sort of ritual to confirm his grisly act? No doubt Butler subscribed to that theory and was sizing up the mourners for possible suspects. Now that she thought about it, there was every likelihood that the murderer *was* sitting somewhere in that room, posing as a grieving friend or acquaintance—just as he had infiltrated Richardson's party.

Struggling to put aside the abhorrent thought, Dani paused for a moment beside the closed casket and bowed her head. Then she walked to the section reserved for the family.

"I'm so sorry, Rebecca." Dani leaned forward to briefly lay a hand on the young woman's wrist.

"Thank you, Dani." Rebecca's lips quivered into a stiff smile. Then she dabbed her flawless peaches-and-cream cheeks with a lace handkerchief. When her hands dropped to her lap, the fingers coiled nervously, twisting the handkerchief into a knot. A solemn light clouded the large blue eyes, giving them a remote, pained expression.

Dani had never seen Rebecca show much emotion, perhaps because the debutante had led such a sheltered life, protected from harsher realities—until now. Whatever the case, Rebecca Pope was visibly shaken by her uncle's death.

"Miss Blake, we certainly appreciate your coming today. This has been such a blow to all of us."

Dani found herself wrenched away from Rebecca by Theo Boynton, who had seized her hand. Everyone in town knew that the younger Boynton had political aspirations. Dani guessed that he had perfected his forceful handshake to that end. Theo was a handsome man, with the same brand of society-page good looks that Rebecca enjoyed, but something in his eager, low voice, in the studiously grieved looks he cast at the bier repelled Dani. She chose the first opportunity to extract her hand from his grasp and move down the row of chairs.

Pausing, she offered her condolences to Rebecca's mother and nodded politely to the two aged spinsters. Dani was startled when the younger of the Whyte sisters—herself a redoubtable octogenarian—only glared from behind her veil, her face a wrinkled white mask of hostility. The elder sister moved her lips, but as Dani stooped to hear, she realized that the ancient woman was muttering to herself.

Poor Richardson! Dani thought. She could only imagine what growing up in Adele and Sapphira Whyte's household had been like. Although his wealth and success had made him the envy of most people, Richardson's life had been a hard one in many ways, Dani realized. Orphaned as a small boy only to be left a childless widower in his later years, Richardson Whyte had had his share of loneliness and heartbreak. The thought intensified her sadness as she made her way back to her seat.

"They're about to begin the service!" a woman whispered hoarsely behind her.

Dani turned to nod, then suddenly halted in her tracks.

"Excuse me!" The woman pressed past Dani, giving her an impatient frown.

But Dani was too intent on a face she had just glimpsed in the crowd to care. Resuming her way to her seat, she strained for a better look, but the generous brim of a woman's black straw hat maddeningly defeated her efforts. Where had she seen that man before? And what about him had stuck in her mind so firmly that she would start at even a fleeting glimpse? Still frowning, Dani edged along the row of chairs.

"Excuse me, please," she murmured. When she reached her seat, however, she stopped abruptly.

Ken McCabe lifted her gloves off the chair and motioned for her to sit. "I've been saving your place for you," he told her in a husky whisper.

But Dani continued to balk. "What are you doing—" she blurted out and then caught herself.

"Sitting here next to you?" Ken shrugged. "I spotted you when I entered the chapel. Since you were the only person I knew, I thought I might as well sit with you. You don't mind, do you?"

Dani carefully sank onto the chair. "No, of course not." In fact, if she were to examine her emotions, she suspected she would discover that she was actually pleased to see him again. Instead, she folded her gloves and tucked them into her handbag, busying herself to disguise the peculiar feeling his closeness had stirred to life.

"I imagine you know a lot of people here?"

"I remember some faces from the party, recognize a few people I've worked for," she replied. A certain undercurrent in Ken's tone caused her to glance over at him, but his face appeared as guileless as it was sober.

Ken's breath brushed her cheek as he leaned to whisper, "I saw our friend Butler." She felt his head jerk slightly toward the chapel door. "I think he's made note of our presence, as well."

"Regardless of Detective Butler's opinion, Richardson Whyte was a close friend of my family. I've every right to attend his funeral," she told him, a little sharply.

"You don't think much of Butler, do you?"

Dani frowned for a moment before replying. "I think he's ignoring an important clue if he thinks that pin is simply something Richardson latched on to in a struggle."

"I think you're right. You know, I'd be interested to hear your ideas about that pin."

Ken shifted in his seat, his shoulder almost touching hers, but Dani pointedly turned her attention to the front of the chapel, grateful that the minister's appearance would silence his probing, at least for the time being. Richardson's murder—in his own home, among people he considered friends—had shaken her previously benign view of the world, leaving her unwilling to trust anyone too readily. That she found Ken McCabe attractive was only more reason to remain on her guard.

As the minister, a bespectacled man with a cresting shock of white hair, approached the lectern, the organ ceased and a hush fell over the assembly. He was opening his Bible when a loud sob shattered the silence. A chill rippled through Dani, covering her arms with gooseflesh, as the crying grew louder and less controlled. Over the mourners' heads, she could see a woman kneeling beside the bier. Her shoulders were shaking uncontrollably, her face buried in her hands.

From the corner of her eye, Dani saw two ushers hesitantly approach the bereft woman. But before they could intercede, a man stepped in front of them. Encircling the woman's heaving shoulders with his arm, the man guided her away from the casket. Only when he turned did Dani blink in recognition.

"That's him!" she exclaimed under her breath without thinking.

"Who?" Ken asked, rising slightly in his seat.

"The fellow I saw in the crowd earlier." Dani hesitated. If she felt foolish sharing an intuitive suspicion with Ken, she would now feel even sillier trying to pass off her interest with that bland remark. "When I was walking back to my seat, I thought I recognized someone. I couldn't place him. You know how it is with a person you've only seen briefly, but something about him stays with you? Well, now I know where I saw this man before—in Richardson Whyte's kitchen. He was talking with one of the maids while I gathered up my supplies. No wonder I had trouble placing his face—he was still wearing his makeup."

Ken's brow furrowed in interest. "Makeup?"

Dani nodded, her eyes still following the retreating couple. "Apparently, he was one of the Ghostwalk actors. Anyway, he was asking the maid a lot of questions about the murder, and—" She broke off.

"What?" Ken prompted, and Dani felt him move closer to her.

"Maybe I was just reacting to the situation, but he seemed awfully flippant about Richardson's death, as if it were nothing more serious than another act in the play." When Ken said nothing, she glanced up at him. "I guess I can't expect people who didn't know Richardson personally to take his death as hard as I have."

"No, maybe not," Ken began slowly. "But I think this guy probably had more than a passing acquaintance with Richardson Whyte."

The minister had now begun reading a psalm, prompting Dani to drop her voice even lower. "What do you mean?"

"That hysterical woman was Beatrice Lawes, Richardson's secretary. As I hear it, she worked for him for years with absolute devotion. The guy who stepped in just then, the one you were talking about, is her son."

"How do you know all this?" Dani demanded, now looking him square in the eyes. Before she could prod an answer out of Ken, however, the minister enjoined the assembled mourners to join him in prayer. For the remainder of the service, Dani forced herself to put her nagging questions aside. Only when they had filed out of the chapel did she once more confront Ken.

"How did you learn so much about Richardson's secretary? I thought you said you didn't know anyone here." Dani halted on the sidewalk, pulling Ken out of the stream of mourners.

"Derek Cannaday told me who she was. He's one of the pallbearers. You remember him, don't you?" Ken nodded toward the procession leaving the chapel.

Dani's eyes followed his gesture. As Ken had indicated, Cannaday was escorting the casket, walking between Powell Boynton and another man whom she didn't recognize. "Yes, I remember him. Richardson had introduced us before...earlier that evening." Dani quickly looked back at Ken. Although she could not specifically say why, she had the funny feeling that he was trying to sidetrack her. "But you really haven't answered my question."

Ken's even gaze was like a deflective shield. "What do you mean?"

Dani shook her head, resisting the distraction of those deep blue eyes. "You seemed very interested in what I knew about Bea's son."

"I'm a curious man." A slight smile played on Ken's lips, but looking into Dani Blake's gold-flecked brown eyes, he could tell she was not thrown off one bit. "If I recall correctly, you were the one who got all excited when you recognized Lawes."

"I told you I had seen him in Richardson's kitchen after the murder." Her low-pitched voice held firm, without a trace of telltale defensiveness.

"Yeah, but what was so remarkable about that? There must have been close to three hundred people cooped up in that house once the police arrived. So he was in the kitchen. So he was talking about the murder in a less than respectful tone. What does that prove?" He watched her with the anticipation of a tennis pro awaiting a worthy opponent's serve.

"It *proves* nothing." She straightened her long neck that in another day would have been called swanlike. When she tossed back her head, the sun caught the fiery glints buried in the dark auburn waves, igniting them to match the sparks in her eyes. "But even you've indicated you think someone at the party committed the murder."

"If Lawes was one of the actors, wouldn't he have been downstairs in the courtyard when Richardson was murdered?"

"Yes, but you know how dark it was. Almost anyone who was supposed to be in the yard or on the piazza could have slipped away unnoticed—for instance, an actor who didn't have a speaking part." She hesitated, drawing a deep breath. "Look, I'm not accusing Lawes of murder. But there was something about that man that made me uncomfortable. Of course, if you're like Butler, you'll discount anything less than a smoking gun."

"I'm not like Butler." Ken was startled by how earnestly he made that contention, by how much he wanted Dani Blake to believe him. "And I think your feeling about the pin is probably on target. Any thoughts on how Lawes and the pin might be linked?"

Dani regarded him warily. "No."

"Didn't you say your father and Richardson Whyte sailed together? Maybe the pin—"

Dani interrupted him abruptly. "Wait, Ken. I haven't drawn any conclusions about anything."

"No, but your mind is running like a computer at top speed right now. I can tell." The moment he had said that, he knew he had chosen the wrong words. Dani Blake was too intelligent to accept that kind of baiting without protest.

"Please don't try to manipulate me," she warned him. "I cared very much about Richardson, enough to want to make sure that no stone remains unturned in the investigation of his murder. But I'm afraid I don't quite understand your angle. You're asking an awful lot of questions for a bartender who's just hit town."

Ken cleared his throat. Although he would normally have offered the first rebuttal that came into his head, he felt compelled to be honest with Dani—as honest as he could afford at this point. "Richardson Whyte was a good man. I didn't know him as well as you did, but I respected him. In my own way, I'm as angry as you are at the thought that the killer might be right under our noses."

Her full lips quivered, signaling that she recognized his sincerity, but she remained silent.

"I guess I'm just feeling frustrated with the police. Like you are. I was hoping that you'd share any bits of info you'd picked up, maybe shed some light on this thing." Ken waited, praying that he hadn't pushed his luck too far. He felt his building anticipation sink when she finally shook her head.

"There's nothing else I can tell you, Ken." She took a couple of steps backward, her lovely face a palette of conflicting emotions. Then she turned and hurried down the walk. Ken could only watch as she climbed into her van and joined the long funeral procession.

Chapter Four

"One white chocolate cake, two Huguenot tortes and five dozen assorted fruit tarts." The red-haired woman surveyed the back of the open van, pointing to each of the white boxes carefully anchored between the cases of champagne. "That's everything you ordered for today, isn't it?"

Dani checked her list before replying. "That'll do it. Thanks again, Meg." As she closed the rear door of the van, she smiled at the friendly bake-shop proprietor.

Dani climbed behind the wheel of the Aerostar and took another look at her calendar's daily schedule. She had made efficient use of the morning, a miracle considering her nagging preoccupation. She needed to make only two additional stops, to pick up a couple of smoked hams and a fresh supply of premium coffee beans, before heading back to the Moveable Feast's tiny kitchen headquarters. In spite of her efforts to concentrate on the day's tasks, her eyes drifted, unbidden, to the adjacent calendar page with its single entry. "Funeral, St. Paul's Chapel, 10:00 a.m." Dani closed the spiral-bound book and let it drop onto her lap. Recoiling from the memories that solemn calendar notation evoked, she closed her eyes and pressed her cold fingers into her forehead.

Less than four days ago, she had followed a similar route through the labyrinthine streets of Charleston's old city, stopping at her trusted suppliers of cheese, pastries, produce and prime meats. She had wanted everything to be flawless for Richardson's party—the most complementary wines, the finest smoked salmon, the perfect selection of early-autumn fruits. In the wake of that evening's tragedy, however, such concerns seemed pathetically petty. Only yesterday, they had buried a kindly, generous-hearted man, a loyal friend to her and her family; today, his brutal murderer still walked the streets, free and undetected. Yet she was supposed to resume the mundane activities of everyday life as if nothing had happened. *As if I hadn't held Richardson's hand in his dying moments. As if he hadn't given me the pin...*

Three long, sleepless nights had done nothing to weaken her conviction that Richardson had been struggling to tell her something. But what? Dani frowned, frustrated by the persistent question and her own inability to answer it. Unlike Detective Butler, Ken McCabe shared her belief that the pin was the dying man's last attempt to communicate. At the thought of the lean-jawed bartender and his probing questions, a fresh slate of doubts rose in her mind, some as troubling and irreconcilable as her misgivings about the pin.

Dani straightened herself and then ground the ignition, releasing the clutch so abruptly that the van's tires squealed as it lurched forward. Given her limited contact with Ken McCabe, trying to analyze him and his motives for attending Richardson's funeral was a doomed undertaking at this point. If she hoped to gain any peace of mind, she would do well to concentrate on an area in which she might be able to get some answers.

At the mouth of the alley, Dani braked to allow an open horse-drawn carriage filled with sightseers to pass before turning out into King Street. With a face as grimly set as her purpose, she piloted the van through the narrow streets. At the sight of the shaded piazza of Richardson's house, her fingers tensed around the steering wheel. Her mouth felt dry, as if her tongue were made of cotton, as she parked the van and secured its doors. Nothing might come of it, she reminded herself, but she knew she wouldn't rest until she learned more about those dreadfully fateful minutes separating the last two times she had seen Richardson alive.

As she walked toward the Battery, she had a clear view of the second-story balcony. On impulse, Dani turned into the pedestrian walkway flanking the back courtyard. She had walked only a few feet when the street sounds began to fade, replaced by an almost startling hush. Like most of the historic district's residents, Richardson had probably cherished the privacy of his walled garden. He could not have foreseen that its seclusion would provide his murderer with the perfect concealed escape route.

Dani was studying the balcony's jutting overhang when the rhythmic brush of a straw broom caught her attention. Through the wrought-iron gate set in the courtyard wall, she spotted Mona Sams, Richardson's housekeeper, sweeping one of the brick paths crisscrossing the garden.

"Oh!" The broom handle clattered against the moss-covered bricks as the woman started. For a moment, her large eyes widened as if she had glimpsed a ghost hovering behind the ironwork's lacy pattern. When she recognized Dani, she hastened to apologize. "Excuse me, Miss Blake! I wasn't expecting to see you peekin' through that gate. I guess I'm just jittery, what with all the evil that's come to pass...." She broke off, shaking her head as she unlatched the gate.

"That's okay," Dani assured her. "I'm sorry I slipped up on you." As she glanced around the walled garden, her hands involuntarily chafed her arms as if to banish the insidious chill seeping from the aged bricks.

"Shall I tell Miss Lawes you're here?" The housekeeper paused on her way to the door.

"Miss Lawes?"

The housekeeper must have caught the look of surprise on Dani's face. "Yes, ma'am. She came by today to help Miss Sapphira tidy up Mr. Whyte's study, go through all his papers and important things, I suppose." The dubious look she cast toward the house suggested that she was happy enough to stay out of the secretary's way.

"Please don't disturb her on my account. Actually, I came here to talk with you, if you have a few minutes. About Saturday night," Dani added carefully. She studied the woman's full face, trying to gauge her reaction.

The housekeeper's thick fingers flexed uneasily around the broom handle. "So many policemen have been by here, wanting to talk about all *that*. It's like nobody is willing to let you put those awful things out of your mind and start trying to heal. Poor Mr. Whyte!" She sighed heavily, shaking her head as if its weight were almost too much for her.

"I know what you mean. I haven't been able to think of anything but this tragedy. But that's precisely why I need to talk with you, to see if I can make some sense out of what happened." Dani swallowed and waited for the housekeeper to respond. When the woman only continued to regard her with stoic forbearance, she decided to try her luck. "When you summoned Richardson to take a phone call, I was with him on the piazza. You remember, don't you?"

The woman nodded with effort. "Yes, of course, I do."

"Do you recall anything about the person who phoned, anything he said?" Dani hesitated, her eyes following the tense lines of the woman's face, before she played her hunch. "And did he by any chance mention a pin?"

The housekeeper's frown carved deep grooves into her brow. "A pin?"

"Yes, you know, like a piece of jewelry," Dani prompted. "Actually, the item I had in mind was a little stickpin fashioned in the shape of a boat."

Wielding the broom as if it were a weapon, the housekeeper took a swipe at a weed protruding from between two of the pavers. "No, ma'am. He didn't say anything about any pin, that's for sure. But I remember exactly what he *did* say, mostly because it seemed kind of odd, I guess."

To curb her growing anticipation, Dani forced herself to inhale deeply as she waited for the housekeeper to continue.

The woman rested her hands atop the end of the broom handle. "He said, 'I would like to speak to Mr. Whyte. If he isn't taking the little drama too seriously, that is.'"

"I suppose he meant the Ghostwalk reenactment," Dani suggested slowly, but like the housekeeper, she found the comment strange.

"I reckon so. But Mr. Whyte was certainly never the kind to put stock in a foolish old ghost story." The housekeeper's rounded shoulders rose and fell as she shifted her hold on the broom. "With all that's gone on, though, you'd almost think bad spirits had been at work in this place." Her eyes traveled cautiously to the balcony, as if they feared what they might glimpse there.

"Did you by chance see Richardson while he was talking on the phone or afterward?" Dani asked, but the woman was already shaking her head.

"I closed the library door after him when he took the call. That was the last time I saw him alive," the housekeeper added ominously.

Dani was pondering this last grim bit of information when a figure loomed in the doorway, directly behind the housekeeper.

"Do we have a visitor, Mona?"

The startled housekeeper whirled, stepping back to give Dani an unobstructed view of Bea Lawes standing in the open French doors. In contrast to the emotional disarray she had exhibited in the chapel the previous day, the secretary now appeared tightly composed, her small face fixed in a look of permanent self-control. With her red, bow-shaped lips and precisely bobbed hair, Bea reminded Dani of an aging silent-film star. Although she could not have stood more than an inch or two over five feet, her trim, compact body blocked the entrance as effectively as an armor-clad sentry. Her light blue eyes grazed Dani disdainfully, as if she were an unwelcome intruder.

Motivated in part by sympathy for the bewildered house-keeper, Dani hastened to mollify Bea. "I'm Dani Blake." When the woman made no response, she went on. "I was a friend of Richardson's."

"I know who you are."

Dani started at Bea's hostile tone. For someone who had only met her a few seconds ago, the woman seemed to harbor a distinct dislike for her. Reminding herself that they had all been under a tremendous strain, Dani made another attempt to crack the icy blue glare.

"I'm sorry if I stopped by at an inconvenient time, but I wanted to talk with Mrs. Sams about...about Saturday night." No sooner were the words past her lips than Dani regretted her candor.

"We've had police detectives swarming this house for the past three days, Miss Blake, with reporters trailing behind them, scavenging for lurid details. Every one with his endless questions, stirring things up, making trouble!" Bea's voice rose, revealing the fault lines in her ironclad restraint. "Hasn't enough trouble been visited on this house already?"

Dani was taken aback by Bea's rude—and unnervingly irrational—behavior, but she saw no point in defending herself. Better to take leave as gracefully as possible, before Bea's ire escalated any further. "I'm sorry to have disturbed you, Mrs. Lawes. Thank you, Mrs. Sams." She

managed a courteous smile for the housekeeper before retreating through the garden gate.

Silence clung like damp moss to the brick walls along the
alley, a quiet so oppressive, so tangible, she could almost
smell its stagnant odor. Dani was relieved when she reached
the street. She had not been prepared for the unpleasant
encounter with Bea Lawes, and the woman's unthinking
anger had upset her. Then, too, returning to Richardson's
house had been almost guaranteed to unsettle her still-shaky
equilibrium.

Dani was walking toward her van when she paused to
glance back at the house. What she saw jolted her to a halt.
It was the briefest flutter, a vague shadow on the edge of her
vision, an impression so ephemeral, most people would have
called it imaginary. But as she stared up at the balcony window, Dani knew she had not imagined the white form passing behind the curtain.

THROUGH THE FILTER of the sheer curtain, Sapphira
watched the young woman unlock the blue van and then
climb into the driver's seat. As her eyes followed the van's
progress along King Street, she absently twisted the large
amethyst ring, chafing the gold band against the gnarled
knuckle that held it anchored to her finger. For once in her
life, Sapphira Whyte felt control slipping away from her,
and that unfamiliar state of affairs filled her with an anxiety she could earlier only have imagined.

Stepping back from the window, she glanced around the
mahogany-paneled walls of her nephew's study. Sapphira
had never felt entirely comfortable in this house. Unlike the
Whyte family home she had occupied for over eighty-five
years, Richardson's imposing mansion had sheltered a
hodgepodge of previous owners: out-of-towners, mer-
chants and, briefly, a widow of less-than-sterling repute. All
had left traces that even the most zealous redecorating ef-

fort could not obliterate. The recent invasion of strangers had further disrupted the atmosphere. The aura of policemen with cameras and fingerprint powder and uncouth voices still hung in the air like a stale odor.

They weren't safe anymore, even in the private bastion of their own homes, Sapphira reflected. The police had even dared to invade the Whyte estate, descending on the venerable Meeting Street house like an alien army. They had bullied the servants and tried to intimidate her in their quest for information that was nobody's business but the Whytes'. Only by sheer strength of will had she prevented them from questioning Adele, as if that poor, dazed creature hadn't suffered enough already!

She should have known that the Blake girl would turn up; only wishful thinking had prevented her from expecting the inevitable. They had no one but Richardson to blame for drawing her into their midst, of course. A wave of rancor toward her deceased nephew swept through Sapphira. She had sacrificed so much for him, raised him as if he were her own, but he never would listen to her—at least, not where anything that truly mattered was concerned. Now he was gone, leaving her to finish his unsettled business for him.

Sapphira parted the gauzy curtain to inspect the street below as if she needed to assure herself that the girl was really gone. Sighing, she let the curtain fall back into place and then carefully smoothed the translucent folds. Dani Blake would be back; there was no use pretending she wouldn't be. But next time, Sapphira vowed, she would be ready for her.

IF DANI HAD BEEN fortunate enough to find a parking spot close to Richardson's house, her luck had run out by the time she reached the busy Market Street intersection. Any hopes she had of finding a convenient place to leave the van while she purchased coffee were quickly dashed by the throngs of cars lining the street. A brisk walk would let her

work off some tension, she told herself as she turned into a
small public parking lot not far from the Old Exchange
Building. The unsettling confrontation with Bea Lawes had
abraded her already frayed nerves; that someone had been
watching her from the upstairs window only exacerbated her
discomfiture. Even her conversation with Mona Sams had
raised questions instead of answering them.

Canfield's Coffee and Tea Emporium was located near
the two-block-long market arcade. Skirting the pack of
ambling tourists blocking the sidewalk, Dani decided to take
a shortcut through one of the pedestrian corridors running
beneath the Old Exchange Building. Inside the passage, the
air was still and cool in sharp contrast to the sun-warmed
street. Dani loosened the moss green cotton sweater she had
draped over her shoulders and wriggled her arms into the
sleeves.

A handful of sightseers clustered near the glass display
cases containing historical information about the Old Exchange, but for the most part, the corridor was deserted. A
few of the small shops interspersed along the passage still
had Out To Lunch signs dangling from their entrance
doorknobs. Dani paused in front of an antique jewelry store
to inspect the glittering wares exhibited behind the thick
plate glass. If only she'd been allowed to keep the pin Richardson had given her! A jeweler accustomed to buying es-
tates could have helped her identify the pin's origin, perhaps
shedding light on Richardson's final wish at the same time.
Of course, the police had probably already traced the pin,
but the likelihood of Detective Butler sharing any knowledge with her ranked second only to hell's freezing over.

Dani's eyes roved the display, vainly searching for anything resembling a tiny yacht. She had been studying the
array of jewelry for some time before she noticed the reflection superimposed on the showcase. When she did she

gasped and then quickly sucked in her breath. Wheeling around, Dani stared up at Ken McCabe.

"You startled me!"

"I'm sorry." His smile was genial, but not in the least apologetic. She must have looked more annoyed than unnerved, for he hastened to add, "I waved to you from across the street, but you didn't see me, so I decided to try to catch up with you in here."

"Well, you did." Dani realized her comeback must have sounded rather abrupt, but for some reason, she doubted that he had made much of an effort to hail her from the street. Like McCabe's appearance at Richardson's funeral, the coincidental meeting in the arcade seemed highly suspect.

Ken didn't act at all fazed by her less-than-open-armed welcome. "I'm looking for a restaurant in this part of town. Maybe you can help me. Any idea where I can find Evangelina's? Someone tipped me off that they might be hiring a new bartender."

"Evangelina's is near the big hotel complex, back that way." Dani had to maneuver her hand carefully to point, to avoid touching McCabe. He was standing so close to her, she felt almost pinioned to the heavy glass window behind her. "I'm surprised you didn't see it from across the street," she couldn't resist adding.

Ken glanced the length of her outstretched arm and clucked under his breath. "I guess I'm not as well oriented to Charleston as I had thought."

It was a perfectly acceptable explanation. He was a newcomer, and the heart of old Charleston was a veritable maze of narrow alleys and quirky eighteenth-century streets. Still, there was something about his excuse that seemed almost too plausible, too smooth—something that kept Dani on her guard.

She retracted her arm, again circumventing one of the well-defined shoulders that hemmed her in beside the jewelry store. She glanced at her watch and then scooted to one side, stepping around McCabe. "Oh, dear! I've got to be going."

"Where are you headed?" McCabe didn't hesitate to fall in step with her.

Dani told herself that only the rankest paranoid would bristle at such an innocuous question. "I have to buy some supplies for a party I'm catering tomorrow evening."

"Need a bartender?"

"No, I'm afraid I already have one lined up." Dani picked up her pace slightly and then caught herself. If she wanted to slough off Ken McCabe, she would have to think of a more clever strategy than outrunning him.

Ken snapped his fingers in disappointment. "Well, I hope you'll keep me in mind for the future."

"So you're going to be staying in Charleston?" Dani asked, neatly avoiding a response to his request.

Ken's dark blue eyes traveled up to the corridor's arched ceiling. "Yeah, I think I'm going to stick around and see what happens." His gaze drifted down the time-weathered walls, finally settling on Dani with the graceful precision of an eagle grasping its prey.

"Good." Dani's frown contradicted her comment, and she hastily adjusted her face to a more neutral expression. If she looked at the matter realistically, she was being silly to get so uptight with McCabe. His barrage of questions at the funeral had irritated her, but he had been very kind and supportive on Saturday night when she had needed it most. And if he was one of the last people to see Richardson Whyte alive, well, so was she. "Where did you move here from anyway?" she asked in a more cordial tone.

Ken took a deep breath. "I've lived all over the place."

Dani waited for him to say more, anything to augment that pitifully ambiguous offering.

As if he sensed Dani's perplexity, Ken chuckled. "My last semipermanent roost was in Panama City. Ever been down there?"

Dani shook her head.

"It's nice, especially in the off-season. And as you can imagine, a good place for bartenders. I worked Duffy's, The Sandpiper, Coconut Joe's, all the good places."

"Why did you leave, if I may ask?"

McCabe shrugged. "Boredom. Wanderlust. An itch to try something new." His wide mouth curved into a self-deprecating grin. "I guess that sounds pretty shiftless to an established businesswoman like you."

"No, not really." Dani allowed him a noncommittal smile. She sensed that Ken's last remark, along with his ingenuous grin, was calculated to disarm her—a task that, under other circumstances, would not have been too difficult to achieve. He was very attractive, she had to admit, with the lean, athletic good looks and relaxed manner she found especially appealing in a man. *All the more reason not to ignore my more reliable instincts,* Dani warned herself.

They had reached the end of the pedestrian corridor and were facing the narrow lane separating the Exchange from the enclosed market stalls. As Dani prepared to cross the street, she turned to Ken. "If you're still interested in Evangelina's, you're going the wrong way."

Ken pulled himself up short at the edge of the curb. "So I am. Well, thanks for the directions. And for your company." His hand nicked his brow in a jaunty salute.

"Good luck," Dani called to him as she cut a diagonal path across the street to the coffee shop. A delivery truck pulling away from the curb blocked her view of McCabe;

when she again surveyed the street corner through Canfield's etched glass door, he had disappeared.

An itinerant bartender with a propensity for amateur sleuthing was the least of her worries Dani told herself later that day as she stored her purchases in the Moveable Feast's pantry and then began to prepare appetizers for the upcoming dinner party. The murder of a close family friend was enough to undermine anyone's sense of security, not least of all when the perpetrator could easily have been one of the victim's guests. The thought still made her shiver as she slid the last tray of homemade dinner rolls into the kitchen's big commercial refrigerator before heading home for the evening.

Normally, Dani regarded her well-kept condo as a haven from the pressures of a highly competitive business. Tonight, however, the quiet that normally soothed her nerves seemed to amplify the troubling questions plaguing her. She selected a few CDs of soft background music to fill the void while she nibbled the two slices of leftover quiche she had saved for dinner. As she tidied up the kitchen afterward, she toyed with the idea of phoning one of her friends. Several of her boon companions had called to express sympathy and offer their support. Joan Bradley, her long-time tennis partner, had even invited her to spend the next few days at her house, in case Dani didn't want to be alone.

As she glanced over the list of people whose numbers were programmed into her phone, however, Dani could imagine the well-meaning counsel her friends would offer. "Just try to put those horrible memories out of your mind." "You wouldn't believe modern investigative technology. The police are certain to solve the case." "Maybe you ought to take a few days' vacation, get away from it all for a while." No, anyone who hadn't shared her experience would be incapable of understanding her present frame of mind. The telephone number penciled in a bold hand on the refrigerator's notepad reminded Dani of the one person she knew who had not only gone through Saturday evening's nightmare, but would also be willing to talk about it with her. And she was not going to call Ken McCabe.

Dani was riffling through the collection of CDs stored in the bookcase when she chanced to notice a leather-bound volume sandwiched between two art books. In her excitement, she dropped the disc she had just selected to tug the photo album out of the shelves. So much time had passed since she had leafed through the black paper pages, had looked at the scallop-edged snapshots and yellowed newspaper clippings. She supposed she had avoided the album in part because it had awakened such bittersweet memories for her mother. Only as a teen had Dani realized that the numerous gaps between pictures were her mother's handiwork; after Dan Blake's death, his widow had excised every memento of her lost husband's passion for sailing.

Still, Richardson Whyte had sailed with her father. If the tiny yacht pin had any connection to their mutual interest, perhaps the album would yield a clue to its exact nature.

Dani hurried to her desk and flicked on the pharmacy lamp, the better to scrutinize the fading snapshots. She had examined the album twice before she was willing to admit how thoroughly her grief-stricken mother had purged all remnants of the sailing team. Only one picture of Richardson and Dani's father remained, two then-youthful faces in a group posed on what appeared to be the terrace of a resort hotel or a country club. Dani squinted over the black-and-white photo and quickly realized the futility of trying to pick a minuscule pin out of the grainy shot.

Only the shimmer of water in the picture's background drew her back for another look. It wasn't such a long shot to assume that the men had been photographed at their yacht club; they were dressed in the deck shoes and scalding-white ducks of yachtsmen. Dani studied a third man among the assembly, trying to place the vaguely familiar boxy jaw and aquiline nose. Theo Boynton, Rebecca's fiancé, would have been in diapers, not cotton ducks, when this snapshot was taken, but his face bore a startling resemblance to the hawklike countenance in the picture.

"Powell Boynton!" Dani exclaimed aloud. Of course, it was him, Theo's father! He had been a pallbearer at Richardson's funeral and had known her father as well. Based on the picture, Dani felt almost certain the senior Boynton had either been a member of the sailing team or would know quite a bit about it.

Closing the album's cracked leather cover, Dani pushed back from the desk. Now, at least, she had something to go on, a thread, however tenuous, that might lead to the significance of Richardson's gift to her. She would phone Powell Boynton first thing in the morning and arrange to talk with him as soon as possible.

She must be very tactful in her approach, Dani reminded herself as she changed into a nightgown. Chances were the poor man, like Bea Lawes, had already been thoroughly grilled by the police. She need only remind herself of how Ken McCabe's probing had irritated her to empathize with Powell Boynton.

The thought of McCabe resurrected a host of conflicting feelings in Dani, but the threat of another sleepless night prompted her to take action. She had managed to unearth a lead regarding the elusive pin. By comparison, getting information about Ken McCabe should be a cakewalk.

Seated on the side of her bed with the phone in her lap, Dani thought for a few minutes. What were the names of the restaurants where McCabe had worked in Florida? One had been The Sandpiper; she was sure of that. Another was called Coconut Joe's; no one could forget such a corny name. And Duffy's, she thought exultantly; that was the third place. Armed with pencil and paper, Dani dialed Panama City's information.

"I'm sorry, but I don't show a listing for Duffy's."

Dani bit her lip. Perhaps she hadn't gotten the name right, after all. Rather than go through a litany of Snuffy's-Tuffy's-McGuffy's with the long-distance operator, she decided to try Coconut Joe's. Her misgivings eased slightly as she noted the number. As soon as she had jotted down the listing for The Sandpiper, Dani tapped the receiver's button and then dialed the number. She had to listen to a Muzak version of "Let It Be" while she waited for the restaurant manager to come to the line.

"You need a reference for someone named Ken McCabe?" The manager sounded dubious. "I'm sorry, but no one by that name has worked here. But then, I've only been in this job for the past three years. He could have tended bar before my time," the woman added encouragingly.

"Thank you anyway." Dani felt her heart sinking as she clicked the button and then dialed the remaining number on her notepad.

"*M-C-C-A-B-E*, you say?" Coconut Joe's manager spelled the name after her. "Nope, sure haven't heard of him."

"Could he possibly have tended bar before you started working at Coconut Joe's?" Dani felt obligated to ask.

The man guffawed as if she had just cracked a hilarious joke. "Lady, I *am* Coconut Joe!"

Chapter Five

Patience had never been Ken McCabe's strong suit, and this morning, his personal supply of the virtue was running even lower than usual. Every minor irritation—a shaving nick, a broken shoe lace, a stalled tour bus blocking Market Street—had seemed the work of a perverse demon, calculated to frustrate him when he had the least time to waste. And Ken had felt as if he had been counting the moments since hanging up the phone after Dani Blake had called last night.

She had been so guarded, so close-mouthed during their last encounter in the Old Exchange, Ken had never expected to hear her soft, clear voice when he picked up the phone. He had been even more startled by the bombshell she dropped in his lap. "I've discovered some disturbing information that I need to discuss with you," she had announced.

So far, Ken's investigation of the murder had yielded little more than idle gossip and a memorably unpleasant standoff with Bea Lawes. In light of the way his luck had been going, Dani's revelation seemed heaven sent. As if to bait his anticipation even further, however, she had refused to talk on the phone, insisting that they meet the following morning in Battery Park. His brief experience with her had taught Ken that trying to bully Dani Blake was counterproductive, and he had resigned himself to her terms.

The park facing Charleston's harbor was peaceful at this hour of the morning, the foot traffic passing beneath the embowering live oaks confined to early-rising tourists and a few nannies trundling baby carriages along the paths. As she had promised, Dani was waiting for him on a bench near the war memorial. She had worn her hair down over her shoulders; in the clear sunlight, it flowed back from her smooth brow like a swirling eddy of molten bronze. Despite his haste, Ken paused, indulging himself for a moment in the beauty of her classical profile and that magnificent hair.

When she caught sight of him, he hurried to meet her. "I hope you haven't been waiting too long. There was a damned bus marooned in Market Street."

Dani didn't smile, and something told Ken that the anger reflected in her hazel eyes had nothing to do with his tardiness. "Please sit down." Given her cold tone, she might as well have dispensed with the word *please*. She gestured, rather peremptorily, to the opposite end of the bench.

Ken eased onto the edge of the bench, still watching Dani as if she were holding a gun on him. Whatever he had expected from this meeting, this was definitely not it.

"All right, Ken. I know you've been lying to me and I want to know why."

Ken swallowed hard and looked out across the rough blue water surging along the quay. *How the hell did you find out?*

As if she had read his mental question, Dani went on. "I phoned those restaurants where you said you had worked in Panama City. One of them doesn't exist, and when I asked for a reference on you at the other two places, no one had ever heard of you. I suppose your name *is* Ken McCabe, or did you make that up, too?"

Ken threw up his hands in exasperation. "Wait a minute, Dani! I can explain."

Arms folded across the front of her royal blue sweater, she nodded curtly. "Please do. That's why we're here right now."

"First of all, I really am Ken McCabe." Ken drew a deep breath and warily regarded the woman seated across from him. For all her fresh-faced beauty, she looked as unmoved as the granite statue overshadowing them. Weaseling out of this predicament with anything less than a full confession was not going to be easy. "But I'm not a bartender, at least, not by profession. When you said you'd never been to Panama City, I thought I was safe rattling off the names of a few restaurants I remembered from a vacation years ago."

He tried to gauge her reaction while he wrestled with his own indecision. At this point, his options seemed pitifully limited. He could fabricate another cover, but it would only be a matter of time until she found him out again. Dani had already proved she was too perceptive to fall for the usual ploys. If he told her the truth, however, he risked jeopardizing his entire investigation. Looking into the appraising hazel eyes, Ken realized that regardless of the hazards, the latter alternative was his only real choice.

He studied his hands clasped between his knees, hoping that the truth would sound plausible. "I work for a company called Associated Security. I'm what they call a 'security specialist.' The night Richardson was murdered, I was supposed to be protecting him from a blackmailer."

Dani's lovely face contracted into a horrified frown. "*Blackmail?* What do you mean?"

Ken suddenly felt almost too weary to nod, certainly too stress worn to carry on his subterfuge with her any longer. "Richardson had received a threatening note a few weeks earlier, demanding a half million dollars. His friend, Derek

Cannaday, had used Associated Security in his business, and I was sent in to appraise the situation.''

Her face still drawn in perplexity, Dani interrupted. ''If someone was trying to extort money from him, why didn't Richardson just go to the police?''

Ken's sigh was laden with regret. ''You know the Whytes with their old-family pride. They wanted to keep this thing quiet and settle it with as little outside involvement as possible. To be honest, though, when I saw the blackmail note, I thought we were dealing with a harmless crank. It was pasted up from letters cut out of magazines, with real melodramatic wording, just like the ransom notes you see in old movies. God, was I ever wrong!'' He rubbed his eyes, for a moment blotting out the incongruously cheerful sunlight.

Dani had unfolded her arms and leaned forward slightly. ''So you're investigating the murder now?'' Mercifully, her voice had lost much of its hard edge.

''Yeah. I persuaded Derek to let me stay on. I just can't walk away, not after what happened. It's one thing when you botch a job and people lose money, but Richardson—'' He broke off, unable to bring himself to repeat the self-recrimination that by now had become a personal mantra.

''I don't think you should blame yourself, Ken. After all, you weren't the only person who didn't take this threatening letter all that seriously. But I understand how you feel. I don't know how many times I've asked myself if Richardson would still be alive today had I gone upstairs just a few seconds sooner. That's why I'm determined to find out what he meant by giving me the pin.''

Ken looked up at Dani. The sharp morning light highlighted the green and gold flecks in her eyes, giving them an iridescent quality. ''So you're conducting an investigation of your own?''

She nodded, a little reluctantly, he thought, but then, they both were still testing the waters. One thing was certain: someone as bright and determined as Dani Blake would make a valuable ally, if she could be persuaded to share whatever she knew with him. Then, too, he was honest enough to admit that working with such an attractive woman would not be a distasteful task.

"Maybe we should consider that old saw 'two heads are better than one.' I'd be willing to let you in on whatever I manage to uncover." It was a big concession, but somehow, Ken didn't think he would regret it. "And you have connections with a lot of folks in this town who wouldn't give me the time of day, some of Richardson's guests, for instance. You could get me the access I need to make progress."

She didn't answer right away, and Ken guessed she was dealing with the same sort of quandary he had confronted. "Some of those people are my friends, Ken. I've catered parties in their homes. They trust me," she hedged. "I don't know how I would feel working behind their backs."

"One of them might also be a murderer," he reminded her.

Dani squared her shoulders, the better to meet the unsavory possibility head on. "You're right. Okay, I'll help you if you'll help me. Where do we start?"

Ken was a little startled by her matter-of-fact approach. Although he loathed the chauvinistic attitude that equated female beauty with indecisiveness, rarely had he found a hard-nosed business client this resolute and ready to take action.

"Well, I guess that depends on what either of us has done so far." In an effort to demonstrate his commitment to candor, Ken went on. "I tried to talk with Richardson's aunts yesterday afternoon. The older one, Adele, is apparently too senile to even know there's been a murder, but

Sapphira, the younger, is as lucid as you or I. Unfortunately, I never got past her first line of defense. It seems Bea Lawes has taken up the protection of the Whyte family's privacy as her personal crusade. What a banshee!''

Dani smiled for the first time during their tense conversation. "She was probably primed for you, since I had already locked horns with her that morning. I did manage a brief chat with Richardson's housekeeper. She told me what the man who called Richardson prior to the murder had said, something about wanting to talk with Mr. Whyte if he wasn't taking the little drama too seriously."

"You think he meant the Ghostwalk vignette?"

Dani twisted a strand of burnished auburn hair around her finger, considering his question. "Yes, I think so. Of course, there may be no connection at all between the phone call and the murder, but after Richardson talked with that person—whoever he was—he went upstairs for some reason. I guess it's a long shot, but I'm curious to know what the caller could have meant by his comment."

"With so little to go on, I don't think we can afford to rule out any suspicious information, regardless of how flimsy it may seem."

Dani looked pleased that he hadn't brushed her hunch aside as ill-founded or amateurish. "I've already thought of a way to find out more about that particular skit. The guy who's tending bar for me at the party tonight is an actor. He does TV commercials and small movie parts mostly, but I'm sure he can put me in touch with the right people connected with the Ghostwalk. Maybe if we know more about that particular vignette's content, the caller's remark will make more sense."

For some reason, Ken liked the way she said "we." "Good thinking. What about the stickpin? Any luck there?"

Dani released the twisted curl to shove the sleeves of her sweater up her arms. "Richardson and my father sailed together. My guess is that the pin has something to do with their team. Last night, I just realized that Powell Boynton knew both men and may even have sailed with them. Actually, I had planned to call Powell this morning."

"I'm afraid he's out of bounds for the time being. I wanted to talk with him, too, since he was such a close friend of Richardson's. We had an appointment yesterday morning, but when I arrived at his office, his secretary told me he had suffered a heart attack only a few hours after Richardson's funeral. He's in intensive care right now, no visitors allowed."

Dani's hand shot up to her mouth. "Oh, my God! I suppose it was the strain of everything this past weekend. Have you heard how he's doing?"

Frustrated as they both were by the dearth of reliable informants, Ken was struck by Dani's compassion. "His condition is listed as stable, but Derek says they think he's going to pull through. In the meantime, I plan to learn as much about the other people on that guest list as I possibly can."

Dani thought for a moment. "There's another option, as far as the pin is concerned. I could go directly to the yacht club that Richardson and my father belonged to. Of course, the pin may have nothing to do with the club, but at least I could rule out that possibility." She hesitated for a second before adding, "You could come with me if you think it would be worth your time."

"That's just the kind of entrée I've been looking for." Ken paused, his enthusiasm suddenly tempered by another consideration. "Uh, not that I want you to bend the truth on my behalf, but I'd prefer that these yacht-club people didn't know a security man was snooping around the premises. On second thought, maybe I should let you handle this one on your own," he conceded reluctantly.

He was heartened by how quickly she protested. "We needn't announce your identity through a bullhorn. And we won't have to lie, either. You can simply come along as someone who works with me in the catering business, which is technically true. We've driven out to the club to get some ideas for parties to coincide with the regatta. I'll let them know I'm Dan Blake's daughter, of course, but we're there on business. Okay?"

"It's fine with me," Ken was happy to agree. "You haven't kept up with the yacht club over the years?" Given Richardson's glowing account of Dan Blake's sailing prowess, he was surprised that Dani seemed so unfamiliar with the club and its activities.

"After the accident, Mother swore she'd never set foot in the club again. She kept her word." Dani looked down at her lap, toying with a tiny leaf that had snagged on her corduroy skirt. "I was just a toddler when it all happened, but she never would talk about the club or the boat or sailing, anything even remotely connected with the accident."

"I didn't realize you had been so young. So you don't really remember your dad?" The moment he had spoken, Ken felt like the proverbial bull in a china shop, lumbering his clumsy way onto alien turf.

"No, I don't. When I try to recall his face, there's nothing there. Except what I've seen in pictures." She carefully brushed the little leaf from her lap, avoiding Ken's gaze.

She looked so fragile, so alone in her sadness. Without thinking, Ken reached to gently graze her shoulder with the back of his hand. Given the nature of his business, he had conditioned himself to grapple with hard practicalities, leaving the finer emotional points for others to take care of. If his gesture had seemed awkward to Dani, however, she was too gracious to show it.

She smiled—for his benefit, he was certain—and then straightened herself. "I'll call the yacht club today and see if we can drive out sometime this week. How does your schedule look?"

"Open for whatever you can cook up. I need to touch base with Derek, but he's usually pretty flexible."

"Good. I'm going to be busy with this party today, but I'll see what I can work out." Dani stood, signaling that their meeting was drawing to a close. But as she started for the street, she gave him a smile guaranteed to linger with him until their next rendezvous.

"Call me." Ken had raised his voice to be heard over the distance, echoing his parting comment on Saturday night.

Dani only threw up her hand in a brief wave, but this time, Ken had no doubt he would hear from her.

"LOOKS LIKE WE CAN chalk up another success for Moveable Feast. Home team, one—competition, zero." Ben Carlisle's warm brown eyes swept the milling crowd as he shook out a clean napkin and began to polish glasses.

Dani chuckled at the bartender's complimentary humor. "Just remember that you're the ace forward for my team," she reminded him. All evening, she had been waiting for the party to taper off, giving her a chance to chat with Ben. She nodded cordially to a clutch of guests, waiting for them to pass before she leaned over the bar. "By the way, Ace, I've got a favor to ask."

Ben grinned, holding a champagne flute up for a sharp-eyed inspection. "Shoot, lady."

"Do you know anybody involved with the Ghostwalk?"

Ben's eyes narrowed mysteriously. "Well, as a matter of fact, I happen to be very well acquainted with one of the actors. Why do you ask?"

"I'd like to know more about a vignette they're doing this year, the historical background of the legend and all that.

Do you think this friend of yours would be willing to help me with some research? I mean, if you were to ask him.''

A pleased smile curved inside Ben's neatly trimmed beard. ''Why don't you ask him yourself?'' He flourished the napkin and then bowed slightly. ''At your service, madame.''

''You? But I thought you had sworn off doing fundraisers.''

Ben looked slightly offended. ''You're a caterer, but you still cook an occasional free meal for your friends, right?'' he pointed out.

Dani laughed and shook her head. ''I see what you mean. Okay, when can you tell me about one of those ghost legends?''

''Actually, you'd probably do better to talk with the event's stage director,'' Ben advised her. ''I'm only familiar with the Bedstead tomb legend, which I'm acting in, but Kate knows all the stories inside out. I'm sure she'd be glad to answer your questions if you came to rehearsal with me tomorrow.''

Dani noted the time and location of the rehearsal on a paper cocktail napkin. As soon as she had checked the desserts arranged on the dining room credenza and made sure Elaine had the coffee service under control, she headed back to the kitchen. She dug her address book out of her handbag and dialed Ken's number, willing him to pick up before Elaine returned.

Ken sounded tired, but happy to hear from her.

''Mark your calendar. I have an appointment with the social director of the yacht club on Friday at noon. And tomorrow afternoon at three, my actor friend is taking us along to a rehearsal of the Ghostwalk troupe.''

Ken's receiver thumped against a hard surface, and Dani could hear some rustling in the background. ''Let's see.'' Ken's voice sounded as if his mouth was squashed against the telephone's mouthpiece. "Noon on Friday is fine, but I'm afraid I have to meet Derek tomorrow afternoon before he goes out of town."

Dani was surprised by how disappointed she felt, but she did her best to conceal it. "That's too bad."

"Call me tomorrow evening and let me know what you learn."

"I'm catering a retirement banquet, so it may be rather late when I get home." Dani realized she was beginning to sound as if she were dodging his questions again, the last thing she had in mind at this point.

"Then you can fill me in on everything Friday morning," Ken suggested amiably. "I could use a good meaty chunk of solid information. Believe me, I'm starting to get a little numb, digging through this guest list of perfectly decent, upstanding citizens whose criminal connections don't extend beyond traffic court." When he laughed, Dani could imagine the little lines crinkling at the corners of his mouth, relieving for a few seconds the intense cast of his face.

Elaine had just bumped the service cart over the kitchen threshold and was beginning to load the dishwasher. With cups, sauces and cutlery rattling in her ears, Dani hastily promised to phone Ken and then hung up. As she stored leftovers in the hostess's refrigerator and gathered up her own equipment, however, she had to fight a peculiar letdown feeling that had nothing to do with fatigue.

She had really been looking forward to seeing Ken tomorrow afternoon, Dani admitted to herself later that evening, after she had returned home and was preparing for bed. Of course, less than twenty-four hours ago, he had been the object of her darkest suspicions. After discovering his bogus connections in Panama City, she had been ready to believe the worst about him. When she had called to demand a meeting, she had even taken care to arrange it in a well-trafficked public spot. With a murderer on the loose, she hadn't been ready to take any chances.

Her elaborate precautions now seemed amusing. Then, too, Dani was relieved that her mixed impressions of Ken had not been all that unreliable. His ineptitude behind the bar and his persistent questioning at the funeral had raised doubts in her mind, and she had been right. By the same token, perhaps she had judged his motives accurately when he had escorted her home, offered comfort and support in those dark hours. Unfortunately, there was no one she could call to confirm that aspect of his psyche one way or the other.

Nor should it matter how Ken felt about her, she told herself the following day as she waited for Ben in a bookstore not far from the theater. She had enough serious concerns without letting a momentary attraction siphon her concentration.

When Dani joined Ben on the sidewalk, she noticed that his dark face was still coated with a thick layer of Pan-Cake makeup. He caught her bemused expression immediately. "Anything for art," he professed, dabbing at his brow with a tissue. "Or a car-dealership commercial." He grinned as he turned into an alley and then pushed open the theater's creaky stage door.

The air was close in the ill-lighted corridor. Dani pressed against the wall to allow two men lugging a planter of artificial boxwoods to pass and then jogged up the steps after Ben. Groups of actors were scattered around the big, barnlike theater. Some were lolled in the auditorium's red velvet seats, reading from scripts, while others clustered near the stage footlights to watch the scene being rehearsed. As she followed Ben along the front of the pit, Dani was surprised to overhear a few unmistakable lines from *A Streetcar Named Desire* coming from the stage.

"I didn't know Blanche DuBois and Stanley Kowalski were Charleston ghosts," she whispered.

The actor's well-defined shoulders shook with mirth. "The Ghostwalk performers are just one of the troupes sharing this space. Several community-theater groups hold their rehearsals here, too. Hey, Katie!" He threw up his hand in greeting to a woman dressed in jeans and a knee-length turtleneck. "Kate, I'd like for you to meet Dani Blake. Dani, this is Kate McPherson, fairy godmother to this year's Ghostwalk."

Kate's bright blue eyes twinkled behind her large tortoiseshell glasses when she shook Dani's hand. "Ben tells me you're interested in learning more about one of the legends we've chosen to enact this year." As Ben loped away to join three actors in Revolutionary War regalia, Kate sauntered toward the wooden steps leading backstage.

Stepping over cables and around backdrops, Dani followed Kate into a tiny cubicle furnished with a gray metal desk, two file cabinets and a threadbare swivel chair. The dingy furniture was relieved by colorful theatrical posters covering the walls from ceiling to floor. "Yes. I'd like to know the story behind the vignette performed at Richardson Whyte's house last Saturday."

The woman's merry smile instantly faded. "What a horrible tragedy! Of course, we've dropped that house for the festival's remaining nights. Although we've given the actors the chance to participate in other vignettes, some of them are still too shaken to go on. Actors are a superstitious lot, you know. I have to admit the thought of what happened to poor Mr. Whyte gives me chills. To think that while the actors were feigning a murder, one was—was actually taking place." Despite her bulky sweater, Kate shivered.

"That's why I'd like to know more about the ghost story." Catching the stage director's dubious expression,

Dani realized how morbid her request must sound, but she was determined not to reveal the clue she had gleaned from Mona Sams. Like Ken, she believed the less they publicized their investigation, the better. "I catered Mr. Whyte's party that evening and was questioned by the police later. I couldn't be sure if some of the screams I heard had come from the actors, but if I knew the story, maybe I could offer the police a clearer account."

Kate folded her arms across her chest, propping one hip against the edge of the desk. "The house was built in 1788, by a wealthy sea captain. He was a self-made man, a new kid on the block, if you will, among his neighbors of longer standing in the city. Joshua Parr—that was the ill-fated gentleman's name—had earned his riches running the profitable rum-and-indigo route from Charleston to Jamaica to England and back. Some say he sweetened the pot with a bit of piracy on the side, but whatever the case, by the latter part of the eighteenth century, he was well-heeled enough to woo Abigail Huntington, the beautiful daughter of a prominent rice planter, and build that big house for her."

Kate gazed up at the ceiling as if she were visualizing the story projected onto the peeling plaster. "Problem was, Joshua had to keep going to sea to ensure the hefty income such an expensive wife and home required. Consequently, Abigail was left alone for months on end. Joshua was accustomed to buying whatever he needed and quite naturally thought he could purchase the necessary diversions to occupy his young wife in his absence. He filled the parlor with exotic birds for her amusement. A harp was imported from Italy, along with a lady to instruct Mrs. Parr in its use. Thanks to her husband's extended voyages and the hobbies he subsidized, Abigail Parr became proficient in watercolor, French and the breeding of spaniels. But it was her dance lessons that were to be everyone's downfall. You see, Abigail fell in love with her dance master."

"The murderer in the legend?" Dani interjected.

Kate's smile was enigmatic. "That depends on whose version you believe. Some say the young fellow was so consumed with passion, he challenged Captain Parr to a duel and won. Others claim Abigail had a hand in the plot to murder her sleeping husband in his bed. At any rate, both accounts of the murder agree on one point—whoever killed Joshua Parr covered his nefarious deed by dumping the corpse from the breakwater at the precise point where the Ashley and the Cooper rivers meet to flow out to sea. Just as he himself had in life, Joshua's unquiet spirit now sails a phantom ship, returning regularly from the sea to visit his young wife—or whoever may be occupying the house he built for her."

Dani nodded slowly. Although she needed more time to consider the strange tale from all angles, the ghost's nautical connections seemed to tie in too closely with the tiny ship pin to be strictly coincidental. She would be eager to see if Ken drew the same conclusion. "What about the screams I heard?" she asked, harking back to her professed interest in the story. "Were they from the actual murder or the subsequent haunting?"

"There is quite a bit of shouting while Joshua duels with Abigail's lover. We chose the duel version because the swordplay lends itself well to dramatization and, well, frankly we thought it less sordid than the wife-lover conspiracy," Kate confessed. She pushed away from the desk, giving the hem of her slouchy sweater a tug. "I love delving into the old legends. I only wish this one hadn't acquired such dreadful associations in the present. I hope I've been able to help you clarify your testimony for the police, anything to bring the murderer to justice. You know, if you'd like, I could lend you a videotape of the vignette's dress rehearsal. I don't have one here right now, but . . ." When the desk phone jingled, she grimaced apologetically. "Hello? Yes, can you hold on a second please?"

"I'd really appreciate a chance to review that video-tape," Dani told her.

Kate put a muffling hand over the receiver. "I'll be here around lunch tomorrow, if you can drop by to pick it up."

"I have an appointment at the yacht club tomorrow at noon. Could I arrange to get the tape later?"

"I teach drama classes all afternoon and into the evening. Tell you what. Why don't I give the tape to Ben and you can get it from him?" she whispered loudly, sliding her hand away from the mouthpiece.

Dani lip-synched goodbye and another thank-you to Kate as she turned to go. Ben would be in the middle of rehearsal now; rather than interrupt him, she would phone his apartment and leave an appreciative message on his answering machine. But the first order of business when she got home was to write down every detail of the Joshua Parr legend while it was still fresh in her mind. Kate was an excellent storyteller, and Dani wanted Ken to have the full benefit of her narrative. That they would be able to review the tape of the performance together was an unexpected bonus.

Dani was so wrapped in her thoughts, she almost failed to notice a pair of boots just visible beneath the bottom edge of the partially open office door. Someone was standing close to the door, too close to be simply loitering, close enough to overhear every word of a conversation in the office. Dani halted just inside the doorway and waited to see what the boots would do. She watched as they took a step, hesitated, then took another step. They seemed to be mirroring her motions, anticipating her next move.

Suddenly, Dani stepped through the door. As the man strode away, she could see only his back. The hem of his dark cape furled open to reveal legs encased in knee breeches and leather boots. Over the cape's high collar, she glimpsed the knotted tail of a peruke protruding from beneath a tricorn hat. Dani pulled up short, bridling her initial mistrustful impulses. What proof did she have, really, that the actor had been eavesdropping? More likely, he had only been waiting to talk with Kate McPherson and had grown impatient with the delay.

Dani would have convinced herself that the caped actor hadn't the vaguest interest in her conversation with Kate if his own curiosity had not gotten the best of him. But as he glanced over his shoulder, Dani got a brief yet all-too-clear view of Stephen Lawes's face.

Chapter Six

Ken crossed his legs and refolded his arms across his chest, trying to adjust his rebellious body to the leather armchair's unyielding frame. He had known Derek would want to look over the background material he had gathered on Richardson's guests, but watching the man pore over the copious handwritten notes was grating on his nerves nonetheless. The realization that Dani Blake might at that very moment be garnering useful information from the Ghostwalk's stage director—without him—did nothing to soothe his impatience. Ken lunged forward in the chair when Derek at last looked up from the notes.

The older man couldn't hide his dejection as he ran his fingers through his thinning gray hair. "You've done a very thorough job, Ken," he said.

Ken was out of his seat, unable to curb his nervous energy any longer. "A very thorough job of uncovering nothing. No grudges, no rivalries, not a damn thing that would motivate any of those people to kill Richardson Whyte." He paced the length of the desk, feeling like a wild creature contained in a much too small cage. "I know no investigation is complete without this kind of background work, but since I've drawn a blank in that area, I'd like to try something else."

Derek rolled his chair away from the desk, tipping the seat back on its axis. "What do you have in mind?"

Ken wheeled to study the weary-looking man seated behind the desk. Derek took a conservative approach to investigation; it was anyone's guess how he would react to the revelation that Dani Blake was now aware of the extortion threat and their efforts to thwart it. "I have a lead, through Dani Blake."

Ken was heartened by the interest reflected in Derek's gray eyes. "So you've gained her confidence?"

"Believe me, it wasn't easy. I had to tell her who I am, Derek, and about the blackmail note."

Derek's fingers formed a steeple in front of his pursed lips. "Do you think that was wise?"

"Under the circumstances, yes." Ken planted his hands on the desk to face Derek squarely. "I think there's something to her hunch about that stickpin, that Richardson gave it to her for a reason. Apparently her father and Whyte sailed together. That would tie in with the pin shaped like a boat. Do you know anything about their yacht team?"

Derek's thin cheeks inflated for a moment as he let out a long breath. "That was a long time ago, and I have to confess I never shared their passion for boats. I was a landlubber, and they were the adventurers on the high seas." He chuckled wistfully and then sobered. "After the accident that took Dan, the team disbanded. They felt the boat was cursed, and nobody wanted anything to do with the sport. Especially Richardson."

"Richardson was particularly close to Dan Blake, I suppose." Derek's last remark had aroused Ken's curiosity.

Derek swung the chair upright, suddenly glancing up. "He felt responsible for Dan's death." He paused, waiting for his companion to absorb the full impact of his words.

"Why?" Ken demanded.

Derek focused blankly on the papers strewed across the desk. "I've never told anyone this before...." He hesitated for a lengthy second. When he looked up at Ken, his face was grave. "For all I know, I may be the only person Richardson ever opened up to on the matter. Even now that he's...no longer with us, I feel as if I'm betraying his confidence. You see, Richardson had been drinking on the boat the day of the accident. When the squall came up, he was in no condition to deal with it. Dan insisted he remain below deck, but that left the team a man short. I always counseled Richardson that his presence on deck would not have saved Dan, that he shouldn't blame himself for what happened." His angular shoulders sank heavily. "But who knows, really?"

"Those doubts must have tortured Richardson Whyte for the rest of his life," Ken said. "Did any of Blake's survivors know about this?"

Derek's frown grew skeptical. "I don't think so. Both Dan's widow and his daughter seemed to think highly of Richardson—not the sort of opinion they would have if they held him accountable for their loved one's death. I don't think it would serve any purpose telling Dani Blake at this point," he added carefully.

Ken shook his head. "I'm going with Dani to the yacht club tomorrow morning, but I won't mention any of this to her."

"I know Richardson would have appreciated your discretion," Derek assured him.

Privately, Ken promised himself that he would take pains to shield Dani from such troublesome knowledge, if for no one's sake but her own. She had lost not only her natural father to a horrible tragedy, but also the man who, however limited their contact, had assumed the role of surrogate father in her life. To reveal Richardson's painful secret now would be an exercise in pointless cruelty.

HE HAD BEGUN TO FEEL protective toward Dani. Ken was not ashamed to admit that development to himself the next morning as he sat beside her in the van, content to leave the driving to her. Not that Dani was the helpless sort of woman who collapsed at the first whiff of stress—quite the contrary. In fact, she would probably bristle if she knew he intended to watch out for her, Ken reflected, glancing at her determined profile. Still, they were on a trail that could lead to a murderer. As the trained security professional, it was his job to stay alert—for both of them.

In spite of such somber considerations, Ken felt himself relax as the road wound through dense pine barrens, opening occasionally to reveal salt marshes that bordered the coast. He was accustomed to staying wound tight as a spring, coiled for action; it was a novel experience to ease back in the bucket seat, let his eyes half close behind his sunglasses and simply listen to Dani's animated narrative. There was something very sexy about her low voice, at once soft and resonant. For a fleeting moment, Ken wondered what it would sound like reduced to a whisper, at night, alone with her. He quickly caught himself and snapped to attention in his seat.

"What do you suppose Stephen Lawes was up to?" Dani frowned, swerving the van slightly to avoid a raccoon huddling on the edge of the road.

Ken considered her question for a moment. "I don't know. Nothing, maybe. You said the actors in the Joshua Parr vignette had been assigned to other reenactments, if they wanted to be. Assuming Lawes falls into that category, he could have had a perfectly legitimate reason to be waiting outside the director's office."

Dani shrugged as she flipped the turn signal. "I guess I may be trying too hard to link him with this awful business. Given Bea's fanatical devotion to Richardson, it does seem rather farfetched that her son would wish him any ill.

But there's something that bothers me about Stephen Lawes all the same.'' She glanced at Ken before wheeling the van onto a single-lane road prominently designated Private. Access Limited To Members Of The Breakers Yacht Club.

"Think they put that sign up for our benefit?" Ken remarked, eyeing the palmettoes that pressed the edge of the road like a row of sentries.

Smiling drily, Dani slowed the van as the road opened onto a sweeping vista of the yacht basin. "Don't worry. I'm accustomed to using the service entrance. I'm a caterer, remember."

Ken chuckled. "Good thing you reminded me, since I'm supposed to be your helper today. How did you get into this business in the first place?"

Dani pulled into the visitors' parking area and killed the engine. "As the saying goes, it's a *long* story, but I'll tell you sometime," she promised.

Ken climbed out of the van and stretched his legs, taking the opportunity to scan the club's impressively landscaped grounds. Dozens of sleek yachts dotted the rim of the sparkling blue cove, while a cultivated green sward spread from the marina to the clubhouse. With its white gingerbread woodwork and soaring turrets, the imposing building reminded Ken of a lavishly iced wedding cake.

Despite her wisecrack about using the back door, Dani went straight to the curving steps leading up to the clubhouse veranda. An attendant in crisply starched white coat and trousers greeted them cordially and then hurried to announce their arrival. Dani managed to wink at Ken just before Paul Crawford, the club's social director, appeared in the door.

"Miss Blake, what a pleasure to meet you!" The man beamed behind his horn-rim glasses as he pressed Dani's hand. Apparently, the name Blake still carried enough currency at The Breakers to guarantee its bearer a warm welcome.

"I've been looking forward to talking with you, Mr. Crawford, but first, I'd like for you to meet my assistant, Ken McCabe. Planning functions is one of Ken's specialties," she added, with a trace of mischief that entirely bypassed Crawford.

Despite his unexpected promotion in the Moveable Feast's organization—or more precisely, because of it—Ken made an effort to stay in the background while the social director escorted them through the clubhouse's various gathering rooms. The last thing he needed was to throw an inept monkey wrench into Dani's well-oiled presentation. And she was doing a masterful job with Crawford, asking questions she obviously knew the man would love to answer and complimenting him on the well-run facility. Only when they had adjourned to the sprawling terrace did she breach the topic of the pin.

"I happened across an old photograph of my father the other day that could have been taken from this very spot." Dani braced her hands on the white balustrade and gazed out at the vessels moored along the shore. "I imagine the club has changed a lot over the years, though."

"Not as much as you might think, at least not in the fifteen years I've been with the club." A look of avuncular interest played on Paul Crawford's sun-pink face as he joined Dani at the rail. "Time marches on, of course, but we at The Breakers pride ourselves on maintaining tradition. New boats are still christened with ceremony. We always open the regatta with the boats sailing up the waterway in formation. Some of the teams have even passed their jerseys down through the generations, father to son, for good luck, I suppose."

Dani turned, seating herself sideways on the rail to face Crawford. "What about insignia, caps, medals, things like that?"

Ken suspected that only he picked up on the tension masked by her light, conversational tone.

Crawford smiled, taking the question in stride. "You must be thinking of those little stickpins the teams used to wear."

Ken imagined a tremor passing the length of the balustrade between Dani and him. "Stickpins?" She deserved a medal of her own for managing to sound so ingenuous.

Crawford nodded, narrowing his eyes against the shards of sunlight reflected off the water. "Each team had its own special pin. They were really quite unique. The head would be in the shape of a yacht. The name of the boat was cast in gold and attached to the pin by a little chain. Sadly, that's one of the traditions that's fallen by the wayside in recent years. But I'm sure your father had one," he added delicately.

Dani's eyes followed the terrace floor's intricate brickwork pattern. "I wouldn't know. You see, I never learned much about my father's involvement with the club." Ken realized that she was not feigning the hesitancy in her voice.

Seasoned socializer that he was, Paul Crawford looked decidedly discomfited by the awkward turn their conversation had taken. "Well now, your father was a member a little before my time, so I don't suppose there's much I can tell you. They took his team's boat away shortly after I accepted this position."

Dani looked up. "Who took it?"

Crawford blinked nervously, as if he feared she held him personally responsible for the yacht. "Why, one of the team members did. Mr. Whyte, God rest his soul. The yacht was registered in his name at that time. He thought the boat was bad luck, but as far as I know, it's still docked at his summer home up on Trumbull Island.''

To her credit, Dani managed to prolong the conversation for a decent length of time, asking Crawford about the club's policy regarding outside caterers and mentioning several well-publicized events she had catered in the past. Ken did his part by reminding Dani to leave some business cards and urging Crawford to refer members to Moveable Feast. Not until they were safely inside the closed van did they dare discuss the pin.

''I knew it!'' Dani smacked the dashboard triumphantly. ''That pin must have been of tremendous sentimental value to Richardson. So much for Detective Butler's theory that it belonged to the murderer!''

Infectious as Dani's excitement was, Ken felt bound to play devil's advocate. ''We still don't know why Richardson gave it to you.''

''No,'' Dani conceded as she cranked the engine. ''We still have a puzzle, but we've just acquired a few extra pieces that I think may be critical to constructing the whole picture. We now know that the pin was Richardson's and that it harks back to the sailing team he and my father both belonged to.''

Ken adjusted the seat, stretching his legs as far as the van's compact cabin would permit. ''What I wouldn't give to have a look at that boat!''

The van jolted slightly as Dani braked at the end of the private road. ''Why don't we, then?''

''You mean pay a surprise visit to Richardson's summer house? But do you even know where it is?''

''No, but Trumbull Island can't be *that* big.'' She gave him a brash look that made Ken grateful they were both working on the same side.

''Let's go for it.'' He gripped the edge of the seat, steadying himself as Dani swung the van onto the road. They drove for several minutes without talking, and Ken guessed Dani, like himself, was mulling over the intriguing yet fragmented clues that had turned up. "You know, we've stumbled onto a lot of connections with sailing—even the Joshua Parr legend is woven around a sea captain."

Dani nodded, frowning into the glare burning through the windshield. "Richardson was a sailor, like Parr. And he was murdered. Somehow, that mysterious caller's remark about the 'little drama' seems too close to the mark to be coincidental."

Two weeks ago, Ken would never have believed that a ghost story would have been a pivotal element in any investigation he conducted. In the case of Richardson Whyte's murder, however, standard investigative procedure had gotten him nowhere. In fact, Dani Blake's hunches had yielded the only information that might legitimately qualify as clues so far. Under the circumstances, their search for an unlucky—or haunted—yacht did not seem all that ridiculous.

True to Dani's prediction, Trumbull proved to be a tiny barrier island whose population must have sunk to the double-digit level in the off-season. While Ken filled the van's gas tank at the island's only service station, Dani chatted with the attendant, who gave her directions to the Whyte family's secluded beachfront home.

"This place looks as if it might have a few ghosts of its own lurking about," Ken remarked after they had turned off the county road and followed an unpaved lane for a couple of miles.

His remark had been intended as a joke to lessen the tension they both felt, but given their surroundings, neither of them laughed. Dense woods, filled with darting shadows, enclosed the road from both sides, while Spanish moss drooping from the low branches caressed the van like shredded webs. Ken felt as if they had emerged from a suffocating tunnel when the wall of palmettoes and cypresses at last yielded to low dunes speckled with sea oats.

Richardson's rambling, blue-and-white house was just visible from the road, its upper deck jutting over the tops of the subtropical trees like the crow's nest of a clipper ship. The white-graveled drive forked around a shrubbery island, one branch leading to the house, the other down to the beachfront. At the sight of a red Mercedes convertible parked near the house, Dani slowed the van to a crawl.

"Looks like somebody is home," Ken remarked under his breath.

"We're not burglars," Dani reminded him, but Ken guessed the irritation in her voice stemmed from their shared disappointment. Like him, Dani had probably hoped they would find the house deserted, leaving them free to inspect the yacht unobserved.

As they climbed out of the van and started up the walk, they could hear the yapping of a small, ill-tempered dog from somewhere inside the house. The inhospitable creature's alarm had not gone unheeded, for the front door opened a crack before Dani could press the buzzer.

Rebecca Pope regarded them coolly from behind the screen door, while the frenzied Yorkie lunged around her ankles. As her appraising blue eyes settled on Ken, he smiled. The china-doll eyes widened, but she quickly checked her impulse to flirt, recalling, no doubt, that he was only a bartender.

"Hi, Rebecca! I didn't know if we'd find anyone here this late in the year." Dani raised her voice to be heard over the terrier's shrill barking.

"I simply had to get away from the city for a few days, to settle my nerves. First, Uncle Richardson, and now Theo's daddy in the hospital—" The crystal blue eyes closed momentarily on the world and its cruelties.

"I'm sorry to drop in unannounced," Dani apologized. This was Rebecca's cue to say "that's perfectly all right," but she only held up one splayed hand to blow on the freshly lacquered nails.

Dani apparently sensed that additional pleasantries would be wasted on Rebecca. "I made a business call at the yacht club today, and in the course of the conversation, Mr. Crawford mentioned that the yacht my father used to sail was docked here. I've never seen the boat, and, well, I just couldn't resist the temptation to stop by and have a look at it."

"Oh, *do* hush, Winston!" Rebecca glanced down at the choleric terrier. When she looked back at Dani, she seemed equally irritated with the two human beings standing on the porch. "I'm sorry to disappoint you," she said without the slightest trace of remorse, "but you'll have to talk with Theo about the yacht. Since he persuaded Uncle Richardson to let him restore the thing, he's been absolutely obsessed with that boat. He'd be furious with me if I let anyone tamper with it."

"I have no intention of tampering, Rebecca. I just want to see the boat." Ken could tell Dani was struggling to keep her temper in the face of Rebecca's capricious refusal.

"And I'm sure after you talk with Theo, he'll be happy to let you look all you want," Rebecca cut in. "Now, if you'll excuse me, dear. As it is, I'm rushing to make a hairdresser's appointment in Charleston, and I *hate* being late." Still mindful of the glossy nails, she nudged the door slightly with her knee.

"Thanks, Rebecca," Dani managed to say just before the door closed in her face.

"Rebecca and Bea Lawes must have graduated from the same charm school," Ken remarked after they had returned to the van. Frustrated as he knew she must be, he was pleased when Dani laughed.

"Rebecca and I have never been best friends, even though we're the same age and went to the same college." She sighed as she steered the van back onto the dirt road.

"So you went to Converse College, too?"

Dani cut her eyes at Ken. "I see you've done a background check on Rebecca."

"But not on you. Not yet," Ken added pointedly. This was such a grim business, putting people's lives under a microscope in hopes of finding a criminal germ; it was a welcome relief to engage in a little playful give-and-take with Dani. "Actually, anyone who wants to know about Rebecca Pope need only read the society pages for the past ten years. Except for a nominal job at an art gallery, Miss Pope seems to spend most her time being photographed at fashion shows and charity balls. Your life, on the other hand, would be harder to delve into, I imagine. It might require some direct questioning."

A smile quivered on the lovely face reflected in the windshield. "Is that a friendly warning or a serious threat?"

Ken evaded her question with a grin. "You did promise to tell me how you got into the catering business. Maybe we could work a deal. I take you to lunch today, and you tell me about yourself."

Conditioned as he was to considering every move from all angles, Ken had never allowed himself much spontaneity, even in the meager social life his haphazard career permitted. When they had left Charleston that morning, the investigation had been foremost in his mind, albeit one that he now had the pleasure of conducting with an extraordinarily attractive woman. He had harbored no intention of inveigling a social encounter with Dani. Still, the lunch invitation had popped out of his mouth so quickly, he realized it must have been simmering on some remote back burner in his mind.

Dani looked both ways before turning onto the paved public road, but she seemed to be considering more than the sparse traffic. "You don't have to bribe me, you know, but it might be a good idea to have a bite to eat on our way back to town, if we can find a place that's still serving lunch. It's already past three-thirty."

Both of them recalled passing a roadside diner not far from the Trumbull Island turnoff. Had it not been for a weather-worn billboard touting the best batter-fried shrimp in Beaufort County, they could easily have overlooked the squat, aqua-stucco building.

The pleasantly greasy smell of fried fish and a plaintive Randy Travis ballad playing on the jukebox greeted them as they entered the dining room. The lunch crowd had cleared out by now, leaving only a couple of older men lingering over lemon-meringue pie and coffee.

"Are you still serving lunch?" Dani asked the waitress, who was mopping one of the tabletops with a damp cloth.

"If we're open, we're cookin', hon," the woman assured her. "Just grab yourself a seat, and I'll be right with you."

Dani and Ken chose a table for two next to the streaky window and immediately pounced on the menus. They had been so keyed up, both had ignored the gnawing rumblings in their empty stomachs. Ken now realized that he was famished. Apparently, Dani was, too, for she seconded his order of jumbo shrimp with hush puppies and coleslaw.

"No pâté or escargot on this menu, I fear," Ken remarked after the waitress had delivered their iced tea and paper-napkin-wrapped silverware.

"That's fine with me," Dani assured him as she squeezed a lemon wedge over her tea. "I may serve a lot of fancy food in my business, but I enjoy simple fare, too, as long as it's fresh and well prepared. I can't stand food snobs. In fact, I'm not too crazy about any kind of snob."

Ken chuckled. Little wonder that Dani and Rebecca had rarely crossed paths at their alma mater. "You were going to tell me about yourself," he prompted her.

"The stakes have just gone up, I see." Dani smiled teasingly. "I thought I only had to tell you about my business in return for this lunch."

"What if I throw in dessert?" Ken shot back. His eyes lingered on her face, enjoying the play of filtered light on her high cheekbones, the skin's delicate gradients of color, cream blending to peach with the faintest golden undertone.

Dani looked down at the platter the waitress had just slid in front of her. Although she was handling his scrutiny with admirable equanimity, she seemed grateful for the diversion. "Well, let's see. I always enjoyed cooking, and one summer when I was in college, I worked at a big mountain resort up in North Carolina, helping out in the kitchen. From there, I started picking up odd jobs with caterers during the school year. After I graduated, I thought, why not give it a try myself?"

"So you came back to Charleston and opened your business?" Ken supplied.

Dani shook her head and laughed as she spooned a dollop of cocktail sauce onto her plate. "If it were only that simple! First, I enrolled in a cooking school in New York. After that, I interned for a year at a hotel in the Catskills. And *then* I came back to Charleston, only to find that it takes hours of marketing to find clients, and oodles of money to set up a proper commercial kitchen. I had a nest egg from Mother's estate, but I was really nervous plunking most of it into the business. I kept telling myself that if Moveable Feast turned out to be a colossal flop, I could always work for a resort or a country club, but that would have been a bitter pill to swallow."

"I'm glad you made it."

Dani smiled modestly. "I prefer to say 'doing okay'. It doesn't pay to tempt the gods. And I still have a lot of un-achieved goals. I'd love to have a small restaurant or a bed-and-breakfast place someday. Right now, though, I'll be happy simply to pay the lease on the Feast's kitchen space and continue to build my clientele."

"With that kind of attitude, I'm sure you'll be a success." Ken hoped she recognized his remark for what it was: not an empty platitude, but a sincere compliment. "What about you, when you're not being the proprietor of Move-able Feast?"

Dani carefully dunked a bite of shrimp into the puddle of sauce. "Well, I've never been arrested. I don't drink in ex-cess. I've never used drugs. And as far as I know, I keep company with clean-living types." She watched him with amused interest, taking her time chewing the shrimp. "I don't know. What else does a background check usually in-clude?"

Remind me never to play poker with you, Ken thought as he met the level, hazel gaze. Trying to get the best of Dani Blake in a verbal combat was not a challenge to be taken lightly. That she wasn't prone to babble every mundane de-tail of her life made those details all the more intriguing. Then, too, he realized that, quite aside from professional interest, he simply wanted to know more about Dani, what she ate for breakfast, the kind of music she listened to on a rainy winter night, if the airport scene in *Casablanca* made her cry. Before he could think of a gambit for extracting such tantalizing specifics from her, however, Dani turned the tables.

"What if we split the check and you tell me about your-self?" she proposed. Propping her chin on her folded hands, she looked as if she were settling in for a lengthy narrative.

"Gee, I don't know where to start." Ken made a production of picking through the shrimp tails on his plate in search of an overlooked bite, trying to stall for time.

All the while his curiosity about Dani had been growing, it had never occurred to him that she might reciprocate the interest. Not that he expected her to find him unattractive. Like most aspects of his life, Ken took a rational, objective view of his effect on woman; he was in good shape, decent if unspectacular looking and not an obnoxious creep. That she now wanted him to talk about *himself,* however, was a development for which he wasn't prepared. His life was so complicated, riddled with emotional thickets that he couldn't even explain to himself.

"Where did you grow up?" Dani prompted.

"In Baltimore." Ken swallowed, suddenly aware of a faintly disagreeable aftertaste clinging to his palate.

"Does your family still live there?"

Which one? We have at least six to choose from. Ken crumpled the napkin inside his fist, avoiding her gaze. "We're all kind of far-flung now," he hedged.

Dani's brow knit as she mulled this cryptic response. Her chin pivoted inside her cupped hands as her eyes drifted to the parking lot. Suddenly, her hands dropped and she sat straight up. "Look!"

Ken turned to the window in time to see a crimson red Mercedes speed past. "Better step on it, Rebecca, or you're going to be late for that hairdresser's appointment," he murmured under his breath. When he caught Dani's eyes, he smiled warily. "You're not thinking what I'm thinking?"

"Come on, Ken. What harm could it do? Assuming she's taken the dog with her, the house will be deserted. We can drive up, have a quick look at the boat and then be on our way. No one will ever know. Besides," she reminded him, "that's what we intended to do in the first place."

"I like your logic," Ken remarked drily. As they stood up, he snatched the check the waitress had anchored beneath the hush-puppy basket. At the register, Dani nudged his arm playfully.

"I guess I'm going to have to buy you lunch if I want to find out more about you," she teased.

"I guess so," Ken agreed.

As they drove back to the isolated summer house, however, he was keenly aware of the camaraderie that had developed between them in the short time since they had reached a truce in Battery Park. If he had not been able to get a break in the case as quickly as he had hoped, at least the protracted investigation now offered a consoling benefit: more contact with Dani.

By the time they reached the house, the sun had already sunk low in the sky, inching its way behind the tops of the trees. They could hear the sound of the encroaching tide surging along the shorefront.

"It's going to be dark before you know it. Do you have a flashlight?" Ken asked.

Dani pulled the keys out of the ignition and dangled the pocket flashlight attached to the chain. "I have this baby. There should be a full-grown one inside the glove compartment." She peered through the van's window, alert to any signs of life from the house, before gingerly opening the door.

Following her lead, Ken climbed out of the van and closed the door as quietly as possible. They both stood in the dark green shadows of the palmetto grove, listening for reassurance that they were, indeed, alone. Overhead, a few gulls squabbled over the bounty of fish carried in by the tide. A sonorous chorus of insect voices resounded from the depths of the landward forest. After a few minutes, Ken flicked on the flashlight to check its battery and then snapped it off again.

"Okay, let's go." Dani's hushed voice blended with the wind rippling through the palmetto fronds.

The dock was a good half mile from the spot where they had parked, obscured in part by a stand of live oaks gracing the front lawn of the house. Only when they had cleared the oak grove did they catch their first glimpse of the boathouse and the silver plane of water stretching across the horizon behind it. A mast was visible over the peaked roof of the boathouse.

"That has to be it!" In her excitement, Dani grabbed Ken's wrist.

Suddenly, her hand tightened its grip as the drone of a car's engine carried from the road. Ken looked around, trying to find some cover in the event the car turned into the driveway. They were too far from the live oaks to seek shelter there. At this point, the boathouse was their best bet. Turning his hand to seize Dani's, Ken made a dash for the dock. They pressed themselves against the salt-bleached wall of the structure, holding their breath until the sound of the car's engine had faded in the distance.

Dani was the first to emerge from the boathouse's protective shadow. Despite her careful tread, the heels of her pumps pecked noisily against the dock. As Dani and Ken rounded the corner, Dani gasped.

"Look!"

And for a moment, all Ken could do was stare at the magnificent white yacht anchored in the bay. It was much larger than its stripped-down modern descendants, which Ken had seen in televised clips of the Americas Cup, a solid ocean-going craft as suited for carrying its sailors to distant ports of call as it was for racing. With its sails lowered and its hull dipping gently with the tide, it still carried an air of energy, of the dazzling speed it could borrow at will from the wind.

Dani was already stalking the length of the dock. "How can we get out to it?"

Ken nodded toward the small rowboats tethered at the end of the dock. "We'll be pulling against the tide," he cautioned her. "But getting back to land should be a cinch."

"Why don't we use this one?" Dani suggested, brashly pointing to the powerboat berthed on the other side of the dock.

"What would Rebecca say?" Ken pretended to cluck under his breath, but he could feel his adrenaline rising, spurred on by Dani's audacious spirit.

They exchanged grins when they found the motorboat's key anchored conveniently in the ignition. But as the craft steadily plowed through the gray tide, carrying them to the moored yacht, a sober expression settled over Dani's face, and Ken knew she must be thinking about her father. Following instincts he had forgotten he possessed, he placed a comforting hand on her shoulder. She didn't look at him, but only reached to cover his hand with her own. As the jutting stem of the yacht loomed in front of them, she released his hand, stretching her arm to point to the large script letters arching across the prow.

"There's the name! *Bandeira Branca.*" She pronounced the unfamiliar words carefully, sounding each syllable. "Remember what Paul Crawford said about the pins—the name of the boat was connected to the little gold chain. Now we know what's missing from Richardson's pin."

Ken guided the power boat alongside the yacht, avoiding a string of buoys and a dinghy tethered to the vessel. He let the engine idle, cutting it only after he was able to grasp a metal ladder extending over the edge of the larger vessel. He took pains to tie the powerboat to the yacht's ladder and to pocket the flashlight before helping Dani scale the ladder.

"I had no idea it was so big. Compared to the sailboats I've seen, it seems like a battleship," Dani whispered. She took a tentative step on the deck, running her hand along the rail.

Ken glanced back to the dark mainland. Although he felt certain they had slipped in undetected, no one could be sure when Rebecca would return. She would be spiteful enough to call the police and charge them with trespassing. Of which, of course, they were guilty, technically speaking. The thought that they were treading a thin legal line prompted him to hasten their inspection of the boat.

"Why don't we split up? That way, we can cover the boat in less time," he suggested. "I think it's important at least to get a quick look at the area below deck."

Dani's head jerked in a brief nod. "So do I. Let me know if you find anything interesting."

"You do likewise." He tapped her shoulder lightly in parting.

Ken bent his knees slightly, adjusting his balance to the fluid feel of the deck underfoot. The yacht rolled with the swelling tide, its great body swaying in an easy cadence not unlike the motion of a cradle. The movement was punctuated by equally rhythmic sounds, the odd creaks and sighs of the vessel's sinews.

The deck of the boat appeared to be in pristine condition, thanks, no doubt, to Theo Boynton's restoration. At the stern end of the cabin, Ken paused to inspect a small cupboard and found it stocked with flares and lifejackets. As he was closing the cupboard door, he glanced down the deck. Dani had disappeared from sight. Although he realized she had only gone belowdecks, a strange apprehension gripped him. *The product of too many ghost stories and your weakness for a pretty face,* he told himself. He didn't believe in ghosts, of course, and to characterize the complicated feelings Dani had stirred in him as common physical attraction was oversimplifying things in the extreme.

Ken tested the hatch to the rear cabin. It yielded easily. For a moment, he stood at the top of the stairs. The corridor below was dark and narrow, and he reached for the flashlight in his pocket. The door to a small chamber to his right swung gently on its hinge. Ken descended the stairs and nudged the door wide open. A quick sweep with the flashlight revealed the valves and pistons of the yacht's engine.

A dull noise somewhere at the other end of the corridor caused Ken to retreat. Ken focused the flashlight's beam in the direction of the sound.

"Dani?"

The quiet was unbroken, save for the throb of the tide and the yacht's audible breathing.

With his hand tracing the oiled paneling, Ken made his way down the corridor. He pushed open the first door he passed. Light from the waxing moon streamed through the round window to dimly illuminate the tiny cabin. Ken ducked and put one foot over the threshold. His flashlight roved the cabin, picking out a bunk and built-in chests of drawers in the far corner.

The floor creaked behind him.

"Dani?"

Ken stepped back, lowering his head to clear the doorframe. Just as he turned, a splintering sensation exploded at the back of his head. The corridor expanded and contracted before his eyes. He could see the flashlight tumbling from his hand in slow motion, feel himself reach for it, hear the hollow thud echo through his skull as another blow fell. The cold floor slammed into his face, and everything went blank.

Chapter Seven

"Ouch!"

Dani lurched and then caught herself. Clutching the frame of the cabin door with one hand, she stooped to massage the ankle she had just bumped against the raised threshold. If Rebecca had only been more cooperative, they could have inspected the yacht in full daylight instead of stumbling and groping around in the dark. The sky was still flushed with the setting sun's afterglow, but its meager light barely penetrated the area below deck. Although the corridor and probably the cabins, as well, were equipped with caged light fixtures, Dani dared not test them. Any light bright enough to do her any good was bright enough to be spotted from the shore, and that was the last thing she wanted to risk.

Squeezing the key-chain flashlight, Dani pointed its needlelike beam into the glowering dusk filling the cabin. The room appeared to be an office or a sitting room equipped with a small couch and a couple of chairs riveted to the floor. The weak ray of light traversed the walls. On one side, it picked out round windows shrouded in striped curtains. Gliding across the far wall, the flashlight beam skimmed framed maps, nautical prints and photographs suspended on the panelling.

Dani crouched slightly as she stepped through the door. There was a musty smell to the room, an indistinguishable blend of pipe tobacco, salt and age. Unlike the parts of the boat she had seen so far, this cabin had an untouched feel to it, as if Theo Boynton's stem-to-stern restoration had somehow passed it by.

On closer inspection, Dani could see that the maps and pictures were arranged above a built-in table that must have served as a desk. The captain's chair facing the wall wobbled on loose rivets, squeaking meekly as she sank onto it. Directly in front of the chair hung a photograph of the sailing team, almost identical to the one she had found in her mother's album. She guided the light flashlight along the row of black-and-white photos, pausing on the unlined, optimistic faces of Richardson Whyte and Powell Boynton.

Without warning, the cabin door slammed shut. Dani jumped in her seat. As she released her hold on the flashlight, the room was suddenly plunged into darkness. Her heart still racing, Dani clamped the flashlight with a death grip. With the dim light restored, she managed to steady herself. The yacht was rolling with the waves; its motion, and nothing more, had tipped the door closed.

Scolding herself to quit conjuring specters, Dani turned back to the photographs. The flashlight beam faltered as it grazed a handsome, open face, the countenance of a man accustomed to winning and setting his own rules for life.

"Dad. Daddy." Dani pressed her lips together, overcome with the thought that she had never had the chance to choose a name for her father. She leaned across the table, reaching to trace the face's contours, the fearless smile, the angular, wind-chapped jaw. Something about this forgotten, fading picture, enshrined in the yacht Dan Blake had loved so well, seemed profoundly sad. The weak light began to blur, but Dani only stared at the picture, letting the tears ebbing from her eyes flow unchecked.

From the far end of the deck, she thought she heard Ken call her name, reminding her that he could walk in at any moment. Although Dani felt far more comfortable with him than she would have thought possible in the short span of their acquaintance, discovering the old picture in such an emotionally charged setting had awakened a deep and private pain within her. For now, she preferred to keep her disjointed feelings to herself, at least until she had a chance to come to terms with them.

On impulse, Dani lifted the framed picture off its hook and pulled the photograph from beneath the glass. Dan Blake's picture would be of no sentimental value to Richardson's heirs; she felt almost protective as she slipped the photo into her pocket. Leaning back in the chair, she tugged open the desk drawer. She was sliding the empty frame into the drawer when she happened to spot another, smaller snapshot half hidden by an open deck of playing cards. Pushing the cards aside, Dani was startled to recognize herself as a child, scuff-kneed and minus both front teeth, grinning up into the camera. Another sound from the corridor prompted Dani to tuck the snapshot into her pocket, alongside her father's picture.

The tiny flashlight's battery was nearly spent. If she wanted to give the cabin a proper inspection, she needed the more powerful flashlight Ken was carrying. As she started for the cabin door, the minuscule light failed. Dani shook it and won a reprieve that she guessed would be brief at best.

"Ken?" Dani peered out into the murky corridor. "Yoohoo! I'm down this way!"

Perhaps the wind had only subsided, but the yacht now seemed very quiet.

"Ken?"

She took a step, reminding herself to give the threshold a wide berth. The flickering beam skittered down the panelled corridor to light on the closed hatch. No wonder it was abysmally dark in the hall; the damned door must have swung shut, cutting out the stingy bit of remaining natural light. Dani was swaying along the corridor when she stumbled over something solid and bulky right in her path. She tried to break her fall, clawing at the wall as she pitched forward. She recognized Ken just as the flashlight winked its last.

"Ken! Oh, my God!"

Dani recoiled from his inert body, scuffling backward with her heels. As she scrambled to one side, her hands slipped on the sticky, wet floor. The rich, sweet smell of blood rose in the darkness, and she almost gagged. *Oh, no, not you, please not you, please no, no, no!* Panic swelled in her throat as she alternately shook the unmoving body and pawed the floor in search of his flashlight.

She heard the metal cylinder roll against the wall. Stretching across Ken's body, Dani grasped the flashlight. Her wet fingers fumbled with the switch. When the beam spread across the corridor, she felt another surge of sickness rising from the pit of her stomach.

Blood oozed from a gash across the back of his head. A network of red rivulets trickled over his bruised face and down his neck. Dani knelt over him, placing her face close to his. When she felt an uneven wisp of breath graze her cheek, she began to cry in relief.

"Ken, can you hear me? What happened to you?"

He didn't answer, but the fact that he was alive helped Dani regain her bearings. She sat back on her heels and tried to think clearly. The injury to his head had been deliberate. Whoever had attacked him was hiding somewhere on the yacht. At that thought, the dark shadows at both ends of the corridor seemed to close in on her, filling her mouth and her nostrils, blocking the air she needed to live.

Dani forced herself to take a deep, calming breath. She knew someone else was on board. Unlike Ken, it would be harder to take her by surprise. She stood a fighting chance—especially if she could find a weapon. She had seen a couple of oars near the hatch. She would be better able to defend herself with one of them than with her bare hands. Swinging the flashlight beam from one side to the other as if it were a laser, Dani staggered to her feet and cautiously moved toward the hatch.

At the top of the steps, she pushed against the door. It refused to budge. Dani braced her shoulder against the obstinate wooden barrier and heaved with all her strength. The door remained securely shut. Banking on the faintest hope, Dani dashed to the other end of the corridor. As she had feared, that portal, too, was secured from the outside. The knowledge that they were locked belowdecks took on a more terrifying aspect when the yacht's engine began to rumble and churn.

A low moan from Ken sent Dani racing back to the spot where he lay. She caressed his face with her palm, wiping the blood from his ashen cheek. He squinted; then his eyes strained to open. When he tried to move, she caught him by the shoulders.

"Take it easy! Don't try to get up yet."

He sagged against her involuntarily, and Dani cradled his battered head against her chest. There was no way of knowing how badly Ken was hurt, but at least she could now be sure that his attacker was aboard, piloting the yacht.

"Dan—Dani." Ken's tongue sounded thick and dry. A haze seemed to cover his eyes, blanketing him in a twilight of half-consciousness.

"I'm here." She pressed her cheek against his blood-matted hair, hating herself for feeling so helpless, wishing she could find a gun or a knife or the sheer, raw strength to even the odds with their captor.

The yacht's engine abruptly cut. Gently lowering Ken to the floor, Dani stood up. She strained, trying to follow the muffled sounds on the deck above. Yes, those were footsteps, the quick tread of someone nervous and in a hurry. Dani crept to the hatch and listened hard. Suddenly, she drew back as a pungent smell began to seep into the corridor. Gasoline! Dani heard the motorboat's engine chug, then rev to a frenetic whine. As the motor's drone faded, an explosive whoosh filled the air. A sickening terror filled Dani as she listened to the sinister crackle of encroaching flames.

The yacht was on fire! Dani froze, paralyzed with fear. For a split second, she could only stare dumbly at the locked hatch. A rush of adrenaline jolted her senses, sent her hurtling back down the corridor. Ken was making a groggy attempt to stand. She looped one of his arms over her shoulders, steadying him against the wall.

"Some bastard knocked me in the head. Are you all right?" he managed to get out.

"Yeah, but both hatch doors are locked."

Ken frowned in confusion. "Something smells funny. Is that smoke?"

Dani tightened her hold on his torso. "The yacht is on fire, but I think the blaze is still confined to the stern. We need to get out of here, though." *Before it reaches that gas tank,* she dared add only to herself.

"Let's try to find something to batter through the hatch." Ken still sounded shaky, but it was heartening to hear his tough, practical logic surfacing again.

"One of the chairs in here isn't secured too well." Dani was already standing in the cabin door.

Ken was weakened by the bludgeoning he had suffered, but together, he and Dani were able to twist the captain's chair free of two of its three remaining bolts. The last bolt, however, stubbornly refused to give.

In the flashlight's dim glow, the cold sweat shone on Ken's waxen face. He looked as if the exertion had pushed him beyond his limit and Dani knew he might lose consciousness again at any moment. In a last desperate effort, she yanked the chair, pitting her entire weight against the bolt. The chair jerked free. Dani fell back with it, crashing heavily against the floor.

Scrambling to her feet, she dragged the chair into the corridor with Ken weaving after her. They positioned themselves on either side of the forward hatch, braced their backs against the wall and heaved the chair against the door in unison. After the first blow, a deep crack slashed the paneling. Another, and the wood splintered.

Dani could see that Ken was still on his feet only by the sheer force of will, but by some miracle, he mustered the strength for another blow. The paneling gave way, emitting an acrid cloud of smoke through the gaping hole. Ken struggled out of his jacket. He pressed a handkerchief against his nose, handed the jacket to Dani and motioned for her to cover her lower face.

Together, they stumbled onto the deck. Even from this end of the boat, they could feel the heat of the advancing blaze. Dani raced to the rail and confirmed what she had feared: whoever had set the yacht on fire had cut the dinghy loose. They were stranded. "I'm going to find some life jackets," she told Ken.

As she turned way from the rail, Ken's clammy hands caught her shoulders. "It's too late for that. They're down at the other end. We're going to have to jump and take our chances without them."

Ken started to strip off his shirt in preparation for the dive when the entire boat shuddered from a deafening roar. A column of yellow flame soared from the stern, searing the night sky. Without bothering to doff her outer clothes, Dani grabbed Ken's arm and plunged over the rail.

The cold, salty water swallowed them up. For a long, agonizing moment Dani was surrounded by a smothering darkness that filled every pore. She felt Ken's grasp weaken, and she fought to hold on to his arm. As she broke the water's surface, one thought filled her mind: she must not let go of him. He was trying to tread water, trying to hang on to consciousness, but with every wave that surged over them, he faltered.

"Don't try to swim. Just float," Dani gasped through the salty froth slapping her face. She was relieved when he didn't resist. Encircling his upper body in the lifesaving cross-chest carry, she began to kick, stroking with one arm while the other pulled him with her.

Another explosion ripped through the damp air, followed by a succession of violent blasts. Treading water, Dani watched the massive fireball burst through the yacht's cabin, severing the vessel in two. The yacht was a floating torch now, its aureole of fierce light spreading over the water. Narrowing her eyes against the inferno, Dani turned in the water, trying to protect Ken's lolling head from the cresting waves while she scanned the horizon for any sign of land. The specks of light looked as distant as the stars overhead.

"Dani?"

Her arm instinctively clung to him as his limbs moved in a feeble attempt to fight the waves. "It's gone, Ken. The yacht blew up, but we're safe." It was the sort of pathetically brave platitude you would offer an anxious child, but the words seemed to calm him.

"We're going to make it, baby. Damned if we aren't," he murmured. She felt his arms begin to stroke the water, sculling steadily in rhythm with her.

Perhaps he was simply too spent to consider the worst at this point. Fear and exhaustion had battered her own resources, leaving her prey to a mounting despair. *You must not give up—you can't give up.* Dani scoured the empty horizon for a glimmer of hope. At least the sea wasn't too rough this evening. She was a strong swimmer, and they could both float awhile as long as Ken remained conscious. Someone was sure to spot the burning yacht sooner or later. Sculling with Ken's sagging head rested against her shoulder, Dani repeated these assurances to herself until she lacked the strength even to think.

Her senses had grown so numb, she could not at first be sure if she had heard the steady throb of a motor or had just imagined it. Then she spotted the lights strung along the shrimper's rigging. A boat was approaching them!

"Hallo! Over here! Help!" Dani pumped with her legs in an effort to thrust herself above the waves.

Ken joined her cry, one hand waving desperately.

As the boat drew near, the sudden fear that its crew had not seen them gripped Dani. What if the boat passed them by? Or ran over them? Or snagged them in its nets? She released Ken, flailing with both arms in a frantic effort to attract attention.

"Ho, over yonder!" A sturdy masculine voice carried over the sea's incessant murmur.

Salt stung Dani's lips as sea foam and tears of relief mingled to dribble down her cheeks. In the light of the still-burning yacht, she watched a small boat put out from the shrimper.

"Steady, lady! There's a good girl. Easy there, Orlin. Looks like this fella's hurt pretty bad." The men's drawling voices sounded soothing, capable.

Dani felt warm, strong hands seize her cold-deadened body and hoist it into the boat. She huddled with Ken, cradling his head. His fingers laced through hers, and he closed his eyes, breathing in exhausted gulps.

"Looks like you folks had some bad luck." The younger of the two men glanced from Dani to the guttering yacht.

Dani nodded, hoping they would be spared a battery of questions, at least for the moment. Mercifully, the two fishermen seemed far more concerned with Ken's questionable condition than the circumstances that had caused it. As soon as they had lifted the two castaways onto the shrimping boat, they took them into the cabin and swaddled them in scratchy wool army blankets.

"Need to get this fella to a doctor, Orlin." From her nest on the low bunk, Dani could hear the older man conferring with his cohort. "We best set in for shore. Ain't nothin' much to catch tonight anyhow."

Ken had been listening to the conversation, too. "I don't think my injury is all that serious," he began as the younger of the two men returned to their corner of the cabin.

"Won't know for sure till a doctor's seen it," the man told him philosophically. "My name's Orlin Poole." His thumb gestured toward the deck, indicating the man who was now piloting the boat toward land. "That's my daddy, Ned Poole by name."

Ken and Dani introduced themselves and shook Orlin's big, calloused hand.

"We'll never be able to thank you and your father," Dani told him. "I don't know how long we could have held out."

The tall, powerfully built man shrugged like a little boy fending off an embarrassing compliment. "We saw the fire burnin' a couple miles off. If we hadn't spotted you, someone else sure 'nough would have. You just rest now." He backed toward the door, angling his big frame into the narrow opening. "You might ought to get out of that wet jacket, Miss Blake," he suggested delicately before disappearing onto the deck.

Dani took Orlin's advice, peeling off her ruined blazer and rolling it into a soggy navy blue bundle. As she wrapped the blanket around her again, she settled it over Ken as well.

"Who do you suppose was on that yacht with us?" Ken said under his breath, shifting closer to her beneath his blanket.

Dani let her head rest against his. The reminder that their would-be murderer was still at large tempered the unmitigated relief of being rescued. "I don't know. How did this happen anyway?" Her fingers lightly stroked his tawny hair, avoiding the angry red seam running through it.

"Someone slipped up behind me after I had gone below-decks at the stern. I never even saw him. If I'd only been more alert..."

"Neither of us expected to find anyone on the boat," Dani consoled him. She hugged his shoulders, liking the feel of him safe and warm within her embrace. She was pleased when his eyes closed and his body relaxed against hers.

Dani realized that she, too, must have drifted off to sleep, for the next thing she knew, Orlin was standing over her, tapping her shoulder apologetically.

"We've docked at Daddy's place. He's gonna take you all to the hospital."

Dani and Ken let Orlin guide them above deck and onto a weather-beaten gray dock. Ken's gait looked fairly steady, an encouraging sign. All the same, Dani was glad when Ned Poole hustled them into the cab of his pickup truck and set off for the hospital without delay.

The elder Poole was a sixtyish version of his son, with the same ruddy, pitted face and thick reddish blond hair, albeit liberally streaked with silver. Orlin had apparently inherited his taciturn nature from his father, as well, for Ned spoke scarcely a word as he steered the pickup over the rough back roads and then sped along the interstate highway to Charleston. If he had any curiosity about the conflagration aboard the yacht, he gave it second priority to the well-being of his passengers.

In the emergency room, Ned hung back, watchful but discreet, while Dani and Ken talked with the nurse behind the glass barrier. After Ken had been whisked out of sight, Dani headed for the phone she had seen near the entrance.

She had only a vague idea of how much time had elapsed since the mishap occurred, but with every passing hour, their assailant's trail grew colder. She dialed 911 and gave the police clerk a report of their harrowing ordeal. After the clerk promised to dispatch an officer to the hospital to talk with them personally, Dani returned to the waiting area. She found Ned sitting anxiously on the edge of his seat, billed cap clasped between his large hands.

"They're gonna look after you, too, I hope." The fisherman eyed the white-uniformed personnel with suspicion.

Dani was quick to reassure him. "They're afraid Ken may have a concussion or may even still be in shock. I'm not injured, but the nurse said they wanted to check me over just to be sure."

"You're gonna catch a real bad cold." The big man shook his head in fatherly concern.

Dani gave him a grateful smile. "Don't worry. If a cold is the worst I have to show for this mess, I won't complain."

"What happened to ya'll out there, anyway?"

Ned had been so reserved so far, Dani was startled by the directness of his question. She started to say "the yacht caught on fire," but then, that would be obvious to any fool, and certainly to a sharp-eyed man of Ned's experience. Still, gossip traveled fast and indiscriminately in rural communities. A harmless comment from the fisherman could conceivably reach the wrong ears—even those of their attacker. For now, it was best to let the well-meaning Ned believe they had been the victims of an accident. "The gas tank exploded," Dani told him. While she was weighing her next comment, Ned caught her by surprise once more.

"You some kin to Mr. Whyte?"

"Y-you mean Richardson Whyte?" Dani stammered.

The shock of fading red-blond hair dipped in affirmation. "That was his boat, wasn't it?" He read her incredulous expression without missing a beat. "I'd know that boat anywhere. *Should* know the old *Bandeira Branca,* I'd say. You see, after he hauled it out to Trumbull, why, any time anything needed fixin', a little dry rot or what not, Mr. Whyte'd call me in to do it. That boy, Theo, was of a different mind. Got himself all kinds of *experts* to polish up the yacht once he had his hands on it. But Richardson, he and I thought highly of each other."

"I had no idea you knew Richardson. He was my friend, too. He and my father sailed together a long time ago."

Now it was Ned Poole's turn to look surprised. "You're Dan Blake's girl? Lord, when you said your name was Blake, I had no idea you were talkin' about *that* Blake. Your daddy was a legend around these parts," he added almost reverently.

Proud as she was to hear that her father was so fondly remembered, Dani did not want to squander the chance to talk about Richardson with someone who knew him and the yacht well. "Did Richardson ever talk about his sailing days with you?"

"Only if you pressed him. Mostly, we just fished and generally took it easy without too much talkin'. He liked to come down to Trumbull to find some peace and quiet. To tell you the truth, Miss Blake, I got the feelin' that Richardson was a real sad man. I know a lot of folks might of thought he had it made, bein' as how he was so rich and all, but I do believe money and power didn't mean all that much to him. In fact, he once told me only one thing in the world mattered a whit to him."

Dani regarded Poole's weathered face curiously. "What was that?"

The fisherman's pale blue eyes looked directly at her. "Why, his child. His only child."

Chapter Eight

"I've never slept in a hospital since the first week of my life, and I'm not about to break a thirty-two-year record to-night." Ken managed to look capable of carrying out his threat in spite of the white bandage crisscrossing his head and the puffy bruise crowding his left eye. His lips quivered, betraying his emotion as he smiled at Dani. "You must be exhausted. How are you doing?"

"I should be asking you that question." Dani pushed up from the green vinyl chair in which she had stationed herself in the emergency-room waiting area for the past two hours. Despite her fatigue, she had passed the time restively, alternatively worrying over Ken's condition and chafing for the opportunity to tell him about Ned Poole's shocking revelation. "The worst they could say for me was 'suffering from exposure,' which means I'll have a case of the sniffles, I suppose. When the police were here, I over-heard the nurse tell them you had a mild concussion." She regarded the incongruous bandage doubtfully.

"And, fortunately, that's all there is to tell." He settled a weary arm over Dani's shoulders. His grip tightened for a long moment, as if to satisfy himself that she was actually standing there, flesh and blood, and not merely a figment of his imagination. "What say we get out of here before they change their minds and decide to find something else wrong with us.''

Like Ken, Dani was eager to be free of the bright lights and sterile, impersonal smells of the emergency room. As they pushed through the swinging doors, Ken pulled her closer to him, and she responded by slipping her arm around his waist. The brush with death had galvanized the tenuous bond growing between them, given them insights into each other's souls that went beyond common words and gestures. Now that they had been reunited, she felt strangely empowered, almost as if she had regained a part of herself. Only when they reached the curb did they pull up short.

"I had almost managed to forget that the van is thirty-five miles away and my keys are floating around somewhere in the Atlantic. We'll need to take a taxi. Do you have any money that's still negotiable?" Dani asked Ken.

Pushing aside his ragged shirttail, Ken dug in his pants pocket and produced a wallet that looked remarkably well preserved, given the thorough soaking it had received that evening. He counted several damp bills and then nodded.

The cabby eyed his bedraggled fare skeptically, but only responded with a resigned "yes, ma'am" when Dani gave him directions to her condo. When the cab pulled into the drive, Ken loosened his hold on her shoulders and an uncertain look passed across his face.

"Since you suffered a concussion, I don't think it's wise for you to go home alone. You can spend what's left of the night here," she told him matter-of-factly.

While Ken paid the taxi driver, Dani unearthed the house key she kept secreted in a hanging planter and unlocked the front door. Never had her neat little home seemed more secure and welcoming. After dispatching Ken to the guest bath, Dani retreated to her bedroom. Her clothes were stiff with dried salt and algae, and she was glad to discard them on the bathroom floor. After a hot shower, she slipped into her oldest, softest sweatsuit and headed for the kitchen. By the time Ken emerged from the bath, dressing in a robe fashioned from safety pins and two large beach towels, she had warmed soup and rolls in the microwave.

"Feel better?" Dani ladled hot vegetable soup into two giant mugs and then scooted one across the breakfast bar.

Ken sniffed the aroma rising from the mug appreciatively and nodded. "We're going to have a lot of explaining to do tomorrow, but right now, I don't want to think about any of it." He took a small sip of broth. "I'm just glad we're both here, both still..." His voice faltered, prompting Dani to reach across the counter and hold both his hands with her own.

"It doesn't matter what might have been, Ken. The important thing is that we did make it." She looked up into his face so earnestly, he had to meet her eyes.

"I've never felt so helpless, Dani," he confessed in a low voice choked with emotion. "After we dove off the yacht, I kept telling myself to stay alert, to swim, to hang on to you. But there was always this awful slipping feeling, as if I were sliding down the side of a cliff, losing my hold inch by inch. You saved both of us, Dani. If you hadn't been brave enough and tough enough for two people—" he looked down at their intertwined hands and a tremor rippled through the fine muscles of his face "—we wouldn't be sitting here right now."

"I don't think either of us would have had much luck alone. If you hadn't come to, I don't know if I would have been able to break through the hatch and get us off the boat in the first place." She smoothed his hands, taking comfort in the rugged, vital texture of them.

Ken rolled her hands over, squeezing her wrists lightly. "I guess we sort of make a team, don't we?" For the first time since she had met him, cool-headed, self-possessed Ken McCabe sounded shy.

"I guess." Dani's voice was as soft as the mellow light warming their small corner of the kitchen.

For a few moments, neither of them spoke, as if both mistrusted the words that might give shape to equally revealing thoughts. They had wandered onto untested ground, Dani knew, emotional territory with no safe, predicable paths to follow. Ken eased the tension by giving her hands a gentle shake and then leaning back slightly on the bar stool.

"This is turning into quite an investigation, isn't it?" A smile lightened the haggard lines of his face.

Dani lifted the mug, grimacing over its rim. "I'll call Theo about the yacht, although I'm sure the police have already contacted him. I told them we had gone on board just to have a look at my father's old sailing vessel. That's true enough, and I think Theo will understand. You know, now I'm convinced we were on to something with the boat. Too bad that any evidence we might have found literally went up in smoke."

Ken nodded, dejectedly toying with his mug's handle, and Dani guessed he was confronting the frightening thought haunting both their minds. Her hunch was confirmed when he at last broke the silence. "The person who knocked me on the head and set the yacht on fire also killed Richardson Whyte. Tonight, he intended to kill us."

Dani crumbled a chunk of the roll into her soup, poking at the makeshift croutons with the spoon. "But how did he know we would board the yacht in the first place? It seems more likely that he was looking for something on the boat when we showed up unexpectedly."

"He couldn't afford to be seen, so he panicked," Ken went on, picking up her train of thought.

"Exactly. And he set the yacht on fire to destroy the evidence and any embarrassing witnesses in the process."

Ken sighed, folding his arms on the counter as he slumped over the empty soup mug. "If we'd only beat him to whatever it was he wanted to get rid of! I didn't get very far before he slugged me. I don't suppose you found anything even remotely suspicious?" He cast a hopeful glance at her.

Despite the crushing fatigue that had by now almost paralyzed her limbs, Dani folded her arms and smiled. "On the boat, no."

Ken was on to the bait in an instant. "What do you mean?" he demanded.

"Richardson Whyte had a child." She announced her discovery with as little fanfare as Ned Poole had.

To judge from Ken's amazed expression, the revelation had hit him with earth-shaking impact. "Where the hell did you hear that?"

"Ned Poole told me while I was waiting outside the emergency room. He used to do maintenance work on the yacht. He had even recognized the boat when he fished us out of the ocean. Anyway, it seems that one time, Richardson let slip something about a child of his. He clammed up afterward, wouldn't tell Ned anything about it. As Ned put it, Richardson seemed 'too torn up to do much talking on the matter.' Ned assumed Richardson was referring to a baby that had died at birth, and I let him go on thinking that. But I'm not so sure. As far as I know, Richardson and his wife were childless."

"So you think Richardson had an illegitimate child?"

"It's something I would never have suspected, but..." Dani shrugged dubiously. "That isn't the sort of admission a prominent man like Richardson would want to trumpet about."

Ken nodded agreement. "Especially given the Whyte family's obsession with appearances. The last thing they would have been able to handle was the scandal of an illegitimate child. I imagine they would give almost anything to keep that skeleton locked safely in its closet.''

Dani gathered up the soup mugs and slid off the stool. ''The person who wrote that extortion note could have been banking on just that.''

''Precisely what I was thinking!'' Ken adjusted the makeshift bathrobe as he followed her to the sink. ''Of course, Richardson never said anything to Derek or me about having fathered a child.''

Dani rinsed the mugs under the tap, frowning at the water swirling down the drain. ''He was a very private man, Ken. I thought the world of him, but, when I spent time with him, I often felt there was a part of himself he held back, a corner of his soul that even his closest friends would never be allowed to see. I don't think it entirely incredible that Richardson would have continued to guard such a painful secret, even when his life was threatened.''

''Maybe you're right. At any rate, this information certainly opens up a whole new area for investigation.'' Ken drew a wary breath and glanced up at the kitchen clock. ''Geez, it's three o'clock. I think that investigation can wait another few hours.''

His fingers seemed to know exactly which muscles most needed a deep massage as they plied the back of her neck. Dani rolled her head slowly and stretched, pressing into the deliciously slow and deliberate strokes. As quickly as it had begun, his hand halted its work. Ken stepped back, and Dani straightened herself. For a moment, another of those self-conscious silences hung between them.

''We need to get some sleep. I'll fetch some sheets and make up the sofa bed.'' Dani smiled as casually as she could and hurried out of the kitchen.

When she returned to the living room with the sheets and a thermal blanket, Ken had removed the sofa cushions and was in the process of unfolding the bed. Together, they tucked the bed linens into place, carefully avoiding bumping into each other as they scooted around the narrow bed.

"I'll see if I can scrounge up a couple of pillows." Hands folded behind her back, Dani backed toward the hall door.

Ken stood by the bed, looking as if he couldn't decide whether he should climb into it or not. Without waiting for him to make up his mind, Dani turned on her heel and headed for her bedroom.

In the past few hours, she had escaped being blown to bits only to come near drowning. Never before in her life had she taken such a battering, mentally and physically; her emotions had been strained to the limit. Right now, she was so tired, her arms and legs felt as if they were deadened clumps of wood. Under the circumstances, it was unrealistic to expect herself to be as levelheaded, as clear thinking as usual. If she were her normal self, she wouldn't be reacting to Ken this way at all. Of course, she was attracted to him, more so as time went by. But the thought that had just crossed her mind for a split second—no, make that a very long second—was something she would *never* have considered at this stage of a relationship.

As she rummaged through the bathroom linen closet, Dani examined the unpredictable feelings Ken's presence in her home had unleashed. Although the atmosphere between them was charged with sensuality, she had to admit that, to some degree, that had always been the case. Ken was a very sexy man, and she had responded to him on that level long before she had begun to like him so much. No, the yearning he had awakened tonight had more to do with closeness. She wanted to be close to him, feel his arms around her, strong and secure, put her arms around him and hug him as tight as she could. Then she would put her head on his chest, he would rest his cheek against her and they would sleep, safe in each others' embrace.

Unfortunately, adults aren't allowed to cuddle, Dani reminded herself as she shook the pillows out of their plastic bags. If we're not wrapped in a passionate clinch, we have to stay at arm's length. Of the two, she knew she must opt for the latter tonight.

She was on her way out of the bathroom when her eye fell on the sad pile of ruined clothing. Stooping Dani picked up the soggy blazer. She had completely forgotten about the photographs she had taken from the *Bandeira Branca*'s cabin. Now that the yacht had been destroyed, her saving the pictures seemed almost providential.

She found Ken sitting on the edge of the bed. Tossing the pillows onto the bed, she sat down beside him.

"Look what I found while I was snooping around the boat." She placed the two pictures on her knees, smoothing the wrinkles out of the damp paper. "That's my father."

Ken's hand rested on one of her shoulders, while his chin hovered near the other. "I'm sorry you never got to know him. Sorry for him, too. He looks like a man who lived life a lot. He would have loved you with all his heart."

Dani edged closer to Ken, grateful for the simple yet heartfelt empathy.

"And that's you?" Ken's bare arm grazed her as he pointed to the gap-toothed little girl.

Dani laughed softly. "It was so long ago, but I must have been seven. That was the year I kept the tooth fairy working overtime, if I remember correctly. Yep, I'm sure I was seven. See? My nose still has the little bump in it." Her fingernail traced the nose's contour in the picture. "I broke my nose playing volleyball when I was eight, and the doctor who repaired it ironed out the bump. Well, now you've seen me at my ugliest. You'll have to show me some childhood pictures of you, just to even the score." She glanced up at him and was surprised by his pensive expression. Ken was looking at the picture as if it were far more important than a faded, grainy snapshot of a pigtailed tomboy with no front teeth.

"I wish I had some to show you—" Ken broke off so abruptly, Dani sensed he wished he could have retracted his words.

"Something happened to your family pictures?" Dani asked gently, imagining a fire or some natural disaster had wiped out the McCabe family's treasury of memories.

Ken shook his head, but his eyes remained fixed on the photograph. "No." He drew a deep, resigned breath. "You see, we weren't much of a family, Dani. Mom died when I was about your age in that picture, and, well, my dad wasn't very good at keeping things together on his own. He'd drink, lose a job, get depressed over that and drink some more. He used to disappear for days on end and finally, one day, he disappeared for good. It was decided to put me in a foster home until my dad showed up again. Most of the foster families I had were all right, I guess." She felt him shrug. "Anyway, that's all in the past. I didn't mean to dump on you. I never talk about this stuff with people, really."

Dani swallowed, trying to find words that were commensurate with the deep, still-throbbing ache reflected in Ken's solemn face. At the same time, she had to choke back her anger at the callous adults who had hurt the lonely, bewildered child still hiding inside Ken.

Following an instinct more trustworthy than any words of consolation, Dani reached up to stroke the lean cheek so close to her own. She caressed the tanned skin, smoothing away the tight lines. Then she turned and in a gesture of the purest concern, of one human being reaching out to another's pain, she pulled his head down, cradling it against her chest. Ken's arms slipped around her, holding her as if they were the only two people left in the world. As they stretched back against the arm of the sofa bed, Dani reached to turn out the light.

A soft haze of fatigue settled over them like a blanket, melding their nestled bodies as they drifted off into sleep. In the dark room, they were two lost children who had at last found each other.

Chapter Nine

The intermittent buzz would not go away. Still in a fog of sleep, Dani pressed her face into the pillow while her hand groped the nightstand in search of the offending alarm clock. She frowned at the pillow's hairy texture, at the relentless alarm that still managed to elude her grasp. When the pillow moved of its own volition, her eyes shot open, gaping directly into the tawny mat of hair covering Ken's chest. As she sat up, she recognized the sofa's end table where she had vainly searched for her clock.

"Phone?" Ken murmured groggily, lifting his hand from her shoulder to rub his eyes.

"I'll get it. For a second, I thought I was in my bed and the alarm had gone off." Dani mumbled an apology as she padded into the kitchen to silence the phone's irritating buzz. She lifted the receiver, taking a deep, bracing breath before putting it to her ear. Whatever was coming, she wanted to be awake for it.

"Hello?" Dani gripped the receiver with both hands and waited for Theo's opener.

"Whew! You had me worried for a minute there, lady." Ben Carlisle's chuckle tempered his good-humored scolding. "When you didn't pick up and your answering machine didn't kick on, I was beginning to wonder if something was wrong."

"Everything's okay right now." An old friend like Ben deserved at least a marginally honest answer. "What's up?"

"Kate gave me that videotape you wanted to see. I have a few errands to run this morning, and I could drop it off at your place if you're going to be home for the next half hour or so," Ben volunteered.

Dani glanced up at the kitchen clock and then down at her rumpled sweats, mentally computing the time needed to make herself presentable. "Around ten will be fine."

"Great! See you shortly!"

Dani hung up the phone and returned to the living room to see what kind of progress Ken was making. He was sitting on the side of the fold-out bed, looking tired and achy and befuddled—exactly the way she felt.

"Ben is on his way over with the videocassette of the Parr legend dress rehearsal. Why don't you make some coffee while I get dressed?" Dani told Ken in passing. "The coffee beans are in the refrigerator door," she called as she ducked into the bathroom.

Just before she closed the door, she heard him mumble, "Beans?"

Dani adjusted the shower head to a refreshingly brisk jet. The prickles of water peppered her body, reminding her of each and every bruise she had earned the previous night. She could only imagine how Ken's head must be throbbing, given the abuse it had endured. They should both feel better after a substantial breakfast. Dani turned off the water and toweled herself gingerly. She threw on a sweater and a pair of slacks, pausing in front of the mirror only long enough to comb out her wet hair. When she reached the kitchen, she found Ken bent over the coffee maker, examining it as if it were a Chinese puzzle.

"How's the coffee coming?"

Ken's skeptical glance suggested that it had not come very far. "Well, I finally figured out which part of this thing grinds the beans. I'm not used to these high-tech kitchen gadgets. Up until this morning, I thought coffee was some dry stuff that you poured hot water over.''

''I like cooking from scratch. Why don't you let me take over here?'' Dani smiled as she seized control of the coffee machine. ''Want to try your hand at scrambled eggs?''

''All depends on how much from scratch you do 'em around here. Do I have to gather the eggs from the scratching chickens?'' Ken quipped.

''No, just from the fridge,'' Dani replied primly, but she was grateful for the good-natured bantering. Joking and laughing as they prepared breakfast helped to ease them through what might have been an awkward situation. Waking up in the arms of a man with whom she had narrowly escaped death was a new experience for Dani, and she suspected that Ken, too, had been caught off balance by the rapidly accelerating intimacy of their relationship.

They had just seated themselves in the sunny dining alcove when the doorbell chimed. Dani took a quick sip of juice before excusing herself. ''That must be Ben.''

''Having a late breakfast?'' Ben eyed the glass of juice Dani held as he sauntered through the doorway.

''Umm, yeah. Gee, thanks for bringing this tape by. I really appreciate it. Did Kate say when she needed it back?''

Ben's attention was now clearly focused on the strange man wearing a head bandage and a beach-towel toga seated at Dani's table, and he took a few seconds to answer. ''You can keep it as long as you like,'' he replied absently.

Dani inadvertently glanced over her shoulder to catch Ken raising his juice glass in a jaunty greeting.

Always equal to the occasion, Ben nodded politely to Ken and then checked his watch. ''Well, I guess it's time for me to get going. That's a six o'clock setup for the anniversary dinner tomorrow night, right?''

"Six o'clock. And thanks again, Ben." Dani closed the door so quickly, she almost caught the tail of his jacket.

"Ben is the actor who arranged my meeting with Kate McPherson," Dani explained as she returned to the dining nook. "I'll introduce you two sometime when you're more..."

"Introduceable," Ken provided helpfully.

Dani held the videocassette up for his inspection. "Why don't we pop this into the VCR and have a look at it while we eat breakfast?" she suggested, but Ken had already collected the plates and was headed for the living room. He folded up the sofa bed and then arranged the coffee table directly in front of the entertainment center. Dani and Ken perched on the edge of the sofa, nibbling at the scrambled eggs while they waited for the Ghostwalk tableau to appear on the screen. The color bars dissolved into a rainbow of squiggles and were then replaced by a shot of the theater's stage.

"That's the place where the troupe rehearses," Dani explained to Ken between bites of toast.

They watched intently as the costumed players assembled on stage and the action began. The story was easy to follow, thanks to the thorough grounding Kate had given Dani. The dramatic content of the enactment was of only secondary interest to Dani and Ken, however, for their attention was focused on one minor character hovering on the sidelines.

Dani pointed with her fork to the picture's foreground. "Lawes is dressed in the same costume he was wearing when I saw him at the theater Thursday afternoon." She suddenly jumped in her seat, almost choking on a corner of toast. "Oh, my God! He *knew* about the yacht!" She grabbed the remote control and hit the freeze-frame button.

Ken swung around on the sofa to face her, his bruised brow knit in a puzzled frown. "What do you mean?"

Dani coughed into her napkin and then cleared her throat. "I just remembered something from my meeting with Kate. I told you that I caught Lawes hanging around outside the office. Well, when we were trying to work out a time for me to pick up this cassette, I mentioned to Kate that I had an appointment at the yacht club on Friday. I'm sure Lawes heard me. If he suspected I was on a trail that could lead to the *Bandeira Branca,* he might have figured he needed to beat me to the boat—to destroy whatever he feared I would find there."

Ken studied the caped man frozen on the television screen. "The next logical assumption is that Lawes is responsible for the extortion note and the murder. That means he somehow found out about this child of Richardson's that Ned Poole alluded to."

"Remember that Lawes's mother worked closely with Richardson for almost twenty years," Dani said. "She could have learned about the child in much the same way Ned Poole did. Bea would have been too loyal an employee to broadcast such a revelation about her boss, but she might have inadvertently let it slip in front of her son."

"I can go along with that line of reasoning, but that still doesn't answer the question how Lawes managed to kill Richardson."

Dani reached for the remote and released the actors hanging in suspended animation. "Let's look at this tape very carefully. Lawes's role wasn't a major one, so no one's attention would have been riveted on him. See, they're du-elling right now, and you scarcely notice Lawes over there to the side."

"It was dark on the piazza," Ken agreed. "He conceivably could have slipped into the shadows. But would he have had enough time to circle around to the back of the house, shinny up onto the balcony, commit the crime and then get back downstairs before anyone was the wiser?''

Dani frowned as she rewound the videocassette. "I don't know." The admission made her feel profoundly dejected.

Ken reached for the remote control. "Why don't we do a little experiment? Got some paper and a pencil.''

Dani went to the kitchen and returned with a notepad and a felt-tip pen. She sat back down next to Ken, eager to continue.

"Okay, draw a big square on that paper. That'll be our diagram of the stage. Now let's track Mr. Lawes's position. I'm going to move through this tape very slowly. We'll stop the action every time he changes places on stage and make an X on the diagram. I'll time each shift so we'll know approximately how long Lawes could linger on that mark.''

Following Ken's suggestion, they reviewed the tape four times. Although the actor remained toward the front of the stage for the first half of the performance, his position gradually shifted to the rear as the action between the protagonists heated up. By the time the young dance master challenged Captain Parr to a duel, Lawes had drifted to the back of the stage, near the periphery at the left of the screen.

Dani surveyed the black Xs arranged on the pad, along with the time noted next to each. She had been so elated with the lead she thought she had uncovered yet now, their hopes of substantiating it seemed frustratingly remote. "All we've really proved is that Stephen Lawes should have been standing somewhere near the back of the piazza at the end of the performance." She tossed the notepad onto the coffee table and slumped back against the sofa. "Too bad we don't have a tape of Saturday night's performance.''

Ken retrieved the discarded notepad. "We could still give this a dry run. What's to stop us from going to Richardson's house and pacing off Stephen's part in the vignette?

We could even see how long it would take someone to sprint around back and try to get upstairs.''

Dani liked the sound of the plan, but after the debacle of the previous evening, she had written off clandestine operations for good. "What if Bea or Sapphira are at the house? Somehow, I don't think either of them would be thrilled to have us bounding all over the piazza and the back garden."

Ken smiled wryly. "Then I guess we'll just have to wait until they aren't there. It's worth a try," he added, rightly interpreting Dani's ambivalent expression.

Dani shoved herself up from the sofa. "I agree, in principle at least. Why don't we drive over to the house right now, before I come to my senses and back out?"

"Uh, I think we may need to stop by my apartment on the way." Ken stood up, holding the folds of the beach towels out to each side as if he were about to curtsy.

Dani chuckled. "Good thinking. We're going to attract enough attention as it is. And while we're trying to reestablish ourselves as respectable citizens, I ought to give Theo a call. Before he calls me," she added ominously.

Ken followed Dani to the kitchen, posting himself in the doorway to lend moral support. Praying that she hadn't exhausted her entire supply of luck the previous evening, Dani crossed her fingers in the fervent hope that Rebecca wouldn't be visiting her fiancé and chance to pick up the phone. Dani was relieved to hear Theo's cultivated voice answer. Far from expressing any rancor over Dani's presence on the yacht, the younger Boynton was full of gentlemanly concern for her well-being. After empathizing with her interest in seeing the *Bandeira Branca* firsthand, he filled her in on his most recent conversation with the police.

"They haven't charged anyone yet, but I'll continue to press them. To think that such a malicious act of vandalism might have cost two people their lives!" Theo heaved a disgusted sigh.

"Please let me know if there's anything I can do to help further the investigation," Dani urged him. She smiled at Ken and gave him an optimistic thumbs up.

"As a matter of fact, I would appreciate your talking with Richardson's insurance man, Art Prevost. I'll be in Father's office tomorrow morning, trying to catch up on some of his business while the phones are quiet. Art offered to drop by around eleven. If you could be there, it would be very helpful."

"I'll be glad to talk with the insurance agent. In fact, I'll bring along the bartender who accompanied me to the yacht club yesterday. He was injured by the person who set the yacht on fire, you know."

At the word *injured,* Theo swallowed audibly. "Yes, of course, bring him by all means."

After Dani had said goodbye to Theo and hung up, Ken unfolded his arms and followed her to the living room. "Sounds like you aced that one," he complimented her. "Am I going to have to dust off Bartender Ken again tomorrow?"

"Uh-huh, but it's the least we can do for Theo. Besides, who knows what we may learn if we can get him talking about the yacht. Apparently, my luck is on a roll right now. I suggest we head for Richardson's house before it takes a reverse."

Ken disappeared into the bathroom to change into his salt-caked pants and shirt before he and Dani set out on foot from the condo. His apartment was less than five blocks away, closer than Dani had imagined, a tiny furnished efficiency that would almost have fit into her living room. In a record five minutes, Ken had dressed in clean clothes. Another five, and they were in his car, headed toward King Street.

The thoroughfare in front of Richardson's house was lined with cars, but it was impossible to tell if any of them belonged to someone inside the imposing Federal Period home. Ken parked on South Battery, within sight of the house. He and Dani watched for several minutes, alert to any sign of activity behind the bare windows. Finally, Dani reached for the car door latch.

"We're going to sit here until we have cobwebs on us, and we still won't know if anyone is home. I'm going to find out once and for all." She snapped the door open impatiently.

"How?"

Hand still on the car door, Dani stuck her head through the open window. "Knock and see."

If Bea or someone equally forbidding answered the door, Dani would simply say she wanted to apologize for the earlier intrusion. It would be hard to fly into a rage at someone trying to say she was sorry. Still, Dani hoped no one would respond to the horseshoe-shaped brass knocker she was rapping against the door. She knocked three times, waiting a generous interval between each attempt, before she was satisfied that the house was empty. She tried not to feel like a prowler as she waved to Ken, motioning for him to join her.

They both felt faintly silly as they referred to their diagram and began to measure Stephen Lawes's progress around the piazza. Without the crush of guests spilling out of the house and onto the lawn, it was hard to estimate how much space the Ghostwalk troupe had actually occupied. Then, too, a spot that seemed blatantly visible in broad daylight might have afforded the actor plenty of cover at night. By the time they had located and timed Lawes's positions over the entire performance, neither Dani nor Ken felt they had reached any iron-clad conclusions.

"Let's see how long it takes to sprint around to the back of the house from that corner of the piazza," Ken suggested. His eyes followed the sweep hand of his watch as he counted under his breath. He signaled with his hand, and both he and Dani rushed down the piazza steps, past the thick stand of trimmed shrubs and into the rear alley. They were racing toward the wrought-iron gate when they spotted a heavyset woman trudging toward them, a bulky parcel clutched to her chest like a shield. Dani managed to brake just as Mona Sams blinked over the edge of the brown-paper-wrapped bundle.

"Miss Blake! Well, it's certainly nice to see you again." The friendly housekeeper smiled at Dani from behind her burden. "Just had Mr. Whyte's draperies cleaned, and I thought I'd get them hung before they close the house up for good. It's quite a chore, I'll tell you." Her graying head nodded toward a Ford station wagon parked at the end of the alley. The rear of the vehicle sagged, packed to the ceiling with more brown-paper bales.

"I'll get those for you," Ken was quick to offer.

Mrs. Sams smiled in a grateful benediction. "Why, that would be right nice of you." Dani imagined the woman almost added "sonny" before catching herself.

While Ken trekked back and forth between the station wagon and the courtyard, the housekeeper invited Dani to have a seat at the white patio table. Without the threat of Bea Lawes suddenly appearing to put a damper on things, Mona Sams seemed relaxed, even chatty.

"Just make yourself comfortable, Miss Blake. Nobody's here to mind a visitor or two today," the housekeeper confided with a wry smile that left no doubt which somebody she had in mind. She disappeared into the house for a few minutes. When she returned with a rosewood tray decked with minted iced tea and sesame-seed cookies, Ken had just deposited the last of the packages on the brick patio steps.

"When I'm doing housework, I always keep a little something cool in the refrigerator." She dispensed the refreshments with the grace of one practiced in fine service. "Though I don't imagine I'll be doing much work around here after today." The housekeeper stiffly eased her substantial frame onto one of the patio chairs. A heavy sigh stirred her expansive breast, a sound that was at once weary and sad. "Sure is going to take some getting used to, after all these years."

"How long did you work for Richardson? My mother and I were invited to an open house here one Christmas. I was only about ten years old, but I remember the lady who served us eggnog and cookies. You must have come after her."

An earthy chuckle rumbled up from inside Mrs. Sams's chest. "Honey, that *was* me. There was just a whole lot less of me back then. No, ma'am, I've run this house for almost thirty years, before you were even born, I dare say."

Dani smiled down at her plate, breaking a chunk off one of the crisp wafers. "But only barely." Her face sobered as she looked up at the sturdy woman sipping tea across from her. "This must be quite an adjustment for you."

Mona replaced the sweating glass on the table. "Thirty years," she repeated, as if she had trouble believing that impressive figure herself. "'Course, when Mrs. Whyte was still alive, I only came in for part of the day or to help out when they were having a big party. That was just fine with me. I didn't want to work full-time anyhow when my young ones were still at home."

"Richardson never had any children, did he?" Ken asked.

The housekeeper shook her head as she reached to refill his glass. "No. To tell you the truth, I don't think his missus wanted 'em—that was just one of the things they didn't see eye to eye on. She was high-strung—you know, the kind that always has to have everything just so in its place. Believe me, that's not easy when there are children about." Her large dark eyes traveled from Dani to Ken as if she were offering them a bit of cautionary advice. "But I do think Mr.

Whyte wished he had done different on that count when he started to get on in years, all alone by himself.''

Ken casually fished out a mint leaf floating on the tea's amber surface. ''How do you know?''

Mona's strapping shoulders rose in a shrug. ''I just know how I'd feel right now if I didn't have a bunch of grandkids to fuss over and spoil. But, no, I believe Mr. Whyte made a big mistake not taking another wife.''

''Maybe he never met the right person,'' Dani suggested, helping herself to another cookie.

''Could be, although there were lots of ladies who wouldn't have minded becoming Mrs. Whyte, I can guarantee that.'' Mona's voice dropped to a confidential hush. ''Especially that secretary of his.''

''You mean Bea Lawes?'' Ken's dark blue eyes widened in interest.

Mona Sams pursed her lips, making only the flimsiest attempt to conceal her distaste. ''I've never approved of a woman chasing after a man, mind you, but I know sometimes a person just can't help herself. Even so, Beatrice Lawes went too far. Taking advantage of a grieving man when he's most likely to have a weak moment!'' The housekeeper clucked disapprovingly. ''Why after Mrs. Whyte passed away, wasn't a week gone by when Bea was in this house trying to take over. I let her know, plain as I could without being rude, that I could manage Mr. Whyte's house without any of her help, thank you. But, oh, she was a trial! Always 'dear Richardson this' and 'poor Richardson that,' always meddling in his affairs, looking after what he ate and wore, telling him what to do like he was a little boy. I could see clear as anything that she was trying to get him so dependent on her, he'd *have* to marry her.''

''Did Richardson seem to chafe under Bea's attention?'' Dani asked.

Mona heaved another of her eloquent sighs. "I think he was a bit flattered by it," she conceded. "But you know how men are when women fuss over them." She hastily cast an apologetic glance at Ken before going on. "Still, I think Bea Lawes was one reason Mr. Whyte would hightail it off to Brazil for months on end, just to get free of her for a while. Now if it had been me, I would have given her a big hint to start looking for another job. Mr. Whyte was too good-hearted for that, though, especially after Bea's husband had up and left her with a child to raise all by herself." Mona's gaze shifted to the empty serving dish. "Would you care for some more cookies?"

"No, thank you, Mrs. Sams." Dani exchanged glances with Ken, but she could see that he, too, was eager to have a private talk. "This was really lovely. I hope we haven't kept you from your work." Smiling, she stood up, and Ken followed suit.

"Not at all. To be honest, I don't much care to spend a lot of time here by myself since everything happened. This house just has a funny feel to it." For the first time that afternoon, a shadow of uneasiness passed across Mona's face. "I'm going to make quick work of those drapes and then be on my way home. I've got a grandson that's turning ten tomorrow, and I want to bake him a big chocolate cake."

Dani wished Mona an enjoyable birthday celebration with her grandson. After she and Ken thanked the kindly woman again, they let themselves out of the wrought-iron gate opening into the alley. As they turned into King Street, Dani plucked at Ken's elbow.

"You know what I think?" Even though the traffic from South Battery effectively muffled their conversation to all but the most attentive passerby, Dani held her voice to a hoarse whisper.

"Stephen Lawes is Richardson Whyte's son?" Ken looked as if he still needed some convincing.

Dani nodded emphatically. "Just consider what we learned from Mona. Richardson's marriage didn't sound all that happy. In a weak moment, he had an affair with his secretary. He came to his senses, decided he wanted to save his marriage and broke off the extramarital relationship. In the meantime, Bea discovered she was pregnant and insisted on having their child."

"That would have raised a lot of eyebrows, don't you think?" Ken put in. For once, Dani found his clear, analytical tone slightly irritating.

"That all depends." Dani knew she had advanced a daring proposition, but she was prepared to defend it. If she could use Ken's own research to that end, all the better. "How much did you find out about Bea's personal background?"

"I can't remember everything, and I gave my notes to Derek. But I recall she was married for three or four years to some guy in sales. Stephen is her only kid."

"She was working for Richardson while she was still married?"

"Uh-huh."

"How old is Stephen?" Dani prodded Ken's elbow again as they sprinted across South Battery.

"Twenty-five, twenty-six."

Dani halted beside Ken's parked car, her face set in a grimly triumphant smile. "Then it would have been entirely possible for Bea to have passed Stephen off as her husband's son."

"You think Stephen learned about his parentage somehow and decided to blackmail a half million dollars out of the father who had never acknowledged him?" Ken frowned, and Dani could tell he was repulsed by the scenario he had just painted.

Dani felt her own stomach turn as the obvious corollary occurred to her: Stephen Lawes had murdered his own father out of spite. "We have to consider the possibility."

Ken was taking his time unlocking the door. "It's a compelling theory, *if* we're willing to accept a couple of assumptions. First, that whoever phoned Richardson that night had nothing to do with his murder, and second, that Lawes was physically capable of slipping away from the performance and invading the upstairs office," he reminded Dani as he held the door open for her. "Don't forget, too, that Stephen would have had to find out the truth about his parentage somewhere along the way. That's the really big question—how?"

Dani paused in the door of the car, turning to look directly into Ken's eyes. "I don't know yet, but I think it's our job to find out."

Chapter Ten

Sometime in the night, a low bank of clouds had rolled i
from the ocean to settle over Charleston like a suffocatin
gray blanket. Deprived of the sunlight that normally re
lieved the shadows of its close alleys and walled gardens, th
old district seemed somber, its usual gaiety subdued by th
moody sky. Even the mingled bells of St. Michael's and S
Philip's sounded faintly mournful as they performed the
centuries-old task of summoning the city to Sunday wor
ship.

Her own frame of mind was doing nothing to counter
balance the melancholy atmosphere, Dani reflected as sh
and Ken paused to check the number of a Tradd Stre
mansion that had been converted to office space. Since the
conversation with Mona Sams, the implications of th
housekeeper's revelations about Bea Lawes had dogge
Dani's thoughts, tormenting her with spectral clues an
half-formed conjectures. Even the usually powerful di
traction of getting ready for a big party had failed to di
place her preoccupation. While Dani had wandered aroun
Moveable Feast's kitchen the previous evening, mechan
cally preparing Beef Wellington and lemon mousse, she ha
continued to ponder the case against Stephen Lawes—an
the difficulty of proving it.

Ken paused on the house's narrow stoop, holding the carved oak door half-open. "Let's stay on our toes with Theo. Who knows? After that unexpected windfall of information Mrs. Sams dropped on us yesterday, I don't think we should write off anyone as an exhausted source."

"I agree." Dani led the way down the hall, following its Oriental carpet runner to a door bearing the engraved brass plaque Powell E. Boynton, Esq., Theodore R. Boynton, Esq., Attorneys at Law.

The indistinct murmur of men's voices on the other side of the door caused Dani to knock lightly before testing the knob. She opened the door slowly and surveyed the neat, well-equipped secretarial station. Against the backdrop of ornate molding and Federal Period antiques, the computer and fax machine looked like space-age anachronisms. The door to one of the two private offices was ajar, revealing a man seated in a leather wing chair with a briefcase open on his lap. Ken slipped in behind Dani, closing the door behind him loudly enough to announce their arrival.

"Dani!" Theo Boynton appeared in the private office door and then charged across the room to greet them. "It's so kind of you to come by this morning. Art and I were just going over Richardson's insurance policy covering the boat." He hastened to get on with introductions, acknowledging Ken with the automatic smile and handshake of a political hopeful.

Dani and Ken followed the two men into the inner sanctum of Powell Boynton's office. Bearing in mind Ken's admonition to be on the lookout for clues, Dani listened attentively to the details Theo offered about the *Bandeira Branca*'s wreckage.

"Definitely arson, the police say." He gave Art Prevost a prompting look and the insurance agent duly nodded.

"Any idea who would want to destroy the yacht?" Dani asked.

Theo lifted both hands in a nonplussed gesture and then let them drop onto the leather blotter covering his father's desk.

Art Prevost tapped the tablet of preprinted forms propped on his knee with the air of a man accustomed to fielding such questions. "Sometimes, it's kids acting on a dare. Or, as seems most likely in this case, young hoodlums with a few too many beers in them, out to prove how tough they are. Their buddies egg them on and before they know it, they're in over their heads."

"There was only one person on that boat," Dani told him.

"Did you see him?" Art Prevost slid his glasses down his thin nose and rubbed the bridge thoughtfully.

"No," Dani replied. "But I heard only one person's footsteps. If there was anyone else on board, he never moved."

Ken didn't hesitate to throw his support behind her argument. "When we first boarded the yacht, we didn't hear a sound that would indicate someone else was there. A bunch of punks tanked up on beer is simply incapable of being that quiet."

Art Prevost readjusted his glasses, the better to inspect the two people who had just shot holes in his theory. "It could have been the work of one malicious individual, of course," he conceded huffily.

"Was there anything of value on the yacht? Something that the intruder might have wanted to steal before he set the boat on fire?" Dani ignored Prevost's perturbed glance that clearly suggested she was invading his bailiwick.

Theo clasped his hands behind his head, leaning back in the big, leather-upholstered executive chair. "Well, there were small things, navigational equipment, a radio and the like. Sailing is not an inexpensive hobby, you know. I must admit I'm a little stunned since I've had to reckon up the amount of money I've put into restoring that yacht. Of course, this would all be a lot simpler if Richardson had agreed to sell me the boat outright in the first place.'' His eyes drifted to Prevost to reinforce the point. ''But to get back to your question, the only thing we're certain was stolen is the motor boat.''

''Have the police recovered the boat?'' Despite the calm, collected manner she had adopted for the interview, Dani leaned forward in her eagerness to hear what might be a telling clue.

Theo shook his head as he tipped the chair upright. ''Their guess is that whoever used it to escape pushed it out from shore and sank it once he—or they—reached land.''

Dani said nothing, but as she exchanged glances with Ken, she could tell that he, too, was convinced that such a careful effort to cover tracks would never have occurred to a pack of drunken vandals. For the next half hour, however, she and Ken kept their suspicions to themselves as they responded to Art Prevost's battery of questions. Yes, Ken was scheduled for a follow-up medical exam the following week, but, no, the doctors didn't think he had anything to worry about. Yes, Dani had inspected her van thoroughly since Ken had driven her out to recover it the previous afternoon, and it appeared to be unharmed. The further they progressed through Prevost's form, the more Dani felt as if she were being questioned about a routine fender bender rather than a life-threatening assault. She was relieved when the insurance agent flipped his black vinyl folder closed and returned it to his briefcase. Theo, too, seemed happy to conclude the interview, although, Dani suspected, for very different reasons.

As soon as he had ushered Prevost out of the office, Theo returned to his remaining visitors. ''This incident with the yacht was really the last thing I needed right now.'' He regarded the fat legal-size folders stacked on both sides of the desk as if they were ticking time bombs only seconds away from exploding in his face.

"I was terribly sorry to hear about your father. How is he doing?" Dani had been intending to ask about the elder Boynton's condition earlier, but this was the first opportunity the meeting had afforded.

Theo ran his fingers through his hair, still staring at the threatening desktop. "Much better, although they still won't say when he'll be allowed to come home. Of course, even then, work will be out of the question, at least for the early stage of his convalescence. I'm his partner, so I'm familiar with a lot of his cases. Still, he has some really sticky wickets in progress right now. Richardson's will alone is enough to give a Supreme Court justice a headache."

Dani blinked in surprise. "Why is that?"

Theo looked as if his last comment had slipped out by accident and that he now regretted the lapse. "It's a complicated estate." The cagey explanation only underscored his hesitancy.

"I suppose because he left no direct heirs." Dani watched Theo, studying the bland, clean-shaven face to gauge the impact of her remark.

"Well, yes, of course." Was it her imagination, or was he the least bit flustered? When she met his eyes, she was startled by the hard glint that had supplanted their customary ingratiating expression. "Actually, Richardson thought of Rebecca as a daughter, especially since her father passed away. Although I'm not aware of the details of his will—nor would I, understandably, be free to discuss them if I were— I fully expect him to have left her the bulk of his estate, with the remainder going to loyal employees, servants and charity."

"Knowing Richardson, I imagine he would have wanted to ensure Mrs. Sams a comfortable retirement—and Bea Lawes, as well, for that matter," Dani remarked.

Theo opened one of the legal folders at random and frowned over its contents. "Yes, I suppose he would have. By the way, if you have a few minutes, I'd like to discuss the Hospital Auxiliary costume ball with you. I've assumed responsibility for coordinating the event since Father was hospitalized." He sounded pleased to be rid of the subject of Richardson's will as he reached for the desk calendar. "Would it be possible for us to meet at the Old Exchange sometime this week? I could walk you through the space we've reserved and explain exactly how it will be set up."

Dani dug her calendar out of her handbag and opened it. "I always like to get a good advance look at the room where I'll be catering a party. It's really the best way to guarantee that service will flow smoothly. Would you be able to do it on Wednesday or Thursday afternoon?"

Theo riffled the pages of the calendar and then replaced it on the desk. "Excuse me while I check my own calendar." He headed out of the office, muttering something about the difficulty of keeping track of two schedules. As he disappeared into the reception area, Dani heard the front door of the office slam.

"You said you would be finished in time for lunch!" Rebecca Pope's voice wove itself into a whine that was at once wheedling and confrontational.

"I've had a lot of business to take care of for Richardson and Father. You know that, sweetheart." Theo's term of endearment did not entirely conceal his irritation.

"Well, it's almost one o'clock!" Dani could imagine Rebecca's determinedly downturned mouth, the challenging look of a spoiled child in her big blue eyes.

"Please just have a seat. I'll only be another moment," Theo cajoled.

"Oh, very well then!"

Dani and Ken looked at each other and shook their heads in silent commiseration with poor Theo. As Dani leaned to one side, she saw Rebecca perched impatiently on the edge of the green leather chaise. When her eyes met Dani's, they darkened. Dani smiled cordially and then sat back in her chair, withdrawing from Rebecca's sight. When Theo returned to Powell's office, the skin above his collar was flushed and he looked slightly embarrassed.

"Is Wednesday afternoon at three o'clock all right with you?" He sounded uncertain, as if he almost expected the same contrariness from Dani that he by now must take for granted with Rebecca.

"Perfect." Dani marked her calendar and then stood up. "I have a big dinner to cater tonight, so Ken and I really ought to be going. Is there anything else you need from us?"

Theo shook his head. "Thank you again. You were both a tremendous help." For once, the slick manner of the professional campaigner had been replaced by an expression of genuine gratitude.

"The-*o!*" Rebecca stood in the doorway, apparently ready to take the matter of speeding the visitors' departure into her own hands.

"Hello, Rebecca." Dani gave the young woman another serene smile.

When Rebecca only glared at Dani, Ken nodded. "It's a pleasure to see you again, Miss Pope."

"Hello." Rebecca must have intended her single, terse greeting to suffice for both of them.

At least we've had a touch of humor to relieve an otherwise depressing morning, Dani thought as she exchanged parting handshakes with Theo. Rebecca was obviously beside herself that her rebuff had failed to keep them off the yacht; for all her storybook-princess prettiness, the woman was a bully, pure and simple. Even now, she was launching another volley of petty complaints at Theo.

Dani hurried toward the door, eager to get away from the scene of strife. It was only by chance that she happened to look at the calendar sitting sideways on Powell's desk. It was lying open to the previous Monday, the day of Richardson's funeral. But it was the cryptic notation that grabbed her attention and held it with a throttling grip.

"Richardson's office, 9:00 a.m. Transfer title *Bandeira Branca*."

"WHAT DO YOU SUPPOSE Richardson was planning to do with the yacht?" Dani did a sideways double step, the better to look Ken in the face.

Frowning, Ken carelessly kicked at the crisp layer of leaves covering the sidewalk. "Maybe deed it to Theo? It certainly sounded as if Theo had invested quite a bit of money in a yacht that wasn't even his. Perhaps Richardson had decided to give him formal ownership. After all, Theo is going to be an official member of the Whyte family pretty soon."

Dani brushed off his suggestion. "Then Theo would surely have known about it. Even assuming that Richardson wanted to transfer the title secretly, as a surprise to his niece's future husband, there's no way Theo wouldn't have discovered what was afoot since he's taken over his father's work load. At the very least, he had to have seen that calendar notation." When Ken made no comment, she stepped in front of him, effectively halting him in his tracks. "Well?" Her intelligent hazel eyes prodded him to respond.

Ken settled his hands on her shoulders. "I don't know what the hell it means," he confessed. He began to smile, feeling his mouth widen in a mirror image of Dani's own slow grin.

"I guess I keep expecting to find *the* clue that will explain everything, but that doesn't happen very often, does it?" When Ken shook his head, she grimaced wryly.

"Maybe I don't have the patience to be a good investigator."

"You think I do?" Ken chuckled as he gave her shoulders a light squeeze.

She felt so slight inside his grasp; a man who knew her less well could be deceived by her delicate frame. Yet Ken had seen firsthand the formidable will housed inside the slender body, the dauntless spirit that had confronted fear and refused to succumb. He had never known a woman like her before, but the union of such frank femininity with unconquerable strength exerted a powerful attraction for him. For a moment, he wanted to put the whole sordid business of Richardson's murder aside, forget they were standing on a street corner in the middle of Charleston and take her in his arms, hold her like the treasure she was, never let her go.

"How can we find out what Richardson intended to do in that meeting with Powell?" Dani's gently insistent voice pricked the rosy bubble forming in Ken's head, catapulting him back to reality.

"Sooner or later, we'll be able to talk with Powell himself. In the meantime, I'll see what Derek thinks. I'm going to drop by his place tonight. I had left a message for him and he called me as soon as he got back into town last night. I think he was pretty upset about the business with the yacht."

"So was I," Dani remarked drily. She fell in step with Ken's ambling gate that was calculated to give them more time before they reached her van.

"I'll fill him in on everything we've been considering." Ken paused a few car lengths short of the blue Aerostar. "All the same, I wish you could be there."

"So do I." Dani reluctantly glanced at her watch. "As it is, I fear duty is calling already. I promised Ben and Elaine we'd set up by six, and I still have some last-minute preparations to take care of in the kitchen." She fingered her car keys, resuming her way to the van.

Ken followed her. After she had unlocked the van and climbed behind the wheel, he closed the door behind her. He leaned toward the open window, gripping the frame with both hands. "I'll be in touch, if not tonight, then sometime tomorrow."

"Good." Dani nodded, but her hand on the ignition key didn't move.

She looked exquisitely beautiful with her wealth of soft, waving hair billowing around her shoulders, her eyes muted to the shade of gold-brown agates in the sunless light. Framed by the open window, she reminded Ken of a portrait of some regal beauty, at once captivating and out of reach.

"I need to go now." Dani smiled, looking down at his hands clutching the door as she cranked the ignition.

Ken stepped back from the van. "Good luck tonight." He saw her mouth the same words as she rolled up the window and pulled away from the curb.

DANI'S PERSONAL ACCOUNT of their harrowing experience aboard the *Bandeira Branca* would have given Derek a broader perspective on the incident, Ken lamented as he drove to Derek Cannaday's Meeting Street residence that evening. Dani had been aware of the intruder's activity while Ken himself had lain helpless and unconscious in the corridor of the hold. She had also had more direct contact with Stephen Lawes, both immediately after the murder and later at the theater. As Ken wedged his compact rental car into a parking space, however, he admitted the most compelling reason he wished she were with him: he missed her when she wasn't.

Ken tried to remind himself that this was no time to get sidetracked by an infatuation—only to run up against the undeniable truth that his relationship with Dani had long since passed the point where it could be written off as a trivial crush. Dramatic events had a way of heightening emotions, Ken knew; surviving the near-fatal episode at sea would have created a bond between a far-less-likely couple than they. But Ken realized that something more powerful than a shared adventure now linked them, something that made him feel more confident and secure when they were together, almost incomplete when they were apart.

In the cool, covering darkness, he felt his face warm at the memory of how he had opened up to her. He never talked about his awful childhood, never expected anyone to understand, never wanted to revive the old ache that, left alone, was content to lie dormant most of the time. He was still only dimly aware of the impulses that had prompted him to spill his heart's pain in front of her. He had felt spent afterward, but strangely eased, too, like someone whose fever has broken after a long illness. The recollection of her soothing embrace calmed him now, gave Ken a sense of not being entirely alone as he approached Derek Cannaday's home.

The three-story house was a fine example of the Charleston "single-house," a term, Ken recalled with a pang, first introduced to him by Richardson Whyte. Characterized by a frontage that was only one room wide, the single-house usually compensated for its narrow breadth by rising two or three stories high and extending several rooms deep. As with most homes of the type, the front door of Derek's house was positioned to one side and actually led to an open piazza.

Through the latticework fence, the piazza lights cut a lacy pattern on the sidewalk. Outside the closed door, Ken could hear voices coming from the piazza. He was about to knock when the precise yet drawling intonation of one of the speakers brought him up short. Ken took a cautious peek through the fence and confirmed that Theo Boynton had just risen from one of the piazza's wicker chairs.

Derek's unexpected company forced Ken to do some quick thinking. Theo, of course, knew him only as a bartender, a guise that he and Dani might want to use again in the future. Then, too, Theo looked as if he was getting ready to leave. Ken decided to take a walk around the block and give Derek a chance to see Boynton off before his next visitor put in an appearance.

Ken had no intention of eavesdropping, but as he walked past the lattice barrier, he couldn't help but overhear a snatch of Theo's conversation. "We can't afford a scandal, I tell you. My family can't and I can't!" The young attorney sounded agitated. "Voters don't forget this kind of thing, Derek."

Instantly on alert, Ken crouched next to the fence. A freshet of adrenaline coursed through him as he strained to catch Derek's response.

"This will all be laid to rest soon," Derek was saying. "I spoke with the police—"

"Damn the police!" Theo cut in with a violence Ken hadn't suspected he possessed. "If this goes too far, Derek, I swear..." He swallowed his unspoken threat.

To his credit, Derek was at least managing to sound unruffled. "We've all been under a terrible strain, Theo. You especially, having to deal with Powell's illness. Go home and get some rest. Everything will be all right. I'm certain."

The men's footsteps resounded hollowly off the wooden floor of the piazza. Ken sprang up and dashed around the corner just before the front door opened.

A scandal! Theo's prediction rang in his ears, echoing with a dire resonance. He had to be talking about Richardson's illegitimate child! No wonder Boynton had gotten so stiff and testy when Dani had mentioned Richardson's lack of direct heirs that morning! Ken realized he was walking at almost a jog, and he hastened to slow his pace to a less-conspicuous speed. He took a deep breath, bridling his ex-

citement as Derek's house once more drew into sight. He
waited outside the door for a few seconds, making sure Theo
had departed before ringing the bell.

"Ken! I was just having a sherry on the piazza. It's such
a lovely, mild evening. Would you care for something to
drink?" Derek ushered Ken onto the piazza.

"Sherry would be fine." Ken seated himself in one of the
white wicker chairs and waited while Derek went into the
house to fetch his drink.

"After what you've been through, I imagine you need
this." Derek smiled as he handed the glass to Ken. The uneven light of the hurricane lamps softened the drawn lines
of his face, making him look a little less harried than usual.

Ken took a sip of the fruit-and-nut-scented liquid. "I went
with Dani Blake to talk with Theo and the insurance guy this
morning. Everyone still thinks I'm the bartender, of course.
Theo seemed to take it all in stride, as much as he could be
expected to." Ken paused, giving Derek a chance to segue
into a discussion of Theo's concerns about a scandal.

"Theo is an ambitious young man, but basically decent"
was Derek's only comment.

Cannaday was a friend of the Whyte family, Ken reminded himself. He might be unwilling to discuss an issue
that Richardson's kin would regard as personal dirt to be
swept out of sight under the carpet. Hadn't Richardson
opted to handle the extortion note through private chan-
nels, without involving the police? The sobering thought of
how badly awry that attempt at guarding family privacy had
gone prompted Ken to take a more direct approach with
Derek.

"I learned something that I believe has critical bearing on
this case," Ken began. "Did Richardson Whyte ever intimate that he might have had an illegitimate child?"

Derek's fingers tapped the rim of the sherry glass for a
long moment before answering. "I imagine there are a lot

of people who wish they could lay claim to Richardson's estate, but no, he never said anything of the sort to me. Why do you ask?''

Ken recounted Dani's conversation with Ned Poole, along with Stephen Lawes's suspicious behavior that Dani had witnessed. "I know we don't have any real hard evidence against Lawes," he concluded, anticipating Derek's objections. "But you've got to admit, he keeps cropping up in this mess with amazing regularity. He was at Richardson's house the night of the murder, and he eavesdropped on Dani the day before we traced the yacht-club pin. And now we know his mother was in love with Richardson."

Derek cleared his throat before speaking. "The police have any number of suspects, Ken. You know, you're not alone in this investigation." Ken tried not to let the brief smile Derek inserted irritate him. "We have to be careful making unsupported accusations, however. Let's look carefully at the case against Lawes. What do we have really? The gossip of a fisherman and a housekeeper. A few remarks and dark looks to which Miss Blake took exception. But nothing that any prosecutor would ever dream of introducing before a jury."

Ken resented Derek's dismissal of Dani's role in the investigation, but he forced himself to stay cool. He should have realized that no one close to the appearance-conscious Whyte family would welcome with unqualified enthusiasm a scenario involving an illegitimate child. The fact that Derek had made no mention of Theo's visit only underscored his suspicion. He sensed that Derek would be furious if he knew that Ken had overheard part of the conversation, however inadvertently.

"Look, I know none of Richardson's family would want something like this splattered all over the newspaper, especially if it turned out to have no connection with the murder. The public will remember a scandal long after they've forgotten the proof that it wasn't true after all. But we can't let a murderer go scot-free just to save face." He paused, giving his words time to soak in. "What if I brought you some hard evidence?"

Derek studied the play of the lamp light on the sparkling sherry glasses. "Then I'd go straight to the police." The admission seemed to require a great effort from him. "Exactly what do you have in mind?"

"I'm going to have a look in Richardson's private office and see if I can find anything in his personal papers."

Derek shook his head and chuckled softly. "Ken, I can guarantee you that Sapphira Whyte would never hear of such a thing."

"Sapphira Whyte won't know, Derek. No one will. I still have the house key Richardson gave me when he hired me." Ken regarded Derek steadily, waiting for him either to ask for the key back or to relent.

A serious expression settled over Derek's gaunt features. "Sapphira would still consider it trespassing." He stared into the dark garden, not looking at Ken. "When do you plan to carry out this . . . operation?"

His plan had been conceived so quickly, Ken had not actually had time to consider the logistics of its execution. Now that Derek was warming to the idea, however, he couldn't afford to waffle. "Tomorrow night."

Still avoiding Ken's gaze, Derek nodded. He lifted the empty sherry glass and examined the flowers etched in the crystal. "Then I suppose you must. But let me remind you, everyone has taken a benevolent view of your escapade on the yacht with Miss Blake. Rest assured, however, that they won't be as quick to forgive this. If you're caught, you will be on your own." He replaced the glass on the table and turned to face Ken. "I like you, Ken, and I admire your guts. But I don't want my name associated with anything il-

egal. As far as I'm concerned, we never had this conversa-
ion. Do you understand?"

Ken met the opaque gray eyes without blinking. "I understand."

DEREK SAT WITHOUT MOVING, watching the oil lamp's wick
gutter inside its crystal cage. An enervating heaviness had
descended on him, pinioning him to the chair. *The weight
of so many mistakes,* he thought, *mistakes that will outlive
those who made them.* A bitter laugh welled up in him and
died unvoiced.

When the lamp expired, he finally roused himself, taking
strength from the unbroken darkness. Inside the house, he
walked to his desk. Without bothering to turn on the desk
lamp, he reached for the phone. He listened to the monot-
onous ringing, counseled himself to be patient, to wait. The
servants would have long since retired, but she never slept.
In time, she would answer.

"Good evening, Sapphira."

"Good evening, Derek." Her voice had an eerily calm
quality to it, as if she had been expecting him to call and
knew what he would say.

"The secret isn't safe anymore." Derek fell silent, knowing that, for Sapphira, the simple, ungarnished statement
would suffice.

She was quiet for what seemed a very long time. Derek
thought he detected the faint murmur of her breath, surging and receding beneath the silence on the wire. When she
at last spoke, her voice was flat, all the more forbidding for
its lack of expression.

"I cannot allow anyone to know. I simply cannot."

Chapter Eleven

The stout salt breeze gusting off the harbor lifted Dani's hair, whipping a few fine strands free of the barrette binding them. Turning her back to the wind, she rested her elbows on the barricade rising above the breakwater.

"Just how do you plan to get into the house?" She posed the question matter-of-factly, as if she were asking him what he wanted for lunch or which television program he preferred. "Even with a key, you could trip a burglar alarm and have the whole city police force down on you in minutes."

From the embankment, Ken could just make out the white-columned piazza through the urban forest of Battery Park. "When Richardson first hired me, I did a thorough security check of his house. The place has no alarm system. Charleston has a very low crime rate, so I suppose no one ever saw the need to fortify the house. Anyway, I should be able to unlatch the courtyard gate and let myself in through those French doors in less than five minutes. All in all, I'm confident it'll be a piece of cake." Despite his bravado, Ken frowned, squinting into the midmorning haze. For all his eagerness to inspect Whyte's office, he was having trouble adjusting to the role of housebreaker.

Dani was, too, apparently. Lines of consternation pleated her brow as she shifted to face him. "It *sounds* workable enough. And you're sure Derek couldn't persuade Sap phira to give him access to the house. She wouldn't have to know you were going to accompany him." Dani's less-than-hopeful tone suggested that she knew Ken had already explored this idea and discarded it.

He shook his head. "To be honest with you, Dani, I think Derek is a little intimidated by the Whyte family's concern for privacy. He never even mentioned his conversation with Theo before I arrived last night."

"And you didn't bring it up?"

"What could I have said? 'By the way, I pressed my ear to the fence and overheard you and Theo talking about a scandal'?" Ken laughed briefly. "There's no way I'm going to get an invitation into that house," he concluded.

Dani sighed as she glanced toward the park. "We have a new moon tonight, so it will be dark as pitch. If we wear black clothes, that will give us some cover, too."

"We?" He should have seen it coming, Ken knew. A spunky woman like Dani was not going to want to miss out on this critical stage of the investigation.

Dani's fine eyebrows rose in surprise. "Well, of course. You don't think I'm going to let you pull off a stunt like this by yourself, do you?"

"It's too risky, Dani," Ken protested.

"Since when? You just said it would be a 'piece of cake.' You'd better make up your mind." Her tight little smile needled him—and he could tell she knew it.

Ken heaved an exasperated sigh. "Okay, I made this thing sound easier than I really expect it to be," he confessed. Before he could go on, Dani jumped to make her point.

"And that's why there should be two of us. I can keep watch while you're getting into the house and actually searching the office. We could have a signal that I would give if anyone showed up unexpectedly."

Ken knew he needed to move fast before he succumbed to her tempting—and very logical—argument. "Dani, please listen to me. I fully expect my plan to come off without a hitch. But I have to consider the possibility that something will go wrong. If there is a mess-up, Derek isn't going to stand behind me. As far as the Whytes are concerned, I'll be a common prowler, caught in the act.'' He took her by the shoulders, holding her firmly but gently. ''I can't let you risk everything on this scheme. Look at all you have to lose— your business, your position in the community, everything.''

''And you have nothing to lose?'' Dani lifted her head, thrusting out her chin in a challenge.

His hands flexed uncertainly on her shoulders. Ken swallowed, looking out across the harbor's billowing silver-gray waves. There had been a time in the not-too-distant past when he would have defiantly shot back ''Yes''; at a time when the premium he placed on each day of his life had seemed hardly worth reckoning. Yet now, he was struck by how sharply his perspective had changed, how greedy he was for life now that Dani was a part of it. That something could happen that would irrevocably separate them sobered him more than any danger he had ever faced.

''Please, Dani. Try to understand.'' He looked into the hazel eyes that today seemed to reflect the frothing water of the harbor. Surely she must know a little of what he felt, why he was pleading with her, how much he really cared about her.

''Please promise you'll call me as soon as you get home.'' It was the closest she could bring herself to relenting, Ken knew. Her voice dropped, its defiance displaced by undisguised concern. ''And take care of yourself.''

''I will.'' He pulled her forward, letting his lips graze her forehead lightly. ''I promise.''

TO HAVE ALLOWED DANI to come with him would have been an act of utter irresponsibility. Ken remained convinced that he had made the only possible decision under the circumstances, even as he approached the forbiddingly dark house that night. At the same time, he wasn't ashamed to admit how much he had come to depend on her clear thinking, her calm manner and, most of all, her simply *being* there.

But this was one time he must act alone, Ken reminded himself. He took a last, quick survey of the deserted street before slipping into the unrelieved shadows of the alley. He hugged the brick wall, cloaking himself in its penumbra until he reached the wrought-iron gate. His gloved hand looked sinister, as if it should belong to someone else, as it worked its way between the black iron curlicues. The latch lifted easily, without a sound.

Ken tested the gate. His face contorted at the painful squeak he provoked from the hinges. He eased the gate open, taking a deep breath as if he could somehow absorb the grating sound within himself. The courtyard was even darker than the alley. Ken closed the gate and then paused, giving his eyes a chance to adjust to the ill-defined shapes surrounding him. He listened, mistrustful of the silence pervading the humid night air.

It's now or never, McCabe. Ken prodded himself into action. The moss-covered bricks muffled his footsteps as he walked to the curtained French doors. He crouched beside the lock, carefully inserted the key and turned it. The lock snapped open with a modest little click.

Now that his invasion of the house was underway, Ken didn't intend to waste a second. Stopping only long enough to pull the doors closed behind him, he fished the flashlight out of his pocket and made his way quickly through the big receiving room. The last time he had seen this room, it had been bright with sparkling chandeliers and gaily dressed revelers. Tonight, the ghosts of that evening's tragic conclusion seemed to hover in the unlighted corners, among the sheet-draped furniture, behind the shrouded mirrors.

Ken hurried into the hall and up the stairs. He hesitated midway, alert to any vestige of movement, any wisp of sound. He glanced over the rail into the dizzying vortex formed by the curve of the free-flying staircase. Looking down at the dark hall was like gazing into a bottomless pit, its unseen region full of secrecy and foreboding. Ken hastily turned and cleared the remainder of the stairs two at a time.

The second floor was even quieter than the first, its polished wood floors shielded by antique carpets, its chambers isolated from what little sound carried from the street. Although common sense told him he was alone in the house, Ken instinctively listened outside Richardson's study before noiselessly turning the knob. In contrast to the ground floor rooms, the study furnishings had been left uncovered. Books still filled the shelves; a cluster of potted palms still stood in a corner near the balcony doors. As his flashlight swept the room, Ken was startled by how normal it looked, as if Mona Sams had simply tidied it up to await her employer's return from a trip to Brazil.

Ken followed the flashlight's beam to the big desk. He skimmed the light over the brass paper weight, the engraved letter opener, the Mark Cross pen set in its leather holder. When he found the desk calendar, he bent to examine it. No one had bothered to turn the page since that fateful Saturday night. Ken thumbed past Sunday to Monday. There it was, a notation similar to the one Dani had discovered on Powell Boynton's calendar! "Transfer *Bandeira,* 9:00 a.m."

If Richardson had been expecting to conduct this as yet undetermined business with his attorney within a couple of days, he might have already assembled the necessary papers or material within easy reach. That thought sent Ken on a methodical examination of the desktop. He pawed through the in box, but its contents amounted to no more than a couple of business magazines and a letter soliciting Richardson's help with a charity drive.

Of course, Bea Lawes had been on hand the previous week to help Sapphira organize Richardson's effects. Her zeal had probably extended to storing away anything of importance. Ken glanced around the room and located a credenza as well as two built-in cabinets beneath the bookcases. Propping the flashlight against the telephone, he decided to begin his search with the desk itself.

The first drawer he tried was unlocked, a lucky break that Ken tried to interpret as a good omen. Unfortunately, the drawer contained nothing more interesting than a stock prospectus and a few statements from a brokerage firm. Ken moved on to the next drawer. This one was fitted with hanging files filled with alphabetized folders labeled in a neat, fastidious hand that he guessed to be that of Beatrice Lawes. Seating himself on the floor, Ken inspected the files. In the limited light, the work was slow and painstaking, made all the more so by the routine nature of the material. He leafed past letters to customers, letters from customers, duplicates and triplicates of the myriad forms generated by an import-export business. As he neared the *F*s, Ken was tempted to give the remaining files a cursory once-over, but he resisted the urge. His conscientious attention, however, yielded nothing of value.

At least the next drawer was easy to scan, filled as it was with a few small boxes. One contained business cards; another, some postage stamps that had long since glued themselves together. Ken was beginning to feel as if he had embarked on a very risky wild-goose chase when he discovered a flat box, bound with an elastic ribbon, underneath the stamps and business cards.

The expanding ribbon was so old, it had lost much of its elasticity. The once-gilded coating crumbled in his hands as Ken slid it off the box. A rush of anticipation washed over him when he opened the box. The envelopes and folded stationery were discolored with age, the flowing script that graced them full of the blots and calligraphic flourishes that only an old-fashioned fountain pen could attain. Ken lifted the envelope resting on top of the stack and reached for the flashlight. Just as his hand closed over the metal cylinder, he froze.

Ken snuffed the flashlight and huddled behind the desk. He imagined he could hear the blood thrumming through his own body as he listened, every sensory fiber of his being pressed to its maximum. His mouth went dry as he followed the labored footsteps climbing the stairs one at a time. He had no idea who was in the house, but one thing was certain: the person was coming too close for comfort.

Easing the drawer shut, Ken moved out of his crouch and made a split-second evaluation of his surroundings. The balcony was the only escape route open to him, but he could hardly expect to open the doors, climb over the rail, and drop to the courtyard below without making considerable noise. There was a good chance that the interloper might be headed for one of the other upstairs rooms. If that were the case, Ken could hide in the office and wait for the opportunity to exit the same way he had entered.

That he had no time for hesitation became clear as the footsteps grew more pronounced. Their soft *pat-pat* on the hallway's carpet runner was coming dangerously close to the study. Shoving the flashlight and the envelope into his pocket, Ken looked frantically around the dark room for a hiding place. He groped the drawn draperies in search of an opening. Ken stepped behind the heavy damask, flattening himself against the floor-to-ceiling window just as the study door opened.

When the light came on, Ken involuntarily flinched. His eyes moved down to the bright band of light running the length of the draperies' hem. Tensing all his muscles, he cautiously inched his feet outward into a splayed semicircle. No one should be able to see them—he hoped. He was awfully damned close to the break between the two drapery panels. They touched, but only barely. He could even make out a thin sliver of the room through the narrow gap.

The person was moving around the office with an abandon that Ken envied, opening and closing cabinet doors without the slightest thought to the noise they made. He closed one eye, straining for a glimpse of the figure that had just hurried across his line of vision. Only when the person paused to stoop over Richardson's desk did Ken get a recognizable view of Beatrice Lawes.

What the hell was she doing here at this hour of the night? The thought reminded Ken that she would probably ask herself the same question about him if she knew he was secreted behind the draperies. Now that he had a chance to observe Bea, she did appear to be rather nervous. After slamming a briefcase open on top of the desk, she began digging impatiently through the drawers, wrenching them open and banging them shut.

Oh, no! Ken's fingers twitched, powerless to intervene, as he watched her remove the box of letters from the bottom drawer, check its contents and then deposit it in the briefcase. Apparently, the single box was all she deemed worthy of removing from the desk, for she now hurried across the room, out of his sight. What was she up to now? Emboldened by his nagging curiosity, Ken risked edging a little closer to the split between the draperies. The heavy fabric stirred slightly, causing him to hold his breath for a second. When he dared spy on Bea again, however, he found her far too busy to have noticed his movement.

She had removed an oil portrait of a mid-nineteenth century Whyte from the paneling and was now poring over the digital keypad of a wall safe. "There!" he heard her exclaim under her breath as the lock clicked. Ken watched her scoop the contents of the safe into her arms. He was startled when she carelessly tossed several fat rolls of cash back into the safe. Bea was kneeling over the pile of legal folders and bound documents, digging through them as if she were excavating buried treasure. She sat back on her heels, flipped through one of the folders, and then put it to the side. Gathering up the remaining papers, Bea thrust them back into the safe and quickly secured the door. Pausing only long enough to adjust the oil painting, she snapped the briefcase shut and rushed out of the office.

Now that the room was once more dark, Ken's ears felt sharper. He listened hard, pushing himself to follow the departing footsteps. After they had died in the distance, he waited what seemed an eternity before he dared to emerge from his hiding place. Reaching for the flashlight, he hurried to the desk. The box of letters was gone, of course, but she could have overlooked something else worthwhile.

Hoping against the odds, Ken finished searching the desk. Anger mingled with frustration as he rummaged through the credenza and then the bookcase cabinets. Finally, Ken flicked off the flashlight and sank down onto the big desk chair. Bea Lawes' clandestine visit had proved his hunch: Richardson's office had contained something of great importance. Unfortunately, she had beat him to it.

BEA FELT FOOLISH LUGGING the bulky briefcase. She hated its clumsy feel, the way it banged against her leg when she tried to walk fast. And tonight, she was walking much faster than she normally did. Of course, she had a perfect right to pay a visit to Richardson's office anytime she pleased. She still had her key, would still be called on to help out for some time to come. As far as the peculiar hour was concerned, hadn't she worked late into the night many times in the past, transcribing the long tapes Richardson would forward from

Brazil, screening his mail to protect him from trivial annoyances, keeping everything filed just so?

All the same, Bea would just as soon no one took note of this particular nocturnal visit to the Whyte house. Tonight, she had a mission. The gravity of this thought caused her to tighten her grip on the briefcase's leather handle that was by now damp with perspiration. She halted on the corner, trying to appear nonchalant as a lone taxi cruised past. She waited until the cab had turned onto South Battery before dashing across the street to her parked car.

She straddled the briefcase awkwardly, supporting it between her knees while she plundered her purse in search of keys. The call had left her jittery, full of a creeping anxiety that hampered her usual efficiency. Bea snatched the keys out of her bag and promptly dropped them into the gutter. She knocked the briefcase onto its side as she knelt, frantically digging her hands through the leaves collected next to the curb. When she found the keys, she thrust one into the car door lock. Yanking the door open, she shoved the heavy briefcase into the front seat and climbed in behind it.

Bea sagged in the seat, letting her forehead rest against the steering wheel. Now that she was in her car, she felt safe, inconspicuous. Her fears had been silly, when she thought about them. Who on earth would pay her any mind, much less question the contents of her briefcase? Nonetheless, Bea shoved the case onto the floor, just to be on the safe side until she had made her delivery.

Bea had just inserted the key into the ignition when she heard steps on the sidewalk. She glanced in the rearview mirror and saw a figure moving between the trees lining the street. As the pedestrian stepped onto the street behind the car, Bea almost panicked. Then she recognized the person approaching the car. Lucky thing she hadn't let her nerves get the best of her. She floorboarded the car and squealed out of the parking space leaving a trail of peeled rubber behind her! She would never have lived that down.

Bea cranked the window down and smiled. ''I didn't expect to see you...'' The words died on her lips. For a moment, her mouth was a gaping, empty hole in her colorless face, her eyes wide, horrified mirrors of the gun pointed straight between them.

Chapter Twelve

If he had searched Richardson's office just one day sooner, he would have found the critical link that connected all the fragmented, conflicting clues surrounding the murder. Ken was as convinced of that as he was certain that Bea Lawes would do her level best to conceal whatever she had taken from the office—or even destroy it. The sobering implication of that last possibility weighed on him as he descended the winding staircase in the dark house.

He would call Derek as soon as he got home and tell him about Bea's nocturnal plundering of the office. The Whytes would listen to Derek, as much as they paid anyone any heed. Ken tried to feel encouraged, but he knew he was grasping at a few very ephemeral straws. The proverbial circle of wagons had been drawn around the Whyte household, and the odds of Derek's penetrating their resistance did not look very favorable.

Reminding himself that he would have plenty of time to consider these unpleasant thoughts later, Ken hastened to the curtained French doors opening onto the courtyard. Tension and the stuffy, close house had given him a raging headache. Right now, he wanted nothing more than simply to get home in one piece, take a couple of aspirin and call Dani. She would be as angry and frustrated as he when she heard about Bea's eleventh-hour raid on Richardson's office. Given her resilient spirit, she would probably start formulating alternative approaches to the case. For his part, he could certainly use a good dose of positive thinking to counterbalance his own sense of defeat. Increasingly, Ken was beginning to feel as if Dani Blake were the only person other than himself who was really interested in unmasking the murderer.

The second Ken opened the French doors, he realized he should have peeked between the curtains beforehand. But he had blundered into the open doorway in plain view of whatever had stirred in the shrubs clustered along the wall, and there was no going back. At least he felt sure a cop hadn't made that noise; the police would have long since yelled "freeze" and taken control of the situation. Ken stared at the thick tangle of oleander and crepe myrtle, straining to penetrate its leafy depths. For the moment all was still. If it was a cat, it would spook, but, of course, it was up to Ken to spook it.

He was weighing his options when a blinding beam of light suddenly landed on his face. Throwing a hand up to shield his eyes, he struggled to make out the figure that had just stepped into the open. The light cut, leaving a kaleidoscope of yellow and orange dots dancing before his eyes.

"Sorry!" Ken heard Dani's soft voice apologize from somewhere behind the screen of Technicolor dots. "I suspected you might have heard me when you stood back in the door, but it took me a few seconds to be sure it was you. I didn't want to startle you by leaping out of the bushes all of a sudden."

Shaking his head, Ken pawed at his blitzed eyes. "This was hardly a gentle introduction."

"Are you okay?" Dani was at his side now, looking up at him with a sheepish smile.

"I'm fine. But just what on earth are you doing here, if I may be so bold as to ask?" Ken fixed Dani with the toughest stare his assaulted vision would permit.

Dani pursed her lips in dismissal. "Come on. You didn't really think I'd be willing to hang around the kitchen making cream puffs while you were prowling around this house, did you? All I could think about was what could go wrong, and finally, I knew I had to do something. On the way over here, I kept asking myself what you would do if someone walked in on you."

"I can tell you exactly what I did—hid behind the drapes," Ken interposed. Despite the evening's depressing outcome, he almost laughed at the startled look on Dani's face.

"You mean someone *did* surprise you?"

Ken nodded. "You didn't happen to pass Bea Lawes on the street?"

"Oh, my God! *Bea* showed up?" Dani groaned in dismay. "No, I didn't see her, but then, I got here only minutes before you opened the French doors. What on earth was Bea doing in the house at two o'clock in the morning?"

"Looking for the same thing I was, I'm almost certain. I'll tell you all about it, but first, I suggest we find a less-compromising spot to talk. I've managed to avoid detection so far tonight, but I don't want to press my luck."

"You're right," Dani agreed. "Let's get out of here."

Ken depressed the spring-lock button and closed the French doors behind him. Moving as stealthily as the prowlers they felt like, he and Dani checked the alley and then slipped through the gate. They didn't risk speaking until they were a good half block up King Street.

"Where did you park?" Dani was asking Ken when he suddenly gripped her arm.

"Do you see that car across the street, the dark red Honda Accord?" he whispered hoarsely in her ear. Ken felt her arm stiffen inside his grasp as she stole a surreptitious look and then nodded. "I could almost swear Bea Lawes has one just like it," he went on as they continued walking toward South Battery. "Remember the afternoon I tried to talk with Sapphira at Richardson's house? Bea was doing her watch-dog number, but after she sent me packing, I hung around the park for a while. I was hoping to see her leave so I could make another stab at getting to Sapphira. Well, she did leave, unfortunately with Sapphira in tow. I felt so frustrated when she pulled her car up to the front of the house and helped the old lady into it. But I got a real good look at her car."

"And that's it?"

"I can't be sure. It's certainly not the only one of its kind in Charleston," Ken admitted. He resisted the urge to turn and gape at the parked Honda. Although the street appeared deserted, the houses lining it dark, experience had taught him he could never be sure no one was watching.

"Then let's have a better look up close. At the very least, we can get the license number and check the owner's name through the motor-vehicle registration office." At the corner of South Battery, Dani stepped off the curb, pulling Ken with her as she walked toward the parked van. "We'll drive around the block and slow down a bit as we pass her car," she explained, unlocking the van. "That way, we won't look like car thieves sneaking around on foot."

"I've had enough of playing at thief for one night," Ken quipped, but as he slid into the seat next to her, he welcomed the normal, respectable feel the van and her company gave him.

Dani waited for a small station wagon to pass before pulling out into South Battery. She circled the block slowly.

As they approached the dark red Honda, she shifted down into second gear.

"I keep a pad and pencil in the glove compartment. Can you make out the tag number yet?" Dani leaned forward in the driver's seat, craning for a better view.

"Got it." Ken jotted the letters and numbers on the pad and then did a quick check of the rearview mirror. "There's no one around. Stop a second and let's have a look inside...." He gasped, slung forward against the harness restraint as the van jolted to a tire-squealing stop. "What the heck..." His voice faded, his eyes riveted on the horrific sight he glimpsed through the Honda's open window.

"Oh, my God, Ken!" Over the hands she held clapped to her mouth, Dani's eyes were wild with terror. "Is it Bea?" she finally managed to get out.

"I'll have a look. Stay in the van." Ken's hand felt weak, unreliable as he fumbled to unlatch the door.

He swallowed hard and succeeded in holding at bay the queasiness roiling in his stomach. *So this is what it means to have your head blown off.* The thought passed numbly through his mind as he stood looking at the mess of bone and blood and tissue that had once been a human face.

Disregarding his command, Dani had scrambled out of the van and rushed to his side. He felt her cold hand slip inside his sweaty palm, trying to steady them both. "It's Bea." She tightened her grip, pulling him back from the ghastly scene. "We need to get the police." Still clutching his hand, she scanned the empty street, trying to orient herself. "There's a bed-and-breakfast on the next street. We could use their phone."

Ken curled her hand inside both of his. In the vaporous streetlight, her face had a damp, yellowish look to it, like molten wax. "Let me stay here while you go call the police. If I see a patrol car in the meantime, I'll flag it down."

"Okay." She gave his hand a resolute squeeze and then hurried to the van.

Ken waited until the Aerostar had disappeared down South Battery before turning back to Bea's car. He had no appetite for what he was about to do, but he knew he had to have a closer look inside the Honda. As he circled the car, he avoided looking at the pathetic, bloodied body sprawled on the gear box. The windows on the passenger side were rolled up. Ken stooped to peer through the glass and immediately had to force back the heaving sensation that filled his throat. The briefcase that Bea had carried with her to Richardson's office lay open on the passenger seat. It was empty, as far as Ken could tell. Unlike the car's interior, the lining of the briefcase was completely devoid of any blood stains. Whoever had opened it and removed its contents had done so after Bea was shot.

The shrill cry of approaching sirens signaled Dani's success in contacting the police. Suddenly, the sleeping street was filled with flashing lights, the sound of brakes slammed to the floor, of brusque voices and rushing feet. Already a few lamps had winked on behind curtained windows as the unsuspecting neighbors awakened to the alarm.

"You the one who found her?" A uniformed policeman with close-cropped black hair immediately collared Ken.

Ken followed the policeman back to the Honda. "My friend and I spotted her as we were driving past the car."

The policeman nodded, but he seemed not to be paying much attention to anything but the mangled creature slumped behind the steering wheel. "Whew-ee!" He massaged the back of his muscular neck, shaking his head slowly. "Ernie, we need to get Forensic over here on the double," he shouted over his shoulder before turning back to Ken.

"Okay, I'm gonna need to ask you some questions." The policeman seemed as relieved to put some distance between himself and the awful scene as Ken had.

They had just paused beside one of the patrol cars when Dani's van hove into sight. While he waited for the police officer to respond to a radio dispatch, Ken waved to Dani. She quickly double-parked the van and then dashed between the patrol cars.

"All right, kid?" Ken put his arms around her, hugging her securely to him.

Her head nodded against his chest as her arms clasped him in an equally fierce embrace. Then Dani pulled back a little to look up into his face. "How about you?"

"Not doing too badly." Ken touched her cheek lightly. She was too beautiful, too good to be involved in such a sordid mess. For a moment, all his other concerns faded, superseded by the overweening desire to shelter her from the wretchedness of human behavior gone haywire. His attention was abruptly refocused by the policeman's return.

"Officer Joe Simpson, ma'am." He nodded briefly to Dani. "Okay, now I need to get your names and then you can tell me exactly what you saw."

Ken and Dani gave Simpson their names and addresses. Dani described how they had been driving past the parked Honda when they discovered Bea's body.

"We thought we recognized the car." She hesitated and glanced at Ken. He could tell she was torn by conflicting impulses: the desire to offer the police every fragment of helpful information without exposing Ken's unauthorized visit to Richardson's office. "As it turns out, we were right. The woman is Beatrice Lawes. She was Richardson Whyte's secretary for many years."

At the mention of the prominent murder victim's name, a visible twitch passed across Simpson's lips.

"Did you notice anyone near the scene of the crime?" Simpson's probing dark eyes moved quickly from Dani to Ken and back again.

Both of them shook their heads. "The street looked absolutely deserted. At this hour it usually is." Dani fell silent, hoping, no doubt, that they would not be required to justify their late-night prowling.

Officer Simpson made a few terse strikes through the blank spots remaining on the police report. His lips moved as he glanced over the completed report. "And you say you found her about a half hour ago?"

"Yes, I think so," Dani said.

Simpson's husky shoulders rose in a world-weary shrug. "There's really no telling how long she'd been lying there like that. If you people hadn't been up high in that van, *you* might not have seen her. Guess we won't have anything to go on as far as time of death is concerned until Forensic has had a chance to run some body-temperature tests. Well, thanks for your cooperation. You may be hearing from me if we have any more questions." He turned toward the medical van that was parked diagonally across the street. "Two homicides in two weeks is two too many!" Ken heard him mutter to himself.

Two homicides that may have been prevented if the Whyte family's damnable pride had not put secrecy ahead of common sense. Ken's indignation flared at the senselessness of it all. Who among Richardson's relatives would allow any hint to be revealed of what poor Bea Lawes may have been carrying in her briefcase that cost her her life? Certainly not Sapphira. Theo, if he had any idea, would be more concerned with political damage control than with justice. Even Derek, for all his hard-headed business sense, would never dream of defying Sapphira. The realization taunted Ken, not least of all because he had let himself wander into the distasteful quagmire.

Dani's hand closed over his wrist. "Ken, we need to talk."

"You're right." He followed her to the van, which offered them some privacy from the grim activity surrounding the Accord.

"The police need to know what you saw in Richardson's office." Dani's eyes held him as firmly as her hand.

Ken took a deep breath. He knew she wasn't going to offer an easy, painless way to do what was right because there was none. In the back of his mind, he had been trying to rationalize a way out, but Dani's even, straightforward gaze told him he wouldn't be able to live with any decision other than that of telling the police everything he knew.

Dani accompanied him, offering her tacit support, as he hunted for Simpson among the police swarming the crime scene. They found him talking with the medic who was securing the rear door of the emergency van.

"Can I speak with you for a moment?"

Simpson seemed surprised, but not half as startled as he appeared when he got a look at the identification card Ken held up for his inspection. "Associated Security? What kind of outfit is that?"

Ken returned the ID to his breast pocket. "We handle private security, primarily for corporations. Richardson Whyte hired me through an associate of his after he received an extortion threat. I'm still technically under contract on that case, still have a key to Whyte's house." He glanced at Dani, fortifying himself with the supportive look she gave him. "I was in Whyte's office tonight when Bea Lawes showed up."

"You're telling me you saw the victim tonight when she was still alive?" Simpson fixed Ken with an uncompromising stare that said he intended to get a straight story.

Ken nodded. Well, they always said courage wasn't being unafraid; it was facing fear and overcoming it. He suspected that before the night was over, he was going to have a chance to see if his own mettle was equal to that old saw.

Simpson shifted his penetrating gaze to Dani. "What about you, Miss Blake? Were you in that office, too?"

"No—" Dani began, but Ken quickly intervened.

"Miss Blake is in no way connected with Associated Security. She came downtown to meet me after I left the Whyte house, for strictly personal reasons." Ken was not about to let Dani deflect any of the heat onto herself. He had hatched the plan to visit Richardson's office on the sly, and he would bear the responsibility for any questionable legal issues that decision raised.

Simpson regarded them both quizzically, as if he were uncertain what he should do with them or their testimony. "I think it'd be a good idea if you folks came down to headquarters. Just let me be sure these guys have enough pictures before they tow the victim's car. Then you can follow me downtown."

Downtown! Dani had thought that only fictional cops used that expression. This was not an old episode of *Dragnet,* however, nor was Joe Simpson merely a well-built version of Officer Joe Friday. This situation was real, deadly real. She needed only one glance at Ken sitting waxen faced and silent next to her in the van to be reminded of that. She knew what must be going through his mind, wished desperately she could think of something to say that would alleviate the sober thoughts oppressing him.

Dani waited for Simpson to climb into his cruiser. When his arm jutted from the open window, motioning them to follow, she pulled away from the curb. The city looked so peaceful, its streets submerged in a dreamy predawn hush. The past week had taught her how cruelly deceptive appearances could be! The shattering experiences surrounding Richardson's death had left her wary and mistrustful; in light of so much corruption, Ken's decision to talk with

Simpson seemed nothing less than heroic. If Sapphira took a vindictive stance, he could find himself on very shaky legal ground. At the very least, the Whytes could make considerable waves with Associated Security, to the point of jeopardizing Ken's job. Yet Dani knew that, whatever the consequences, Ken could never conceal valuable information about the last hours of Bea's life and continue to live at peace with himself—no more than she could.

Following another cue from Officer Simpson, Dani turned into the parking lot flanking the unassuming building that housed the city police headquarters. After she cut the engine, she sat for a moment, giving Ken some time to collect himself.

"I'm going to tell them everything, Dani." Ken's voice was ominously quiet, much like the stillness that precedes a violent storm.

Dani reached to take one of his hands, trying to offer encouragement. "I'll stand by you, Ken. I don't give a damn what Sapphira or any of the others do. Someone has got to speak up before we have yet another murder on our hands."

In contrast to the slumbering city surrounding it, the police station was bright with hard fluorescent light, an encapsulated mill of ceaseless activity. Officer Simpson met them at the entrance, guiding them past the desk clerks and upstairs to a sparsely furnished office.

"Coffee?" The policeman made a beeline for a scorched carafe simmering on a hot plate.

Ken shook his head, but Dani said, "Please." Right now, she needed something to steady herself, something to hold on to, even if it was only a cup full of carbonized sludge.

Simpson leaned over the desk, his large hands carefully rearranging a couple of framed photographs to give Dani a place to park her coffee. Dani guessed that the pictures' subjects—a pretty teenager dressed in cap-and-gown and a grinning boy in a royal blue band uniform—were the policeman's children. As he sank down into the battered desk chair, Simpson took a slug of the coffee and grimaced. "Now let's get back to what you told me at the crime scene. You ran into the victim in Richardson Whyte's office tonight."

Ken leaned forward in his seat, clasping his hands between his knees. "Not exactly. I didn't want her to see me." He drew a deep breath, focusing on the tight ball formed by his hands. "Bea Lawes took a very proprietorial attitude toward her boss's business, and I thought she might resent my being in his office."

Simpson doctored the oily coffee with a generous dose of instant creamer. "Just why *were* you there?"

Ken exchanged glances with Dani before answering. "I wanted to see if I could find the missing link to some information Miss Blake and I had uncovered." Choosing his words slowly and carefully, Ken recounted their tracing of the yacht-club pin and the incident aboard the *Bandeira Branca*. Although he discussed Ned Poole's conversation and the possibilities it had suggested, he omitted any references to Stephen Lawes.

Dani and Ken had not had an opportunity to discuss how many of their as-yet-unproven hunches they could responsibly share with Joe Simpson, and Dani was relieved that Ken had avoided implicating Stephen Lawes. However incriminating the young actor's behavior may have seemed in the past, she was firmly convinced he had not killed his mother. She recalled his protective treatment of the bereaved woman at Richardson's funeral; Lawes might be a trained actor, but Dani's intuition told her his solicitude that day had sprung from the heart. Then, too, quite apart from their suspicions about Stephen Lawes, Bea's shocking death had thrown a wild card into every possible scenario they had constructed to solve the case.

As he concluded his account, Ken looked drained, his energy sapped by the endeavor. "Richardson Whyte hired me to protect him from an extortionist—a measure that, in the end, failed. I've had a few losses in my career—corporate secrets that managed to slip through the security net, thefts that persisted despite the most stringent precautions—but I've never had someone lose his life. I feel personally responsible, feel that I need in some pathetic, inadequate way to do something to make it up to Richardson. I have to see his murderer brought to justice. Do you understand?"

Simpson nodded slowly, his eyes following the emotional currents reflected on Ken's face. "Yeah, I think I do."

"I have to be honest with you, Officer Simpson. If I had announced my intentions, none of Whyte's relatives would have let me within a mile of that office. Even trying to talk with the family is like running up against a stone wall."

Simpson chuckled cynically over the rim of his cup. "I suspect that's what a lot of Butler's guys in Homicide are thinking, even if they won't admit it. Okay, for now, let's forget about whether you bent the rules or not and go over what happened in the office. You stayed out of sight while the victim was in Whyte's office?"

Ken nodded so wearily, Dani suspected he wished he had taken Joe Simpson up on his offer of coffee. "I hid behind the drapes, so I had a good view of her activity. I saw her take a small box from the desk and some papers from a wall safe. She put everything in her briefcase and left right away."

"What time was this?" The desk chair squeaked as Simpson leaned forward to pitch the coffee cup into his overflowing wastebasket.

"About one-thirty, I guess. I really didn't pay much attention to the time," Ken admitted. "After I was sure she was gone, I looked around the office a bit longer, then left the house and met Dani. That's when we discovered Bea in her car.''

''Uh-huh.'' Simpson clutched the edge of the desk, pushing himself back a few feet. ''You know we found her briefcase in the front seat of the car. But it was empty.''

Ken eyed the policeman steadily. ''Whatever was in that briefcase, I didn't take it.''

For a long moment, the room was very quiet, broken only by the *crick-crack* of Simpson's swivel chair as he rocked it slightly from side to side. Then the rhythmic squeaks ceased abruptly. ''I believe you. I don't suppose you have any idea what those papers might have been?''

Ken ran his fingers through his already disheveled hair. ''I think the box contained some letters, but—'' He broke off as the office door suddenly flew open.

Detective Sam Butler filled the doorway, porcine pink face glistening with sweat, BB-pellet eyes ricocheting all over the office. ''I want a copy of that report, Simpson. A positive ID has just come back from the morgue—the woman was Richardson Whyte's secretary.''

Joe Simpson rearranged his muscular frame in the sagging office chair, making himself comfortable. ''I know,'' he remarked in a calm voice guaranteed to rankle Butler.

Butler's perennially flushed face deepened a half shade. Anger spewed from the tiny, dark eyes, quickly finding the perfect target in Dani and Ken. ''What are you doing here?'' he demanded.

''Miss Blake and Mr. McCabe discovered the victim,'' Simpson supplied helpfully.

''Huh!'' Butler snorted. ''You people seem to be cropping up in a lot of interesting places these days. I heard about your little sailing expedition.''

''That 'little expedition,' as you put it, Detective Butler, very nearly cost us our lives.'' Dani's jaw tightened as she struggled to hold on to her temper. Common sense dictated that her desire to defend herself and Ken be tempered by at least a token effort to avoid locking horns with the irascible detective.

Butler gave her a malicious smile. "Then I suggest you avoid such dangerous activities." He looked back at Simpson, jabbing the air with a thick finger. "I'm waiting for that report, Simpson." As he retreated down the hall, his rubber-soled shoes left a trail of angry, squishing steps behind him.

"Right," Simpson muttered to the empty doorway, but he appeared unfazed as he eased up from his chair. "Well, if you folks can't think of anything else pertaining to this case, I don't see any reason to keep you here any longer." He shook hands with Dani and Ken and then escorted them to the door. "Try to get some rest," he advised them as they headed down the hall to the stairs.

"That's the best suggestion I've heard in a long time." Ken's arm felt heavy with fatigue as it dropped over Dani's shoulders. The harsh light had carved cavernous circles beneath his eyes, but he managed a tired smile.

"I'll second that!" In her eagerness to put the taxing interview behind them, Dani had already dug her keys out of her purse. As they crossed the lobby, she scarcely noticed a man hunched, forehead in hand, on one of the lobby's Spartan benches. Only when they were pushing through the doors did the man lift his stricken face, fixing her with a look of mingled grief and bewilderment.

Dani swallowed, forcing herself to meet Stephen Lawes's disquieting stare. She had seen him only once without stage makeup, and then only from a distance. In contrast to the sinister countenance created by his role in the Ghostwalk, however, his rounded features and fair coloring gave his natural face a mild, even timid appearance. Here was the man who had become the focal point of her suspicion, a person she had believed capable of the most heinous sort of murder. Yet now that they were face-to-face in the inhospitable police station lobby, all she could see was a hurting human being, utterly alone in the world.

Extricating herself from Ken's arm, Dani approached the corner bench on which Lawes sat. "I'm sorry," she said quietly.

The young man blinked as if he were in a daze.

"I'm Dani Blake," she went on in an effort to penetrate his shock.

"I know who you are. You were one of Whyte's friends." Lawes's dulled voice carried an accusing undercurrent. He glanced at Ken, who had joined Dani, and then gazed down at his hands tightly gripping his knees.

"I just can't believe what's happened. I had seen her just tonight. We had dinner at Booth's—that was always her favorite place. She was starting to laugh a little again, said we ought to do this kind of thing more often." Lawes spoke haltingly, half to himself, as if he were trying to fit together the ill-fitted pieces of a sinister puzzle. "She said she was a little tired, wanted to go home and get to bed early. If I'd had any idea what she was planning to do, I—I wouldn't have let her go."

Dani sank onto the bench next to Lawes. "What was she planning?" she asked as gently as possible.

"She didn't tell me, of course, because she knew what I'd say. I've warned her time and again that it wasn't safe, a woman being out alone at all hours of the night. But she never would listen. That's where they found her tonight, parked across the street from *his* house." Lawes's expression shifted so abruptly, Dani almost started. An angry white shadow outlined his lips that were now quivering with hostility. "She was so dedicated, such a perfectionist. And what did all that slaving in his office get her? Murdered by some mugger!" In his fury, he spat the words.

Lawes's suffering was so palpable, Dani hated assaulting him with any further questions. "But your mother didn't mention having to go to Richardson's office tonight?"

Lawes's lip curled in contempt. "She knew how I felt about him. I know what you're thinking." His puffy, reddened eyes fastened themselves on Dani. "You all thought he was so wonderful, so generous, such a gentleman. You've all been wringing your hands over him, turning the city upside down to find out who killed him. Well, do you want to know what I think, Miss Blake?" The swollen eyes were defiant. "I don't care if they ever find the murderer, ever! Richardson Whyte robbed my mother of the best years of her life, fed her on lies that poisoned her whole life. She loved him, and he exploited that love. She always held out the hope he would return her love someday if she were patient and loyal enough." Lawes's face contorted in pain. "She lived for his praise, believed him when he said he would take care of us. I remember my mother always saying, 'Richardson will look out for you, Steve. He'll see you through college, even medical school, if that's what you still want later on.'" Lawes's bitter laugh cut to the quick. "I'm not a doctor now, thanks to Richardson Whyte. Sometime over the years, he conveniently forgot his promises to Mom—even while he was asking her to write the checks for the other tuition he was paying while he was in Brazil." He looked at her a little uncomfortably, as if he feared her reaction.

Richardson was only human, and Dani realized that at least some of Stephen Lawes's resentment could be justified. Still, she felt obligated to defend her old family friend. "I think Richardson held himself responsible for seeing Rebecca Pope through college after her own father died. She is his niece, you know."

For a moment, Lawes only gaped at her in disbelief. Then a look of unfolding comprehension spread over his ravaged face. "Whyte didn't pay Rebecca Pope's tuition. He paid *yours!*"

Chapter Thirteen

"I had no idea. Mother, Richardson, no one ever said a word about his paying my college tuition." Dani frowned pensively at the mug of hot cocoa Ken had just placed in her hands. She pulled her knees up, clasping them to her chest with one arm as she edged deeper into the corner of the sofa.

Ken seated himself on the edge of the sofa. As he sipped the hot drink, he opened one of the home-decorating magazines on the coffee table, aimlessly flipping through the colorful pages. "Maybe they thought you would have felt self-conscious about it," he suggested after a lengthy silence.

"But I never even had a chance to thank him!" Dani blurted out.

Ken stared blankly at the magazine for a second before looking up at her. His face wore a curious expression, an ambiguous blend of doubt and apprehension. He had been through a trying ordeal, one that almost guaranteed unpleasant aftershocks, Dani reminded herself. By comparison, her fixation on Stephen Lawes's revelation surely seemed annoyingly trivial. When she looked at it rationally, it was just another manifestation of Richardson's generosity to her and her family, albeit an impressive one. She probably wouldn't feel so off balance if the discovery had not come in the wake of such an emotionally exhausting evening.

Dani scooted out of the pocket she had carved between the sofa cushions and slid her mug onto the end table. "We certainly have more compelling things to think about than my tuition. Poor Stephen! I can't believe how different he looked in the police station. That was the first time I had ever seen him up close without his stage makeup. He seemed so fragile this morning, like a hurt little boy. He's not a killer, Ken."

The sofa springs recoiled as Ken stood up abruptly. "No, I agree with you." He paced the length of the coffee table, then hesitated, as if he had forgotten where he intended to go, before walking to the dining alcove. He adjusted the blinds, admitting flushed stripes of early dawn between the narrow slats. "He doesn't look a bit like Richardson, either. I think it's safe to assume that Bea Lawes's love for Richardson went unrequited."

Dani picked up the mug, remembered that it was empty and replaced it on the table. "Maybe it *is* only unfounded gossip that Richardson had an illegitimate child." She clasped her knees with both hands, waiting for Ken to say something. He was making her nervous, pacing around the room, not able to sit still for more than a few minutes.

Ken continued to gaze out at the just-awakening street, apparently lost in thought. He seemed reluctant to relinquish that peaceful, innocuous view of the world as he turned and slowly walked back to the living room. He paused behind the sofa directly behind her, and Dani felt a sigh quiver through him.

She twisted around to look up at him. "What's wrong?"

Ken said nothing as he reached into his pocket and pulled out a yellowed envelope. He leaned over the back of the sofa and gently laid the envelope on her lap.

A tingling sensation pulsed through her, creeping into her limbs like an insidious chill that stings and numbs at the same time. At first, she could only gape at the envelope and the elegant, feminine script ranging across the front of it. "Where did you get this?" she finally managed to choke out.

Ken evaded her question, his voice tight with uneasiness. "Do you recognize the handwriting?"

Dani felt a wash of heat seeping into her cheeks, a symptom of the fear and pain and anger colliding within her like dangerously volatile chemicals. "Of course, I do! I know my own mother's handwriting. But I want to know how you got this!" She jumped up from the sofa, slapping the envelope with her hand as she glared at Ken.

Ken's dark blue eyes were filled with an exquisite sadness as they met hers. "I found it in Richardson's office, in that box of letters Bea took." He sounded as if those few words were among the hardest he had ever uttered in his life.

"No!" The cry leapt from Dani's mouth unbidden. Shaking her head, she backed away as Ken rounded the sofa. When he reached for the envelope, she was seized by the mad impulse to rip it from his grasp and shred it into a thousand indistinguishable little pieces. Instead, she only stood half dazed while he opened the envelope and held it up for her to see.

"I love you, my darling." The flowery handwriting curling across the inside of the envelope flap seemed to mock Dani's battered emotions.

She felt Ken take her unresponsive hand, pulling her down on the sofa beside him. "I know it's hard to accept, Dani, but there are just too many things pointing to Richardson being..." He swallowed with difficulty, as if something had caught in his throat. "Being your father." He forced himself to finish. "The possibility had never occurred to me until we talked with Stephen this morning. I knew the handwriting on those letters wasn't Bea's, but, well, it could have been any woman's—until you confirmed what I was beginning to fear.'' When he squeezed her hand, it felt alien, remote, as if her whole arm were anesthetized. She watched, unfocused, as he walked to her little desk and picked up a framed photograph. Sitting down beside her, he removed a snapshot tucked into the corner of the frame. ''Richardson kept this picture of you as a little girl on the *Bandeira Branca* for a reason. No wonder Ned remembers him being so melancholy on his visits to the summer house.'' He went on in a voice so gently prodding, he might have been talking to the child in the photograph. ''See, before you broke your nose, it looked exactly like Richardson's.''

Dani stared at the grinning, unknowing girl in the photo. All these years, she had believed what adults had taught that innocent little girl to think, that she was Dan Blake's child, that her adventurous, much-admired father had perished in a sailing accident, that Richardson's interest in her had been for the sake of his old friend. All of it, everything, had been a lie, a deception so fundamental, it cut to the very quick of her soul. They had lied to her about who she was.

''Why didn't he ever tell me?'' she whispered, not expecting an answer, knowing there was none that could offer any solace.

''Richardson really cared about you, Dani. I'm sure he loved you.'' Ken's hand on her shoulder felt as awkward and forced as his words had sounded. She knew he felt he had to say something, at least make a stab at consoling her. Decent as she realized his intentions were, however, the feeble platitudes only seemed like yet another attempt to deny the truth.

''I need to be alone right now, Ken.'' Dani didn't look up from the glossy blur of the magazines arranged on the coffee table.

The hand on her shoulder faltered. "I know you're really upset. This is so sudden and so...so difficult to accept." The hand dropped from her shoulder. "I'll call you, okay?"

Dani nodded, her eyes still fixed on the garish magazine colors melting into one another. She sat there for a long time, long after she had heard the front door close behind Ken and his steps fade on the walk. Her body felt too heavy to move, paralyzed by an inertia so dreadful, it wouldn't respond even if she bade it to.

When she began to cry, it was slow and noiseless, a silent mourning for the child in the picture, the woman sitting alone with herself in the empty condo. Her tears came from a deep, aching well, the secret place where she had kept all the unfulfilled longings of her life. As long as she had believed Dan Blake was her father, the pain had been bearable. A cruel act of nature had taken him from her, but who had a right to rail at fate? Certainly not the little girl in the picture.

Yet now that she was confronted with the truth, everything she had wanted and never had suddenly loomed before her. Dani had never begrudged Rebecca Pope her beauty, her wealth or her numerous admirers, but at that moment, she felt an almost primal envy of the fifteen years Rebecca had enjoyed with her own father. How could Richardson have denied *her* that? Hadn't he realized how desperately she wanted to be Daddy's special little girl, have him tease her about her braces, spy on her boyfriends to see that they behaved themselves, get a suspicious fleck in his eye when she graduated from college? Even now, she would have given anything to have him take her hand, look into those hazel eyes that were so like her own, simply hear him say, "I love you, baby," and give her the chance to say, "I love you, Dad." But neither of them would ever have that opportunity.

A profound sense of aloneness welled up inside her, the feeling of someone who has been abandoned. It was an emotion her reasonable, adult side would never allow, but sitting alone in her home, with the incongruously cheerful morning sunlight flooding the room, Dani acknowledged the full depth of her pain. The men who mattered always abandoned her. Dan Blake had been powerless to defy the sea, and he had been forced to abandon her. Richardson Whyte had been controlled by vastly different forces that had proved no less insurmountable. The somber thoughts touched a new fear hovering in the corner of her consciousness. Ken had become very important to her. Yet in caring for him so deeply, she had surely guaranteed that he, too, would one day walk out of her life, unable to resist the forces that demanded he get on with business somewhere else.

Dani had long since exhausted her reservoir of tears when she finally roused herself from the sofa. As she walked to the desk, she felt strangely calm, for she knew there was an unavoidable step she must take if she were ever to achieve a sense of closure.

She consulted the phone directory, steadying herself with the ordinary, methodical task, and then punched the number. As she expected, one of the servants answered.

"I'd like to speak with Sapphira Whyte." She was startled by how unemotional her voice sounded.

"I'm sorry, ma'am, but Miss Whyte is unavailable."

"Is she at home?" Dani persisted.

The maid hesitated, obviously unaccustomed to resistant callers. "Yes, ma'am. But she's at breakfast with her sister and Miss Pope. If you'd like, I could give her a message."

"I'd like for you to tell her I'm calling. I think she'll want to speak with me now."

The maid reluctantly took Dani's name and then excused herself. A long silence passed before the phone was picked up again.

"Yes?" The rasping voice did not sound quite as imperious as Sapphira Whyte no doubt hoped.

Dani took a deep breath to steel herself for what they both surely knew was to come. "It's time we talked about my father."

"WE'RE NOT GOING shopping?" Nestled among the papery skin that drooped around them like wrinkled crepe, Adele Whyte's bleached blue eyes were as wide and wondering as a child's.

Rebecca Pope got a firm grip on the bony elbow, guiding her great-aunt toward the brocade wing chair facing the bedroom's bay window. "Not this morning, Auntie."

"Why not?" Adele wanted to know.

"Great-aunt Sapphira has business to take care of." Rebecca regarded the unblinking blue eyes looking directly into her face. By now everyone took Adele's confused state of mind for granted, but sometimes, Rebecca was not so sure. What really did go on behind those great, staring eyes? Did Adele spend her days drifting through a mist of half-forgotten memories? Or was she observing them—perhaps more clearly than any of them realized?

"Business?" Adele repeated as if it were a foreign word she was trying for the first time. "What sort of business?"

Rebecca pulled the old lady down into the chair, anchoring her for a moment by the shoulders. "Nothing you need worry about, Auntie." She watched the slightly trembling head, its thin, white hair tinted a pale pink by the scalp peeping through beneath it. When she was sure Adele was not going to pop up from the chair—as she often did—she released her hold on the frail shoulders.

Nothing to worry about, indeed. Rebecca's admonition
followed her as she paused in the bedroom doorway, taking
a last look at the shriveled little creature gazing out into the
garden, and then walked down the hall. Sapphira was the
only one of them with the sense to realize there was something to worry about. Not that she could fault poor old
Adele; the ancient woman had her hands full just dodder-
ing from her bedroom to the dining room and back again.
Rebecca could find no such excuses for her own mother's
attitude. After her brother's death, she had withdrawn to
her big house, emerging from her mourning for an occasional lunch with friends or a brief golf game at the club.
Unlike Sapphira, she didn't seem to realize how threatened
they all were. But then, her mother had never really under-
stood money and the things it could inspire, Rebecca
thought with a tinge of contempt. And unlike herself, Rebecca's mother had always been willing to leave the difficult tasks to Sapphira.

At the end of the hall, Rebecca glanced over her shoulder, checking to make sure that none of the nosy servants
were lurking about. She slipped into the guest bedroom and
silently closed the door behind her. Although the housekeeper was certainly too lazy to bother cleaning a room that
was seldom used, Rebecca took care to survey the chamber's shadowy corners. Confident that she was alone, she
walked to the big four-poster. She knelt by the foot of the
bed, frowning as she lifted the corner of the mattress. Her
hand groped the hard coils of spring until it recognized the
silky-slick feel of glossy paper. Sitting back on her heels,
Rebecca pulled the magazine from beneath the mattress.

She opened it on her knees, turning the mutilated pages
carefully. An entire headline had been excised from one
page, but for the most part, only snippets had been cut, a
single letter from one ad, a few syllables from another. Rebecca gazed at the butchered pages and wondered what she

should do next. Finally, she stood up. Rolling the magazine into a tight cylinder, she left the room and went directly downstairs. She hated the way her heart pounded as she passed the maid on the stairs, but the plodding woman seemed not to notice.

The remains of an early-morning fire was still simmering in the dining room fireplace. Rebecca loathed handling rough things, anything that might chafe her beautifully kept hands, but for once, she was glad Thomas had left a good supply of logs in the wood basket. She piled three stout logs onto the grate and then jabbed the embers with the poker. When the flames began to curl from the dry bark, she shoved the mangled magazine beneath the grate. Rebecca held it fast with the poker inside the devouring blaze, watching until it had been reduced to a meaningless heap of ash.

DANI HAD NOT REALLY expected Sapphira to invite her into her home. That would have been too great a concession. In a way, Dani actually preferred that their meeting take place on neutral turf, a symbolic way of putting them on equal footing. She had raised no objections when Sapphira had suggested they meet at Patriots Point, within an hour of the time of her phone call. The shipyard museum was a public place, but one where Sapphira could safely avoid running into any of her acquaintances.

The big, black limousine rolled into sight at precisely the appointed time, a phantom emerging on the single road leading up to the shipyard. Its dark windows and slow movement reminded Dani of a funeral car, a comparison that made her shiver in spite of the bright sun sparkling off the water. The car stopped well to the far side of the bridge leading to the anchored aircraft carrier *Yorktown,* a good fifty yards from where Dani stood. Dani watched the chauffeur alight, circle the car and open the rear passenger

door. For several moments, nothing stirred inside the dark
cavern of the car. Then a white gloved hand emerged,
clamping itself onto the chauffeur's wrist like a great pale
claw. Sapphira climbed stiffly from the car and then
straightened herself. Across the distance, she looked at
Dani, slowly walked a few feet and then stopped.

She was waiting for Dani to come to her, just as everyone
had for the eighty-odd years of Sapphira Whyte's life. *Not
this time, Sapphira. Today, you come to me.* Dani waited,
not moving as she watched the erect statue of a woman
thrown into relief against the immense gray aircraft carrier
in the distance.

Sapphira turned her head and looked toward the *Yorktown,* hesitating for a small but significant moment. Then
she turned back to face Dani. When she finally took a step,
Sapphira looked as if she were pulling her feet out of the
cement beneath them. The old woman walked with the un-
hurried gait of the conscious aristocrat, slowly traversing the
expanse of drive separating them. She stopped a few feet
short of Dani, lifting her chin ever so slightly to indicate that
she would come no farther.

"You know now. What else is there to say?" Sapphira's
jaw was tight beneath the transparent skin, rigid as a mum-
my's.

"I believe there's still a lot to be said," Dani countered.
"How could my father have kept this secret from me?"

The old woman laughed, the sound of dry leaves rustling
in her breast. "The same way he kept his affair secret from
everyone else. Most people only see what they choose to.
But I knew what was brewing between him and your
mother. Richardson, of course, claimed it was only a
friendship. Dan Blake was away so often pursuing his ad-
ventures, one would have suspected he occasionally forgot
he even had a wife. Richardson never cared for sailing that
much, never was a competitor like Dan. I suppose he and

your mother discovered they had quite a bit in common. One thing led to another.'' Her pale eyes drifted across the harbor, drawn to some unseen point in the distance.

''They had an affair.'' Dani felt almost relieved to at last get that distasteful phrase out of her mouth.

''Yes. I don't believe it lasted very long, actually. Both of them were too loyal to Dan Blake to deceive him comfortably. When your mother realized she was pregnant, I imagine they both panicked. Richardson and your mother knew they had been playing with fire and were in danger of being badly burned. They decided to end the relationship at that point. Fortunately, Dan Blake was willing to believe you were his child.''

''Everyone was, I imagine,'' Dani remarked. A burdensome sadness had settled over her, tinged with a new-found sympathy for the thwarted lovers.

Sapphira nodded slowly. ''Oh, yes. Richardson married right away, to a perfectly hopeless woman who loved him even less than he loved her, I might add. Less than six months after his wedding, Dan Blake was killed at sea, but then, of course, it was too late.''

''He never thought of divorcing his wife and marrying my mother?'' Dani asked.

Sapphira regarded her in a way that made her look much older than her eight-plus decades, that made Dani feel much younger than her twenty-eight years. ''Have you never heard of doing penance for one's sins? Richardson had sinned against his best friend, Dan Blake, and he had to punish himself. Denying himself the woman he loved was the cruelest, most fitting way he could find. That's part of being a romantic, I suppose, suffering grandly, and Richardson was a romantic to the core.'' Her grooved lips curled in a mirthless smile. ''You might as well know that's how he came to attach such significance to that foolish little pin.''

''The *Bandeira Branca* pin?''

"When they ended the affair, your mother insisted on having some memento she could always keep close to her, to remind her of Richardson. He gave her part of the pin and kept the other part for himself."

"That's why he gave me the pin," Dani murmured, her voice so low she was surprised that Sapphira heard her.

"He also wanted you to have something else after his death." Sapphira hesitated before snapping open her black leather purse and pulling out a sealed piece of folded paper. "I must confess I am not happy giving you this, but since you now know, I suppose it can do no additional harm. For all his waywardness, I did love Richardson and would want to honor his wishes."

Dani slit the seal with trembling fingers and opened the letter.

My dearest Dani,

When you read this, I will no longer be able to see you, to talk with you and to share in your life. I pray you will not think too ill of me and forgive my weakness. I have always loved you deep in my heart, as the father I should have been to you. I wanted to give you my name, to be able to take pride in your achievements, to ensure your happiness. Please understand that only love and respect for Dan Blake's memory prevented your mother and me from bringing the truth out into the open. I hope you can find it in your heart to forgive me and know that you will always be my sweetest, best-loved daughter. With my abiding love,

Richardson

A tiny droplet of water spattered onto the velum page, weaving a pale blue smear through the neat, uniform letters. Dani felt her throat swelling with grief, with the great store of emotion she would never be able to share with

Richardson Whyte, the forgiveness for which his still heart had yearned.

"If he had only told me, I would have kept his secret to my death." Dani's voice was full of ragged emotional edges. She shook her head as she carefully refolded the letter.

Sapphira seemed slightly embarrassed by such unabashed tears. "I don't mind telling you we all counseled him against such a move—his sister, Adele, even Derek, they all agreed with me that any acknowledgement of the affair could only lead to difficult complications."

Dani regarded the woman standing in front of her, wondering if she had ever experienced any emotion other than pride. "You would have had him deny his own child?"

Sapphira drew herself up in an attempt to appear insulted. "Rest assured, he has provided well for you. At your birth, he earmarked a special investment for you. When his will is opened next week, you will not be disappointed. The house will be yours."

Dani stared at Sapphira, too dumfounded to comment.

"Yes, his house on the Battery," Sapphira repeated, misinterpreting Dani's silence. "It's quite valuable, really. You've no account to feel slighted."

"You think I only care about my father for the property I'll inherit from him." Frowning, Dani shook her head. "You don't understand at all, do you?"

Sapphira's thin lips tightened into a formidable line. "What is it you want, then? If it's more money, it can be arranged. In return, I would hope we could reach some sort of agreement that you would continue to protect Richardson's name. He escaped scandal during his life. There is nothing to be served by exposing his folly now that he is gone."

Dani felt angry heat suffusing her face. Her unflinching gaze connected with the old woman's cold eyes. "You don't care about Richardson's memory. All you're interested in is saving face.''

''I've made you a reasonable offer.'' Sapphira's tone was as hard and intractable as granite.

''I'm not interested in your offer.'' Dani's mouth felt thick, caked with an insulted fury that made her want to choke. ''I won't be bribed, Sapphira, not by you or anyone else.'' Turning on her heel, she rushed to her car, leaving the ramrod figure standing alone in the shipyard.

Chapter Fourteen

Ken focused on Derek Cannaday's long, bony fingers, watched the way they clamped around each arm of the chair, pressing deep indentions into the tan leather. So far, those fingers seemed to be the only reliable barometer of Derek's anger. Now that he thought about it, Ken hadn't really expected him to shout and swear and bluster. No, Derek's anger was the quiet kind that seethed from every pore like a slow-acting venom. From across the desk separating them, Ken could almost feel the livid fury building beneath the controlled exterior.

"I warned you, Ken." Derek spoke deliberately, measuring each word. "This is the very worst thing that could have happened. Do you realize the position your irresponsibility has put me in?"

"What would you have wanted me to do? Not tell the police I had seen Bea Lawes only minutes before her death? That's called 'withholding information,' not the kind of misbehavior the police take kindly to. No, thanks, I'm more concerned with staying on the right side of the law than in being in Sapphira Whyte's good graces." Ken met the hard, level eyes that were fixed on him like bayonets. If Derek intended to play a war of nerves, Ken was determined to meet him on equal ground. "And don't talk to me about irresponsibility, Derek. You and I both know that if the Whyte family weren't so obsessed with keeping Richardson's skeleton locked in its cupboard, Bea Lawes might still be alive today. For God's sake, Richardson might even be alive.'' He heard his voice rising and quickly checked its modulation. Lose his temper and he had lost this battle with Derek.

''That's preposterous!'' The tapering fingers flexed around the chair's arms.

''I don't think it is, Derek. Look at how difficult it's been even to talk with any of Richardson's relatives. His aunts, his sister, even his niece have all closed their doors in my face. If I hadn't accidentally stuck that envelope in my pocket last night, I still wouldn't have any proof that Richardson had ever had an affair.''

Derek's aquiline nose flared as he drew a short breath. ''I'm surprised that you've allowed this sort of sordid business to distract you so easily.''

Ken lifted his hands in despair. ''How can you sit there and talk about a valuable clue as if it were no more than tabloid gossip?''

''Because it is cheap gossip—''

Ken cut in. ''Then why did Bea Lawes see fit to go to Richardson's office in the middle of the night and take those letters? And why did someone want them so badly, he was willing to kill her for them?''

Derek pinched the armrests and then suddenly released them. ''You don't know that. You said yourself there were other things in her briefcase.''

''Yes,'' Ken conceded evenly. ''But why would anyone want those letters, too?''

Derek's restless fingers latched on to the edge of the desk. ''Maybe the murderer didn't want to waste time sorting through the contents of the briefcase and simply took everything.''

''You don't believe that any more than I do,'' Ken shot back. He had soft-pedaled his views to accommodate Sapphira and her coterie long enough; now that the body count had risen to two, he was not prepared to listen docilely to any more nonsense.

Derek was silent for an unnervingly long moment, leading Ken to wonder if the sleeping volcano were about to erupt. "Perhaps I'm wrong and you're right, Ken," Derek said at length.

The unexpected admission caught Ken off guard. "What do you mean?"

"Sam Butler was here this morning, asking questions about the investigation you've been conducting behind his back. You'll be interested to know that he shares some of your suspicions about the murderer's motives, especially after last night." Something about Derek's dramatic pause gave Ken an uneasy feeling. "He's beginning to believe it's a case of common blackmail, and that you've put yourself in a very compromising position."

"Get to the point, Derek," Ken demanded impatiently.

The thin lips twitched, the telltale sign of repressed anger straining for release. "Dani Blake is now a prime suspect in both murders."

The statement was so unexpected, so totally ridiculous, Ken was momentarily at a loss for words. "That's the most harebrained, half-baked notion anyone could suggest!" He realized he was sputtering, but he was unable to contain his indignation. Dani had been through hell in the past few hours; the thought that Butler now intended to victimize and harass her was intolerable.

Derek's calm agreement only rankled Ken more. "That's what I thought at first, but after Butler laid his case out, I began to follow his line of reasoning. You know, much of the testimony you gave last night has strengthened Butler's feelings about Miss Blake."

Ken jumped up from the chair. "This is insane!"

Derek regarded him skeptically. "Is it? Richardson never said a word to me about having a child, but you seem convinced Dani is his unacknowledged daughter. If that is true, might she not have harbored resentment toward him? He was, after all, a rich man. By comparison, her means are rather modest. You mentioned your suspicions about Stephen Lawes earlier in our conversation. Might not Dani fill his role equally well? She was the last person to see Richardson alive, certainly had easier access to his office than Lawes. After her extortion note failed, she confronted Richardson face-to-face. He resisted, and she killed him to cover her plot. Then she set out to obliterate all evidence linking her to Richardson. This childhood picture you've seen was on the yacht. Who knows what other incriminating things Richardson might have kept secreted there? Dani destroyed that possible source of evidence, after conveniently dispatching you and then engineering your rescue to cover her deed."

"Dani didn't knock me out aboard the *Bandeira Branca!*" Ken almost shouted.

"She didn't? Butler says you claim not to have seen your assailant." Derek maintained his unruffled pose. His hands were now relaxed, looped easily over each armrest. "With the *Bandeira Branca* gutted, she moved on to remove evidence from Richardson's office. Here Butler's theory begins to get rather circumstantial. Possibly she devised a way to trick Bea into removing the offending papers from the office before you could find them. Then she got rid of her in the same way she eliminated Richardson. The letters have now disappeared, and along with them, another damaging clue."

Ken slammed his fist against the polished wood desk, desperate to put an end to the obscene scenario Derek was constructing. "Dani Blake is a decent, honorable woman.

She's incapable of the sort of cold-blooded brutality you've just described.''

"This isn't my theory, Ken." Derek lifted an eyebrow, staring at Ken's red-and-white knuckles pressed against the polished mahogany. "Sam Butler is the person you need to convince that Dani Blake is innocent. I'm merely repeating what he told me. But be forewarned. Associating with a murder suspect is not the best way to maintain credibility with the police."

"Dani did not murder anyone," Ken insisted through clenched teeth.

"I'm sorry, Ken, but as far as Butler is concerned, you've constructed a very convincing foundation for this case. He's simply chosen to insert a suspect you would never have chosen into the critical slot. You may not like the direction your investigation has taken the police any more than I do, but I warned you about getting in over your head. Oh, yes, Ken, I can see how badly you wish the police would just forget Dani Blake and leave things as they were. Now perhaps you can understand how the Whyte family has felt all along." Derek's fingers quivered reflexively on the arms of the chair. "You've botched things, Ken—for yourself, for Dani, for all of us. Also, you've now incriminated yourself in a case of breaking and entering. Fortunately, I think I've persuaded Sapphira not to press charges in return for certain assurances from you."

"Don't threaten me, Derek." Ken leaned across the desk, the better to stab his opponent with each word. "I used a key to enter Richardson Whyte's house. That's not breaking in. Whyte personally gave me the key, as a tacit sign of his trust when he hired me for the job. Our contract was up for renewal at the end of this month. It didn't terminate upon his death. I had every right to enter that house."

Derek pushed up from his chair. A heat field of anger seemed to emanate from his entire body as he stood face-to-face with Ken. "But you are terminated as of now. You're no longer authorized to conduct any activities on behalf of Richardson Whyte's estate."

DANI HURRIED ALONG Queen Street, cutting her way around more leisurely pedestrians who blocked her hasty progress. The tumultuous events of the past twelve hours had skewed her sense of time; she had almost forgotten her afternoon appointment with Theo Boynton at the Old Exchange, and heaven knew what else had slipped her mind. Never in her life had she felt more off balance, less in touch with herself. When she chanced to glimpse her image floating across the windows of the shops lining the street, she was almost shocked to discover that her appearance had not also undergone a radical transformation.

And now she wasn't even sure she could turn to Ken. An emotional pang gripped her when she recalled how she had rebuffed his attempts to comfort her, withdrawn from him, pushed him out of her home. She had been afraid of letting him see so deeply into her heart, exposing such raw, fierce pain to his scrutiny. Yet now, another ache had joined the chorus of hurt throbbing inside her, a gnawing longing to have him hold her close and whisper that everything would be all right.

Theo was waiting for Dani at the entrance to the Old Exchange Building. Word no doubt traveled fast through the private enclave of the Whyte family and their relations, but apparently not fast enough to have reached Theo before their appointment. As she shook hands with the ingratiating young man, Dani felt certain he was still ignorant of her emotionally charged conversation with Sapphira that morning.

"As you know, we've reserved the Great Colonial Hall for the event." Theo ushered Dani into an immense, columned ballroom, replete with tall, recessed windows and striking Palladian arched doorways.

Dani nodded automatically, but after a few minutes, she realized she had registered scarcely a word he had said about the hall's historical background. Reminding herself to pay attention, she pulled a pad and a ballpoint pen out of her shoulder bag. She jotted a few notes as Theo showed her where the dance band's platform would be set up and asked her opinion on various ways to keep traffic flowing comfortably. Fortunately, Dani was so accustomed to appraising unusual party locations, she could rely on instinct to get her through. By the time they had circled the room, she had decided where to place the buffet tables, counted electrical outlets for warming trays and area lights, and plotted an unobtrusive route between the ballroom and the service area.

Theo seemed relieved by her assurances that the elaborate costume gala would run as smoothly as a modest dinner party for six. "Father will be relieved to know that the costume ball is well under control. They're hoping to take him out of intensive care tomorrow, you know."

Dani hadn't heard the good news, but she was glad that the elder Boynton's condition was improving. "Please tell him not to worry about a thing." She took a last glance around the ballroom before tucking the pen and paper into her bag. "I believe you've answered all my questions. Can you think of anything else we need to discuss before the event?"

"Well, yes, now that you mention it. As you know, we're trying to make as much of the Halloween theme as possible. There will be awards for most creative disguise, most unusual costume and so on. To add a bit of spice, we've persuaded the Exchange to include our guests in their annual Halloween tour of the Provost Dungeon. According to legend, a few of the dungeon's former occupants still put in an appearance on All Hallow's Eve.'' Theo's smile was slightly impish. ''The Exchange has volunteers dressed up as historical ghosts wandering about carrying candles on Halloween night. These Ghostly Guests, as they're called, will greet our revelers, so it should be great, spine-tingling fun. Food and drink won't be permitted in the dungeon, but you know how people are. A few guests are bound to forget the rules and leave some napkins and empty cups down there. I'd like for your crew to help police the dungeon after the ball is over, just to make sure the place is tidy.''

''I'll add the dungeon to my post-party clean-up checklist,'' Dani assured him as she followed him to the door.

Theo gave her a sidelong glance. ''Have you ever visited the Provost Dungeon?''

Dani shook her head. ''No. It's one of those hometown tourist attractions I've never gotten around to seeing.''

''Would you like to have a look now?'' With his hands clasped behind him, Theo looked like a smooth-faced little boy making a dare. ''It's really quite fascinating.''

Given her current frame of mind, Dani could think of at least a million curiosities she would rather see than a purportedly haunted dungeon. Theo seemed so keen on giving her a quick tour, however, she would have a hard time declining his offer without appearing ridiculously superstitious. ''Okay, if you have the time.''

''I'll make time,'' Theo told her over his shoulder as he led the way downstairs. He smiled and nodded in his deft political way to the security guard they passed on their way down the second flight of stairs. ''We'll only be a few minutes, George.''

''Take your time, Mr. Boynton.'' The man's words sounded hollow and remote, as if he were calling down to them at the bottom of a well.

It would have been hard to imagine a more stark contrast than that between the light, airy Colonel Hall and the murky, oppressive dungeon lurking beneath it. A damp chill seemed to emanate from the ancient stone walls, along with a musty odor that was hard to place and all the more disquieting. The area was divided into a series of alcoves formed by brick columns arching into the low, vaulted ceiling. Dark pockets of shadow filled the arches, encroaching on the skimpy light.

"Isn't this spooky?" Theo gleefully eyed the musty bricks curving over his head.

"Very." Dani hung back by the door, instinctively clinging to the vestige of adequate light.

"Come on. I'll show you where they kept pirates chained up." Although the ceiling cleared his head by a generous margin, Theo stooped slightly as he disappeared behind one of the columns.

Dani took a few reluctant steps into the cavernlike chamber. She didn't believe in ghosts, of course. But her experiences during the past few days had left her with a marked distaste for ill-lighted places. *This is just a museum. Theo is the only other person here, and whatever his faults, he's certainly harmless enough.* Dani was almost embarrassed by the compulsion to repeat these reassuring facts.

"Theo?" In his schoolboy eagerness, the young attorney had quickly outpaced the less-enthusiastic Dani. Already she had lost sight of him among the beehive nooks shaped by the arches. She bit her tongue, stifling the urge to call to him a bit more loudly.

Dani peeked around one of the arches and instantly jumped back. "Oh!" she gasped, and then caught herself. The figure shackled to the foot of the pillar was only a mannequin dressed in the uniform of a British redcoat, but her heart was still palpitating long after she had sidestepped the inanimate form.

Theo must have heard her cry out, for he immediately emerged from the next alcove. "They're awfully lifelike, aren't they?'' He glanced down at the hapless redcoat. "Here's the pirate I was telling you about."

Dani followed his beckoning and peered into the next alcove. "He does look almost real," she agreed, giving the chained pirate an appreciative enough inspection to placate Theo. She stooped to lightly touch the pirate's homespun jerkin.

The sound of unruly young voices and many feet scuffling down stairs carried into the dungeon's somber recesses. "Sounds like a school group is about to descend on us," Theo commented under his breath. "I guess we'd better get out of their way."

Dani followed Theo back to the entrance, letting him push a path through the horde of youngsters trying to press through the door all at once. When they reached the street, Dani politely thanked Theo for his tour of the dungeon and promised to touch base with him again on Monday morning in case there were last-minute changes in the event's schedule.

She had let herself deteriorate into a more neurotic mess than she had suspected if a museum exhibit calculated to delight children had left her feeling this jittery, Dani told herself on the way back to her house. Her nerves were like a raw wound, able to make her wince under the slightest pressure. Thank God, she didn't have a function to cater that evening! Never before had she felt such a desperate need to retreat into her quiet, serene home, to shut out, at least for a few hours, a world that was taking on an increasingly hostile aspect.

As Dani pulled into the driveway, she acknowledged the one person who would have been welcome in her home that evening. She could, of course, call Ken, try to explain how she had felt last night, make a stab at reconnecting the broken lines of communication. Dani realized that much of her hesitancy stemmed from uncertainty about Ken's reaction

He had suffered severe rejection as a child. Who was to say how he might respond to her now that she had refused his comforting? She could imagine nothing worse than seeing him again, only to find him friendly in a casual, distant way, the intimacy between them hopelessly damaged.

Dani was pondering the disjointed turn their relationship had taken as she walked to the curb to check her mailbox. The usual jumble of junk mail—pizza delivery flyers, magazine-subscription offers and coupon packages—filled the black metal box. "Occupant. Occupant." Dani read the computer-generated address labels as she pitched the unopened envelopes into the garbage can. "Miss Danielle Blake." She paused over a plain white, business-size envelope. Not even her creditors called her Danielle. She turned the envelope over, vainly searching for a return address. There was none. On closer inspection, she noticed that the stamp had not been canceled.

Another of those unsteady, apprehensive feelings surged through her, undermining her fingers' efforts to slit open the envelope. She found a single sheet of white typing paper, folded twice, inside the envelope. When she opened the letter and saw the hodgepodge of unmatched letters pasted to the paper, her head began to swim. For a moment, she couldn't focus her eyes well enough to read the crude message spelled out on the page.

> Mind your own business. Let well enough alone. You cannot change the past. Keep your secret well if you want to see the future.

WHEN KEN SAW the police car pulled up in front of Dani's condo, he panicked. Never mind that an actively dangerous situation—and certainly a homicide—would have warranted at least two cruisers, the official vehicle with its no-

nonsense, black-wall tires was enough to hurl him into a paroxysm of fear. He parked clumsily, the rear half of his rental car still jutting into the street, and scrambled from behind the wheel. His heart was pounding as he cut across the lawn to the front porch. The door opened just as he was about to press the buzzer.

"Ken!" Dani looked as relieved to see him as he was to find her on her feet and apparently unharmed.

Officer Joe Simpson's nod of greeting was friendly, if more reserved. The police officer followed Dani out the front door, anchoring his cap on his head as he cleared the threshold.

"What's happened?" Ken asked. To judge from the tense expressions on both Dani's and Simpson's faces, the answer could not be good.

Simpson held up a plastic bag containing a folded piece of paper. Opening the bag, he carefully removed the paper and unfolded it for Ken to read the primitively lettered message. "Looks like someone's been playing cut and paste again," he remarked drily.

"I found it in my mailbox when I got home this afternoon," Dani explained. Ken could tell she was making a mammoth effort to keep her voice steady.

"I'll have a patrol car keep an eye on your house, Miss Blake," Simpson assured her as he resealed the plastic bag. "And remember, if you notice anything that makes you feel even a little uneasy, don't hesitate to pick up that phone."

"I will," Dani promised. The brave little smile she gave the departing policeman tore at Ken's heart. After Simpson had climbed into his patrol car, she turned to Ken. "I—I wanted to call you. Listen, about last night, uh, I'm sorry if I seemed like a real basketcase. It was all so…" Her small hands rose in a helpless gesture.

Ken took one of her hands and gently guided her back into the condo. "You don't have to explain anything, Dani."

Enfolding her in his arms, he nudged the door shut with his foot. Only when he pulled her close to him did he realize that she was trembling. "There, sweetheart. It's going to be okay." His lips grazed her forehead. Then he rested his cheek against the top of her head, rocking her slowly back and forth.

"Oh, God! I'm glad you're here." Her arms closed around him with a ferocity that almost made him wince.

"I'm here and I'll stay as long as you need me, as long as you like." Ken cradled her head against his chest as he led her to the living room. They sank down into a corner of the sofa. Dani pulled her legs up, snuggling into the protective nest of his arm.

He let her talk, gently caressing her hair as she poured out the pain she had been unable to share with him last night. He listened without commenting to her account of the meeting with Sapphira. Whatever the significance of the encounter at Patriots Point, Ken had no desire to ask questions or draw conclusions at this point. Right now, he was unconcerned with the case, with clues, with the whole frustrating investigation. His only care was for the sensitive woman curled inside his embrace; her needs were all that mattered.

After a time, she fell silent and Ken noticed that the shivering that had rippled through her slender body had subsided. "It feels so good to be here together." She shifted her face against his chest to look up at him. In the muted light filtering through the drawn blinds, her hazel eyes reminded him of two smooth, marbled stones glistening in a pool of clear, fresh water.

Ken bent to kiss first one eye, then the other, closing them with his lips. He shut his own eyes, surrendering to the delicious, tactile sensations freed by his blocked vision. His hand found its way to her cheek; for a moment, he let his fingers savor the liquid softness of her skin, tracing the delicately sculpted framework beneath it. Then his hand drifted across her nose and down the upturned peaks of her lips. He felt her mouth move against his palm, planting dewy kisses on the coarser-textured skin.

Dani's hands were exploring his face now. For a moment, Ken was so distracted by their insinuating touch, he could do nothing but revel in the soft fingertips tripping from his temple to his ear and down his neck. An electric shiver tingled through him as she stroked his shoulders, letting her hands slip into the warm, hidden region beneath his open shirt collar.

A shudder of desire gripped him, startling not only in its intensity but in the complexity of its source. He had never wanted a woman the way he wanted Dani right now, wanted her whole being, her tender heart, her strong spirit, her gentle soul every bit as much as he wanted her exquisitely beautiful face and body. And in yearning for her so completely, Ken realized that he was discovering a part of himself that had lain fallow for many long, lonely years: the part of him that could love.

"I want to make love to you, Dani." His whispered desire brushed her cheek like the feather-light flutter of a hummingbird's wing.

"And I want to make love to you." Dani was surprised by the frankness of her response, how unselfconscious she felt with their increasing intimacy. *Trust.* That was the magic ingredient that elevated their relationship above a mere physical attraction with all the attendant uncertainty.

There was no need for words as they rose from the sofa and walked hand in hand to the bedroom. They stood next to the bed, holding each other, experimenting with the taste and texture of a kiss. The subtle light from the shaded window cast a soft imprint of their embrace onto the quilted coverlet. The muted silhouette swayed against the pastel background, the shadow of hands following the contours of their bodies. Gradually, the outline of their forms grew sharper, free of the cocoon of clothing blurring it.

Ken's palm began a slow passage down her back, leaving a ripple of delightful sensations in its wake. When his hand reached a barrier hindering its progress, it glided beneath the bra to loosen the taut elastic. Dani instinctively pressed against him, responding to the fingers working their way around her rib cage. She moaned softly, nuzzling his chest as his hands slid between her breasts and the lacy bra cups. His fingers massaged her breasts, moving in ever-smaller concentric circles until they reached her rigid nipples. He withdrew his hands, but only long enough to unfasten the bra clasp nestled in her cleavage.

Her senses had been so captivated by the delectable activity of his hands, Dani had been content only to clasp Ken's neck while his fingers worked their magic. Now, however, her hands began an exciting investigation of their own, letting the intriguing contours of his body dictate their path. First, they caressed the cord of muscle sloping from his neck to his shoulders. Next, they wandered over the well-defined biceps, then detoured to the lean rib cage. When she began to stroke his sides, he pulled her to him, pressing her breasts against his bare midriff.

Still molded against each other, they sank onto the bed. Ken rolled onto his side and then loosened his hold on her slightly. "You're so beautiful," he murmured as his hand drifted into the dip of her waist and then over her hip's curve. Dani gasped with pleasure when his touch grew firm, pulling her hips parallel with his own.

The passion that had been kindled inside them flared, sending a thousand sparks of ecstasy radiating through every fiber of their bodies. As their lovemaking reached its rapturous peak, Dani gazed into Ken's eyes and saw the tiny image of her own face residing in the dark blue mirrors. *I am now a part of you, just as you are now a part of me.* The thought settled over her like a soft, sun-filled cloud, filling her with an immeasurable happiness as they drifted off to sleep in each other's arms.

Chapter Fifteen

Dani languidly stretched her legs, easing them out of the warm crevice formed by Ken's bent knees. She had no idea how long she had slept, and right now, the effort required to check the time seemed hardly justified. The flare of Ken's shoulder rose next to her cheek, blocking her view of the bedside clock. Rather than risk waking him—or rousing herself from the seductively comfortable spot next to him—Dani decided to stay put for the moment. Only when his shoulder shifted did she make an effort to crane toward the clock.

"I didn't mean to wake you." Dani's smile drew into a kiss as her mouth grazed Ken's conveniently positioned cheek.

Ken reciprocated the kiss with relish. "You didn't. I've been awake for about twenty minutes, but I didn't move for fear of disturbing you. Of course, I wasn't all *that* uncomfortable." His hands snuggled around her waist, pulling her closer to him.

Dani gave him a teasing grin along with a light kiss on the tip of his nose. "So you were just going to let me lie here forever, thinking you were asleep?"

"Not *forever*." Ken's thumbs kneaded the points of her hip bones suggestively. "I guess you and I need to find a better way to communicate."

"I didn't hear any complaints last night." Dani cuddled against him, happily locking her wrists behind his neck. "What time is it anyway?"

"Dinner time." Ken held up his arm, offering her a look at his watch. "Would you like to get up, shower, dry your hair, get dressed, climb in the car, drive downtown, find a parking place, go into a restaurant, pore over a menu, wait for our order and have dinner? *Or* should we just phone and have some Chinese food delivered?"

Dani pretended to frown. "Gee, that's a tough one!" She ruffled his hair as she sat up in bed. "I'll get the Golden Dragon's take-out menu." She padded to her closet and threw on her robe before going to the kitchen. When she returned to the bedroom, Ken had pulled on his twill slacks and was peeping behind the window shade.

"Do you see something?" Dani froze by the bed, suddenly tense.

Ken reached for the drapery cord and tugged the curtains shut. "Just a patrol car driving past." He walked to Dani's side and put his arm around her shoulders, giving her a reassuring hug. "I've dealt with a lot of cops, enough to know a good one when I see him. Joe Simpson is a straight-ahead guy. He'll have so many cruisers in this area, the newspaper carrier won't be able to slip through their net."

Dani tilted her head to one side, pressing her cheek against Ken's hand. "Let's hope the Chinese-delivery fellow can," she quipped. At this point, joking about the phantom threat seemed the best way to diminish some of the power it held over her imagination. Then, too, she was determined not to allow anything to mar the relaxed, cozy feeling of this special time with Ken.

Seated on the side of the bed together, they perused the selection of Oriental dishes, finally settling on Moo Goo Gai Pan and shrimp with lobster sauce. While they waited for the order to arrive, Dani prepared hot jasmine tea and Ken arranged cutlery and napkins on trays and carried them to the bedroom. Dani had just removed the ceramic tea ball from the pot when the Golden Dragon's delivery man rang the doorbell.

"All set?" Dani smiled around the edge of the bedroom door, her arms laden with enticingly scented paper bags.

Ken proudly surveyed the two lacquered trays positioned on the bed, right next to the freshly fluffed pillows. "I even checked the paper and discovered we have an old Tracy-Hepburn movie for dessert."

"Great! I've got the answering machine on, so the drawbridge is officially raised for the evening. We are *not* to be disturbed." Dani grinned as she sidled onto the bed and began to open the white paper cartons of food.

They had never had much time just to focus on each other, Dani reflected as she and Ken laughed and chatted over the delicious dinner. Discounting the all-too-brief lunch near Trumbull Island, they had never even had a date. The entire span of their relationship had been overshadowed by nerve-racking and often dangerous events. And yet, somehow they had managed to—Dani's mind pulled up short, stymied by the appropriate conclusion to her last thought. Get attached to each other? Well, yes, but there was certainly more going on between them than that bland phrase suggested. Become very close? That went without saying. *Fallen in love.* The idea glowed in her mind like a newly polished gem just released from its obscuring stone.

"'A happy heart shares its joy.'" Ken held up the strip of paper he had excavated from one of the fortune cookies. "Well, I'm certainly not opposed to that." He leaned over, cupped Dani's chin with one hand and bestowed a leisurely kiss on her lips. "What's your fortune cookie say?"

Dani pulled back slightly and cracked the crisp-baked crescent. "'While you're sharing your joy, be careful not to spill sweet-sour sauce on the sheets,'" she pretended to read.

"Oh, sure!" Ken snatched for the paper slip that Dani held just out of his reach.

Giggling, Dani backed off the bed. It really says, 'The man of joyous heart dumps the empty containers into the trash can.'"

"I get the message," Ken grumbled good-naturedly as he began to gather up the remains of their meal.

"If you like, I'll make some more tea," Dani offered, collecting the blue-and-white china pot.

"Sounds terrific." Ken managed to sneak a quick kiss as they headed for the kitchen. The sound of the door-buzzer stopped both of them in their tracks.

"I'll get it," Dani volunteered, eyeing Ken's full hands. Actually, she would have preferred to ignore the intrusive buzz in hope that the unannounced visitor would assume no one was home. She couldn't turn a deaf ear, however, to the possibility that one of Officer Simpson's patrolmen had stopped by for some reason.

When Dani peeked through the peephole, she was startled to see Sam Butler glaring at the closed door. The ruddy flesh of his face looked even heavier through the distorting fisheye lens.

Dani opened the solid door, but not the storm screen. "Good evening, Lieutenant Butler. What can I do for you?"

The detective regarded the flimsy barrier separating them with annoyance. "I heard about the interesting note you supposedly received this afternoon, Miss Blake, and I decided to lend Simpson a little hand in his investigation."

Dani bristled at the word *supposedly*. Perhaps Butler had only been watching too many tough-cop movies, but she definitely didn't like the way this conversation was starting out. "There's nothing to suppose. Someone put that note in my mailbox today between the time I left my house at a quarter of three and my return at four-thirty."

Butler stroked his bulbous chin. "Yeah, but it's funny. We've been questioning people in this condo development, and not one person saw anyone fooling around your mailbox."

"I'd be curious to know how many of my neighbors were even home during that time," Dani remarked evenly. "Most of the people who live here are at work during the day. Just what are you getting at, Lieutenant Butler?"

The burly detective feigned a shrug, but his beady eyes had lost none of their hard luster. "Maybe you want to think over your story, Miss Blake. See if you've left out any important details...." He broke off as Ken appeared in the doorway behind Dani.

"Any problems, Dani?" Ken settled a hand on her shoulder, but he was staring straight at Butler's belligerent face.

Dani shook her head, but she was grateful for Ken's supportive presence. "Not as far as I'm concerned. Lieutenant Butler, I gave Officer Simpson a complete account of my discovery of that note. If I *think* of anything else, as you suggest, then I'll be in touch with him. Now unless you have specific questions, I have other things to do."

Butler looked as if the storm door were the only thing preventing him from pouncing on her and Ken like a rabid bulldog. "You'll be hearing from me, Miss Blake." He made no effort to disguise his parting comment as anything other than what it was: a blatant threat.

Dani closed the door and then leaned back against it. "What on earth does he want from me? Maybe all this stress is making me paranoid, but he sounded as if he thought I had made up the whole incident with the note." A chilling possibility suddenly grabbed at her. "Remember how closely Butler questioned me the night Richardson was murdered? You don't think he still suspects me and be-

lieves I constructed that note to deflect attention from myself, do you?''

Ken's protracted silence was an answer in itself. "Butler
is anxious to wrap up his investigation," he finally said,
"and I imagine he's grasping at just about any straw within
his reach. But he'll never be able to fabricate enough evidence to pin phony charges on you.''

Never before could Dani have imagined she would find
comfort in such a dubious consolation. "You know, there's
one surefire way to put a stop to Butler's scheming.''

"I've thought of a few, but they'd all land us in even
hotter water," Ken remarked drily.

Dani gave him a grimly resolute smile. "We need to find
out who sent me that note.''

Ken whistled under his breath. "That's a tall order. Any
candidates?''

Dani frowned. "I didn't tell you last night, but Sapphira
tried to bribe me to keep Richardson's secret buried. I know
it sounds farfetched that she would pull a stunt like this,
but—''

Ken interrupted, shaking his head. "After what we've
been through during the past two weeks, nothing is unbe-
lievable. I suggest we give Miss Sapphira Whyte a chance to
prove us wrong.''

"ARE YOU SURE you want to be involved in this?" Dani had
posed the question at least a dozen times since she and Ken
had hatched their plan the previous evening to call on Sapphira Whyte. Although he had remained adamant, she was
still concerned that the vindictive old woman might create
problems for Ken in retaliation.

"You sound as if you don't trust me to behave myself."
Ken smiled as he leaned over the dashboard to get a better
view of the stately Federal Period house. When he looked at
Dani seated next to him, in the car, his handsome face so-

bered. "There's no way I can't be involved, Dani, not until we have a clear explanation for all of the bizarre, terrible things that have been happening. Besides, kid—" he patted her hand, which was curled into a little fist at her side "—we're in this together, aren't we?"

Dani opened her hand to give his a grateful squeeze. "Yes, and I think we'd better get on with it before I lose my nerve. Sapphira isn't someone I'd ordinarily seek out for company."

Ken's grin helped to lighten the tension. "Come now. We've given her a chance to have her morning coffee. Who knows? She may be downright hospitable."

Dani chuckled at Ken's wholly improbable forecast, but as they climbed the steps to the mansion's front entrance, a flurry of uneasiness stirred in the core of her stomach. The doorbell was the old-fashioned kind, a pulley cord that jangled a real bell mounted somewhere inside the entrance hall. Dani rubbed her palms together, trying to dispel the nervous film of moisture as the sound of evenly paced steps on polished hardwood drew near.

"Yes?" A tall, slim woman clad in a black dress and starched white apron opened the door just enough to make the uninvited callers feel acknowledged but unwelcome.

"Please let Sapphira Whyte know that Dani Blake is here to see her." Summoning all the dignity she could muster, Dani took a step toward the door. There was nothing they could do if Sapphira refused to see them, but she was determined not to be kept waiting on the porch like an itinerant vacuum-cleaner salesman.

The maid gave them a disdainful look as she allowed them into the foyer. Dani and Ken watched her walk down the corridor past the winding stairs and then disappear behind a closed door. This was Sapphira's private domain, Dani reminded herself, a tiny principality within the city where the older woman's word ruled supreme. If the imperious spinster did not deign to receive them, they would be summarily dismissed without recourse. Their only hope was the chance that Sapphira would believe Dani had come to bargain for money.

"Miss Whyte will see you in the conservatory." The uniformed woman made her announcement from a haughty distance halfway down the hall.

Dani and Ken exchanged glances as they followed her to white double doors. The maid grudgingly held one of the doors open for them, ushering them into a large-windowed room filled with tropical trees and orchids. When Dani caught sight of the spare, erect figure seated in the high-backed chair flanked by two palms, she wondered if Sapphira Whyte consciously planned her dress and surroundings to overawe her guests or if intimidation simply came naturally to her, like the blue blood flowing in her veins. Encased in a high-necked black silk dress garnished only by a single jet brooch, she reminded Dani of a dowager empress holding court.

"I was expecting you to be alone." Sapphira cast a scornful eye on Ken, rearranging the floury-white hands folded in her lap.

Good, Dani thought. Surprise was always a useful element. "I think you may have misunderstood my reason for being here."

Sapphira tilted her head slightly. "I have offered no conjectures regarding the purpose of your visit, Miss Blake."

She was being cagey, due in part, no doubt, to Ken's presence. Dani realized that if she wanted the cards laid on the table, she was going to have to do it herself. "I think you *were* expecting me today. You realized I wouldn't ignore your note."

"Note?" The sparse, silver eyebrows rose in question. "What are you talking about?"

Dani studied Sapphira's face, trying to second-guess the real feelings concealed behind the pallid mask. "The note you had delivered to my home," she replied calmly. Whatever Sapphira's intentions, her attempt to appear puzzled was having a steadying effect on Dani's nerves.

"I did not have any note delivered to you, Miss Blake." A sudden spark of indignation flared in Sapphira's flinty eyes.

Dani shook her head. "When we met at the shipyard yesterday, you asked me to leave well enough alone, to keep my secret. When I receive a threatening note demanding the same concessions, only a few hours later, what do you expect me to think? I'm sorry, but it's just too obvious. I suppose you chose to model it on the extortion threat Richardson received because you thought another cut-and-paste note would frighten me. It hasn't, however." This last statement smacked a bit of bravado, but Dani knew Sapphira would be looking for any sign of weakness—and was willing to exploit it.

Sapphira's fleshless hands gripped the arms of the chair as she half rose in her seat. "I know nothing of this ridiculous note!" Her aged voice quavered, threatening to crack.

"We'll see what the police have to say after they've concluded their investigation," Ken interposed.

The old woman's gaze settled on Ken with the ferocity of a predator sinking its claws for the kill. "How dare you suggest I have violated the law in any way, you—you contemptible meddler!" Sapphira was out of her seat now, jabbing the air separating her from Ken with one crooked finger. Then she pivoted unsteadily toward Dani. "And as for you, no one accuses me in my own home. Do you hear me? No one!"

Both Dani and Ken were stunned by the violence of Sapphira's eruption. Her icy equanimity had shattered much more readily than either of them had suspected. Surrounded by her retinue of servants, she was no doubt un-accustomed to dealing with direct confrontation—and thoroughly unhappy with the new experience.

"I want you out of my house! Now!" Before Dani or Ken could move, Sapphira reached for an embroidered bell pull hanging on the wall behind her chair. Not waiting for her servant to respond, she tottered to the double doors and flung them open. "Monette! Thomas!" Her shrill voice bounced off the hall's hard surfaces. Dani heard feet rushing down the hall, one pair scurrying lightly on low pumps, the other heavy and purposeful. When the two servants appeared in the door, Sapphira pointed a shaking arm at her visitors. "Get them out of here!" she shouted, as if Dani and Ken were a couple of mice that had the misfortune of putting in an appearance at the wrong time.

Dani recognized the chauffeur from the previous morning, a great, hulking red-haired fellow who wore his uniform like a suit of armor. He took a menacing step toward Ken and reached for his elbow.

Ken jerked his arm free of the chauffeur's paw. "Hands off, buddy!"

"Out, I said!" Sapphira repeated her command, this time accompanied by a stamp of her foot.

The chauffeur regarded his enraged employer and then looked back at Ken and Dani, apparently weighing the line of least resistance. Whatever he decided, there was bound to be trouble, and that was a commodity Dani had already seen enough of in the past two weeks.

"Come on, Ken. Let's go." Dani tugged at his sleeve, urging him toward the door.

As they walked past Sapphira, Dani would not have been surprised if the old woman had reached out to strike them, so consumed with fury was she. Mercifully, she only chose to follow them down the hall, hurling a barrage of verbal abuse after them. "Liars! Troublemakers! You'll rue the day you set foot in this house! Accusing me of pasting together an idiotic note! Who do you think you are?''

''Stop! Oh, please, just stop!'' a frail voice pleaded from the top of the winding stairs.

Everyone in the corridor halted simultaneously and looked up, including Sapphira. Dani was startled to see a wraithlike apparition clinging to the bannister.

''Enough. Enough.'' The wizened creature repeated the word like an incantation as she edged down the steps.

For the moment, Sapphira was distracted from her task of expelling Dani and Ken from her home. ''Monette, see Adele to her room.'' She gestured urgently to the maid.

The tiny crone relinquished her hold on the bannister long enough to hold up a hand, warding off the maid's advance. ''No, not until I've had my say.''

Sapphira decided to take matters into her own hands. ''Adele, you're going to overexert yourself,'' she insisted, reaching for her sister's sticklike arm. She looked shocked when Adele pulled away from her.

''You people came here about a note?'' Adele's voice had an undulating, scratchy quality to it like an old phonograph record. When Dani nodded, the ancient woman pressed her thin lips together and looked down. As she lifted her head again, her withered cheeks glistened with tears. ''I only did it to make things right.''

''What do you mean?'' Dani asked. Of all possible developments she could have anticipated during her visit to the Whyte household, this was one that never would have occurred to her in a million years.

''Poor Richardson! I only wanted to help him, you see.'' Through the film clouding her faded eyes, she blinked at Sapphira. ''When you said he was going to tell this girl he was her father, I could only think of the scandal. How awful for Rebecca and Theo! And you, dear sister. So I thought about it. A lot. And I decided the best way to settle matters once and for all was to get enough money to give this girl so that she would leave town and be out of Richardson's mind. I pasted my note together from letters I cut out of a magazine so no one would recognize my handwriting, and then I hid the magazine. And when we visited Richardson one day, I just slipped the note into the mail box when Thomas wasn't looking. He should have listened to my note. I would have just taken that money and given it to the girl. He should have listened to my note," she repeated, shaking her pink-white head. "I never intended for someone to hurt him. Who would have wanted to hurt our dear, good Richardson . . . ?" Her voice trailed off.

The astonishing realization that Adele was talking about the original extortion threat against Richardson jolted Dani. "Did you send me a note, too?"

Adele's milky blue eyes widened. "Oh, no. I only sent one note." She held up a single, pathetic finger. "Just one."

"STRAIGHT UP OR WITH A splash?" Ken held up the bottle of Chivas for Dani's inspection.

Hunched over the nondescript Formica-topped table that filled one corner of Ken's efficiency apartment, Dani frowned at the bottle of Scotch. "My weaker instincts say 'just hand over the bottle,' but my better sense says 'in a small glass with a very generous dose of water.' I'm going to listen to better sense for now."

Ken rummaged beneath the pass-through separating the kitchen from the rest of the apartment and then mixed the drinks before joining Dani at the table. "I think we both need to hang on to our senses at this point. I never dreamed *Adele* was behind that note Richardson got." Shaking his head, he took a sip of the diluted Scotch.

"And the weirdest part is that she couldn't possibly have killed him." Dani cradled the glass between her hands and stared blankly across the room. "Poor little soul, I guess she really believed he would just put the money in a bag and leave it in the church where she could retrieve it. Then she would have handed it over to me, and I would have conveniently resettled in Tibet or somewhere equally out of reach.''

Ken tilted his chair back, stretching his long legs out to one side of the table. ''So now it looks as if we have a murder that has no connection to a bogus murder threat. Plus, we still haven't proved who sent you that note. I don't know about you, but I think old Sapphira might actually have been taken by surprise when you accused her this morning.''

''I still don't trust her,'' Dani maintained. ''But I do feel better about one thing.''

''What's that, sweetheart?''

''Apparently, Richardson was planning to tell me the truth.''

Ken let the chair lurch forward and then leaned across the table to stroke her hand. ''He wanted to do what was right, Dani. Sapphira's already mentioned that he planned to leave you his house. I'm sure he really wanted to make it up to you for not having been there when you were younger.''

''I would rather have had him than a hundred houses,'' Dani whispered, caressing Ken's hand with her thumb.

Ken held her hand for a long moment. Then he gave it a light shake. ''You know, something just occurred to me. Remember the appointment Richardson had with Powell Boynton about transferring the title to his yacht? Maybe he was planning to give it to you.''

''But I don't even sail!'' Dani protested.

Ken shrugged. ''It's just a guess. At any rate, it wouldn't hurt to ask Powell now that he's out of intensive care.''

''That's a good idea,'' Dani agreed. ''If I'm going to pull off catering this costume ball on Halloween, I have to do some big-time cooking tonight, but we could pay Powell a visit tomorrow morning if you're free.''

Ken settled both his hands over hers and smiled. "Right now, I'm as free as a bird."

As IT TURNED OUT, however, Ken had not taken into account the fetters still tying him to Associated Security. When he phoned Dani the following morning, she could tell from the way he said "hi" that something was wrong.

"I'm not going to be able to go with you to the hospital today." Ken's pause hinted that he was not happy about the news he was about to share and was searching for the least distasteful way to say it. "Miles Farrell called me around 2:00 a.m. this morning."

"Who's Miles Farrell?" Dani interjected, wondering if yet another player had been introduced into the mystery enveloping them.

"My boss at Associated Security."

Dani felt her heart gravitating in the direction of her shoes, but she stifled her dismay for Ken's sake. To judge from his tense tone of voice, the conversation with Farrell had not been pleasant; Ken didn't need yet another person pressuring him at this point.

"I have to be in Washington by noon today. I managed to get a flight out in a couple of hours."

"When will you be back?" It was the question she most dreaded asking.

Ken took a deep breath; whether he was trying to collect himself or buy time, Dani couldn't tell. "I don't know," he confessed reluctantly. "Some time next week, I hope. I still have a lot of things to take care of here, the apartment, and, well . . . I'll be back soon."

To pack your things, clear out the apartment and say goodbye. That was the logical sequence of events, even if Ken were too rushed or squeamish or kind to spell it out right now. *You just can't do that,* Dani cried inwardly. *Not after what we've shared. It can't end like this.* Of course, he wouldn't simply chuck her under the chin and promise to write, but the specter of an enforced physical separation was rife with a number of equally alarming pitfalls. They would both have to make an extraordinary effort to nurture the relationship. Spur-of-the-moment get-togethers would be out of the question, and when they did manage to see each other, would they find that the lines of communication had grown brittle with disuse?

"Let me give you a phone number where you can get in touch with me," Ken was saying on the other end of the line. "I don't know where I'll be staying for the time being, but the Associated office can usually find me."

Dani clamped the receiver beneath her chin and scribbled the number on the kitchen notepad. "Got it," she mumbled.

Ken didn't say anything for a moment. "Well, I'd better start throwing a few things into my garment bag if I want to make that flight. Look, take care of yourself. I'll be checking in with you. And, Dani, if anything seems strange, bothers you, I don't care how insignificant it might seem, call Joe Simpson. Promise?"

"I promise."

"Okay." Another of those long pauses intervened. "Bye, then."

"Goodbye, Ken." The phone clicked in her ear.

Just like that, and he's gone. The sobering thought cast a shadow over her mind that refused to be dispelled. *We'll talk soon. He'll be back.* In an effort to boost her sagging spirits, Dani reviewed the more encouraging segments of their conversation as she drove to the hospital. It was the conventional stuff that dating couples offered each other when circumstances drew them apart. *But we're more than a dating couple!* she heard her offended heart cry. Worse still, the very words that Ken had not said weighed most heavily on her: *I love you.*

Inside the hospital elevator, Dani forced herself to shift these troubling considerations to the back of her mind for the time being. At the very least, a recovering heart patient deserved a cheerful smile and the semblance of pleasant conversation. Already, Dani felt slightly uneasy with the prospect of bringing up Richardson Whyte's name. She would introduce the topic of Richardson's appointment with Powell as gently as possible.

Dani stopped at the nurse's station to confirm Powell Boynton's room number before continuing down the corridor. Saturday morning was a peak time for visitors, no doubt; the possibility that Rebecca or Theo might have decided to drop in on Powell prompted her to approach the half-closed door cautiously. When only the faint rustle of sheets broke the silence on the other side of the door, Dani knocked lightly.

"Yes?" The voice sounded weak, strained.

Dani eased through the door. "Mr. Boynton? How are you feeling? I hope I'm not disturbing you." As she neared the hospital bed, she was startled by how gaunt Powell looked. Stretched over his prominent facial bones, his skin reminded her of weak skim milk, thin and bluish. His tired eyes peered from their hollows, struggling for a moment to place the unexpected visitor.

"Miss Blake!" His colorless lips slowly pulled into a smile. "What a pleasure to see you! I hope that son of mine is giving you all the help you need with the costume ball."

Dani returned his smile. "Theo is doing a great job of managing the affair, but, of course, everyone is going to miss you tomorrow night."

"I would make a fine ghost, don't you think?" Powell lifted his hand, raising the sheet draped over it. "Trouble is, ghosts never win any costume awards—those always go to the space aliens and the two-person horses." His dry chuckle dissolved into a cough.

Dani joined in his laughter. She chatted for a few minutes about the awards ceremonies Theo had planned and the Ghostly Guests ritual that was to be a part of the evening's program. Although Powell's illness had sapped his stamina, his eyes brightened and a bit of color returned to his face as he smiled and offered comments. An intelligent man accustomed to leading an active life, he obviously missed participating in the larger world and was eager for news of events outside the confining hospital room.

"I'm giving those doctors another few days to make up their minds, and then I'm going home—whether they like it or not," Powell threatened good-naturedly. "Staying cooped up like this is guaranteed to turn a healthy person into an invalid. Nothing for company all day but that thing!" He gestured contemptuously toward the blank TV screen suspended in front of the bed. "I'd be half mad by now if I didn't have my books and the daily paper. I've been hoping to open the paper one morning and read that the police have apprehended Richardson's murderer," he added, his pallid face growing sober. "They don't seem to be making much progress, do they?"

"No, it's very frustrating," Dani agreed.

Powell shook his head. "And now poor Beatrice Lawes! I've lived most of sixty-five years in this city and never seen such awful violence. It almost seems as if a terrible plague has befallen us. I was very disturbed to hear of your hair-raising experience aboard the yacht. Thank God no one was seriously hurt by that ruthless act of vandalism."

"I'm terribly sorry about the yacht. It was such a beautiful boat. I understand that Theo had put a lot of work into it, too," Dani remarked.

The thin shoulders shrugged beneath the ill-fitting hospital gown. "For my mind, Miss Blake, the old *Bandeira Branca* never looked finer than when she sailed forth from the yacht club with Dan Blake at the helm. I know your fa-

ther would have been pleased that you were the last person
to pay the boat a visit before those ruthless vandals destroyed it.''

To judge from Powell's warm smile, Dani guessed that he
was still blithely unaware of Richardson's secret. Theo
would have learned of the Whyte family's long-suppressed
scandal from his fiancée, Rebecca, but his future in-laws'
passion for secrecy had no doubt prevented him from sharing it with his father. ''I suppose Richardson was going to
let Theo have the boat someday,'' Dani remarked as casually as possible.

Powell pursed his lips. ''Sailing is one of Theo's passing
fancies, and Richardson was willing to indulge the boy. But
I am certain he could never have brought himself to surrender custody of that boat. It simply meant too much to him.''

Dani frowned in puzzlement. ''But wasn't he planning to
transfer ownership of the boat?''

''If he was, he certainly never said a word to me about the
matter,'' Powell insisted.

''Mr. Boynton, I'm almost certain I saw a note on your
desk calendar when I met with Theo last week. Wasn't
Richardson planning to meet with you and arrange for the
transfer of the boat's title?'' In making that admission, she
risked portraying herself as a snoop. Given her suspicions
about the yacht's destruction, however, she was determined
to find out what exactly Richardson had intended to do with
the vessel.

''No, not unless this wretched illness has affected my
memory,'' Powell began slowly and then caught himself. He
smiled apologetically. ''Now I see what you're talking
about—the *Bandeira Branca* transfer! I had almost forgotten it shared its name with the yacht!''

''There are *two Bandeira Brancas?*''

Powell nodded, raising his head slightly off the pillows.
''I suppose we have Richardson's sentiment to thank for the

confusion. When he underwrote the shipping firm in Brazil, he was given the privilege of christening the newly formed company. *Bandeira branca* means white flag in Portuguese. Since Portuguese is the official language of Brazil, it seemed an ideal name for the company, as well as a way of honoring the old vessel he loved—we all loved—so well." As he gazed across the room at the blank wall, he looked as if his thoughts were far from the characterless hospital room, transported back to the golden years of his youth. "If I had known at the time what he ultimately planned to do with his investment, I would have thought the name even more appropriate," he added with a wistful smile.

"Why is that?" Dani asked.

When Powell looked back at Dani, a kindly twinkle glimmered in his weary eyes. "Because the Bandeira Branca Shipping Company was destined to provide for the legacy of the *Bandeira Branca*'s captain. Richardson was going to deed his holding in the company to you, Miss Blake, every penny of it!"

Chapter Sixteen

"What's up, Dani?" A haze of sleepiness blanketed Georgia Fairchild's normally perky voice.

Under any other circumstances, Dani would never have dreamed of phoning her old friend before noon on a Saturday. When they had roomed together in college, Georgia had regarded early rising on weekends as an unforgivable barbarism, something akin to shoving little old ladies and eating raw meat; she had stubbornly clung to the belief through an MBA program and into her professional life as a stockbroker. This morning, however, Dani would have been willing to brave an obstacle far more threatening than a little drowsy grumpiness from Georgia.

"I've got to have some background on a company in Brazil," Dani told her.

Georgia made a token effort to stifle a yawn before answering. "Brazil, you say?"

"Yes. You can get financial information on foreign companies, can't you?" Dani persisted.

"Sure, but it could take a little time. Sometimes inquiries abroad don't get the snap-to attention we give 'em here in the good ol' U.S. of A."

In her desperation, Dani gripped the phone a little tighter. "Georgia, I've got to have this information right away. It's absolutely urgent."

"A hot stock tip, huh?" Georgia swallowed another yawn, but she was beginning to sound interested.

"You might say that. Can you do it?"

"I have to go into the office today anyway. I'll do my best and see what I can stir up," Georgia promised.

That was really the most anyone could offer, Dani told herself later that afternoon as she and Elaine scurried around the Moveable Feast kitchen, putting the finishing touches on six dozen miniature cheese quiches. There was an excellent chance, too, that the information Georgia received from Brazil would do nothing to enlighten the mystery-shrouded circumstances surrounding Richardson's death. Dani was playing a hunch again, she knew, one that might well prove futile. Still, could she afford to ignore the fact that Richardson was murdered one day before he had been planning to transfer a valuable asset to her? Money sometimes inspired heinous behavior, and any number of people could have stood to benefit from the Bandeira Branca investment remaining in the Whyte family. At this point, she refused to let herself speculate on who could have valued wealth greatly enough to kill for it.

If she only had Ken to talk things over with, Dani reflected, her nerves would feel less like a bundle of explosives ready to go off at the least provocation. Even a brief phone call would be better than nothing. With this thought in mind, Dani rang the Washington, D.C., number Ken had given her as soon as she got home that evening.

"This is the night answering service," a bored voice told her on the other end. "Regular office hours for Associated Security are 9:00 a.m. to 6:00 p.m. Monday through Friday, except in cases of emergency."

"This is an emergency." Given her frame of mind, Dani felt that statement was no exaggeration.

"Are you a client?"

"No, but . . ."

"I'm sorry, ma'am, but I'm not allowed to give out the emergency telephone number. That number is reserved exclusively for clients of Associated Security." The phone clerk recited her lines in a flat monotone calculated to discourage troublesome inquiries. When she concluded, Dani almost expected her to drone "next!"

"Look, I've got to get in touch with an Associated Security employee, Ken McCabe. Do you have a number where he can be reached?" Dani struggled to contain her impatience.

"I'm sorry, ma'am, but I'm not allowed to—"

"Give out the telephone numbers of company employees," Dani finished for her. "Surely you can take a message and give it to him when he phones in."

"Yes, ma'am, I can do that." The clerk sounded offended, but she dutifully read back Dani's name as well as her home phone number and the number of the Moveable Feast kitchen.

By noon the following day, Ken had still not called. Dani vacillated between blaming the snippy phone clerk for carelessness on the one hand and worrying about Ken on the other. Of the two possibilities, the latter offered by far the less-palatable possible scenarios. Could Ken have already been reassigned to another city? Was he now involved in a demanding assignment that had superseded the Charleston case in his mind? Had he picked up her message and put it on the back burner, intending to call her whenever time permitted?

The annoying guessing game resolved itself Monday morning—in a maddeningly frustrating way. Dani returned from setting up tables and service supplies in the Great Colonial Hall to find the red message light on her answering machine blinking.

"I'm sorry I missed you," Ken apologized on the recording. "I'll try to reach you later this evening. Hope you're doing okay." He hesitated before saying "Bye."

Apparently, Ken had become so absorbed in whatever he was doing in Washington that he had forgotten tonight was Halloween. Still, Dani had talked so much about catering the costume ball, she was a little surprised—and piqued—that it had slipped his mind so easily. And why on earth hadn't he left a number where she could reach him directly? He had to be sleeping somewhere; these days, even the most Spartan hotels had phones. Her inability to formulate a satisfactory answer for any of those questions continued to dog her throughout the day.

When Moveable Feast's phone rang while Dani and Ben were loading the van that afternoon, she tore back into the kitchen.

"Hello," Dani said, trying to catch her breath.

"Hi, Dani," Georgia greeted her. "I know it's getting late in the day and you probably have a job tonight, but I wanted to bring you up to date on this Bandeira Branca business. I learned that the company is licensed in Rio, but really haven't been able to get anything more concrete than that. You sounded pretty eager to get your hands on this info, though, so I decided to collect on a favor. One of the guys in my MBA class works with an American bank in Rio—I referred some clients to him when he was still stateside, so he owes me one—or two or three, for that matter. He's promised to do the footwork personally on finding out about the company. In fact, I may hear from him as soon as tonight."

"Oh, Georgia, that would be wonderful! Will you call me the minute you have something? I'll give you a number where you can reach me tonight."

"All right," Georgia agreed. "This must be one hell of a red-hot tip. Maybe *I* should consider buying some of this stock."

After Dani thanked her friend and said goodbye, she took a deep, calming breath. She would know soon enough just how much the Bandeira Branca Shipping Company was worth. Then the only question remaining would be who could have deemed that sum worth committing murder for.

For once, Dani was grateful for the inevitable pressure that came with catering a lavish fund-raising event. While she was running back and forth between the service area and the Great Colonial Hall, checking hors d'oeuvre trays and punch bowls, she had little opportunity to ponder the outcome of Georgia's investigation and its possibly sinister implications.

The costumes, too, were a welcome distraction. Most were so well designed they completely obscured the wearer's identity. Dani did not recognize Theo until the swashbuckling pirate, replete with eye patch, twirled mustache and seven-league boots, stopped by the service area to congratulate her on the efficient setup. He was as cordial as ever, even going out of his way to compliment Ben and Elaine, but Dani detected a new note of coolness shading his conversation with her. Of course, it had only been a matter of time until Theo learned of her meeting with Sapphira, but his aloof manner bothered her nonetheless. He was yet another person joining the camp massed against her. In fact, with Ken now in Washington, Dani felt as if everyone were either blithely ignorant of her painful situation or actively committed to making matters worse for her.

As she circled the ballroom, gathering up discarded tumblers and replenishing chafing dishes, Dani had the uncomfortable feeling that some of the eyes peering from behind masks were watching her. She was letting herself get paranoid, she knew, an excusable enough condition, however, considering the Whyte family's united front against her. Even during the best of times, she could have expected little more warmth from Rebecca, who made a point of flouncing her hoop skirt and bobbing away from Dani when they chanced to meet at the dessert buffet.

Dani was juggling an armload of cake plates when the lights slowly began to fade. The dance band's lively swing tune dissolved into a few dissonant chords as the room was plunged into darkness. An undercurrent of murmurs and nervous giggles flowed among the guests. Dani propped her burden against the edge of the table and watched the procession of candle bearers moving through the Colonial Hall's entrance. To judge from their costumes, these were the Ghostly Guests, come to add a spooky touch of history to the twentieth-century revelers' party. Rather than risk bumping into someone and breaking twenty-odd china plates, Dani decided to wait until the performance was over before returning to the service area. When the lights at last came up, she backed away from the dessert table and almost collided with Darth Vader.

"Excuse me," she apologized.

The tall, powerfully built man's breath rasped heavily through the slits of the helmet's mouth shield, but he said nothing. Something about the way the monolithic figure stood facing her, not moving or making any accommodation, annoyed Dani. Who would come to a costume ball dressed as Darth Vader nowadays, anyway? *Star Wars* was old hat. As she hurried back to the service area, however, Dani realized that her irritation was a defense against the unsettling feeling the black-clad giant had left with her.

He was still lurking on the periphery of the room when she returned to watch the awards ceremonies. Now that she had a chance to take a breather and observe the ballroom, several of the costumes struck her as unpleasantly sinister. There was a mauve-faced Frankenstein with a hardware store's worth of bolts protruding from his head and neck, a fanged Dracula in a high-necked cape, and a Rasputin with wild hair spiraling from his mask down the back of his black cassock. Rasputin knew she was watching him; she could tell by the way he stood, back almost turned to the podium, while Theo "Blackbeard" Boynton cited various guests and roused the crowd to applaud.

Determined to curb her overactive imagination, Dani refocused her attention on the more playful costumes. The baggy-suited clown with bright orange hair was definitely more to her liking. She smiled when the surreal, wide mouth curved first into a grin and then into a sad frown.

Dani jumped as Elaine lightly pinched her elbow in passing. "You have a phone call in the service area, Dani," she whispered over the two teetering columns of fresh drink cups she was balancing.

"Thanks."

Dani sprinted to the service area and grabbed the receiver propped next to an unused coffee urn. "Hello?"

"Dani, this is Georgia. I just got a fax from Stuart in Rio." She took a deep breath, suggesting that she was looking over the transmission.

"And?" Dani prompted.

"Well, dear, Bandeira Branca doesn't look all that great. In fact, it looks pretty wretched."

Dani could scarcely believe what her friend was saying. "What do you mean?"

"First of all, the company isn't publicly traded, so that precludes your buying any stock. Not that you'd want to, though. The firm appears practically worthless. I mean, what's a shipping company without ships?"

"No ships! But how can that be?" Dani demanded.

"I know you're disappointed, but based on my experience, I'd say Bandeira Branca exists only on paper. At some point, it probably functioned as a business, maybe experienced a serious downturn and has remained a legal entity for tax purposes. That's just a guess, of course, but it's definitely not something you'd want to put your money into," Georgia advised her.

Dani licked her lips, trying to put the wholly unexpected revelation into perspective. Why would Richardson have wanted to give her a worthless investment? It simply didn't make sense. "Does the company still have an office in Rio?" she asked, buying herself a few moments to think.

"Let me have another look at this fax," Georgia mumbled. "A mailing address is all I see. No correspondent bank listed. Only one officer."

"Does it give the officer's name?" Dani asked on impulse.

"Uh-huh. Somebody by the name of Derek Cannaday. *C-A-N-N-A-D-A-Y.* Sounds American or maybe British."

"Thanks, Georgia!" Dani said with a gasp.

"No problem." Georgia sounded a little startled by Dani's suddenly breathless tone. "I'm just sorry my research didn't yield anything worthwhile."

"I've got to go now, Georgia. I'll catch you later."

Dani slung the receiver down and dashed to the cupboard where she had secreted her handbag for the evening. Derek! He had worked with Richardson in Brazil, would have been the most likely candidate to handle an investment in that country for his supposed friend. No telling how much money Richardson had entrusted Derek with over the years, money that he had earmarked for his daughter's future, money that Derek had squandered. Because Richardson had thought they were friends, he would have been easy to deceive, would have been unlikely to question bogus financial statements or to demand audits.

Dani's mind was reeling as she dug her address book out of her bag and impatiently flipped the pages. She punched out the seven digits and then pressed her lips together, waiting for someone to answer.

A businesslike female voice responded to her call.

"I'd like to speak with Officer Joe Simpson, please." Dani's heart was pounding so thunderously, she imagined the policewoman could hear its reverberation on the other end.

"I'm sorry, but this is Officer Simpson's night off. Can someone else help you?"

Dani thought for a moment. The information she was about to offer was so sensitive, her conclusion so speculative, she had to be careful. The last thing she needed at this point was for Sam Butler to get wind of her suspicions. Prejudiced as he was against her, he was sure to discount her theory, might even spill the news and inadvertently give Cannaday a chance to escape. "No, thanks," Dani finally said. "I'll call him in the morning. Do you know what time he'll be in?"

"Officer Simpson usually arrives in his office around seven."

Dani thanked the policewoman and then hung up. She checked her watch. It was already past midnight. The party would soon begin to wind down. Another hour or so and they could start breaking down. By the time they cleaned up and returned the equipment to Moveable Feast's kitchen, it would be three o'clock or even later. Then she could go home, park herself by the phone and wait another four hours to call Simpson. In the meantime, she would try to stay busy and not let her nerves get the best of her.

"Traffic by the punch bowls is starting to peter out," Ben announced as he rounded the corner into the service area. "A good sign."

"Yeah," Dani agreed. "I think we can start doing some discreet K.P. duty."

"I'll police the potted plants and the window sills for discarded junk," Ben volunteered. "Elaine is keeping a close eye on the food trays so they don't start to look too anemic. Like you always say, we don't want 'em to think we're holding stuff back for ourselves." Ben cackled. "That should just about do it, so why don't you kick your shoes off and take it easy back here for the rest of the evening? You've certainly earned the right."

Ben's suggestion was tempting, but Dani never allowed herself to sit idly by while her helpers worked. Still, she was glad to hear that Ben and Elaine had the Colonial Hall well under control. Given her shaken nerves, she welcomed the chance to stay in the background as much as possible. "Have you checked the dungeon yet for litter?"

Ben snapped his fingers. "Nope, forgot all about it."

"That's okay. I'll give it a thorough patrol." *And stay out of Darth Vader's and Rasputin's sight at the same time,* she added to herself. Right now, the acid flooding her stomach didn't need any additional priming.

Dani armed herself with a large plastic bag before heading down the stairs to the Provost Dungeon. As she passed the rest rooms, she smiled at the jovial clown who was loitering in the hall. Although the Ghostly Guests had long since departed for their earthly homes, the entrance to the Provost Dungeon was still open. The subterranean chamber felt even clammier than she recalled from her prior visit with Theo, its dark cavities even less inviting. Even if she had not been eager to conclude the night's work, the dungeon offered plenty of incentive to make short order of her cleanup.

As Theo had predicted, Dani spotted several wadded napkins and a number of cocktail picks before she had even reached the redcoat mannequin. She was bent over, trying to scoop the remains of a crushed snack cracker into a plastic cup when a shuffling sound stopped her cold.

"Ben?" Dani waited in vain for an answer.

For a second, she could only listen to the throbbing of her own heart as it futilely cast itself against the rib cage that held it imprisoned. Her shaking knees threatened to lock on her as she eased out of her crouch and slowly turned. Dani could see the door, but what stood between her and it? She could scream, but would anyone hear her? She could try to sneak out of the dungeon, but would she be able to elude the prowler? These terrifying questions fastened her with an ice-cold grip. Fear spread through her limbs, paralyzing them with its insidious poison.

The one thing she couldn't do was remain crouched in the dungeon, a sitting duck for the stalker. The thought forced her into action. Dani hugged the brick column, pressing herself into its shadow. She edged around the column, her senses alert to the faintest stirring. Suddenly, a flutter of white from behind one of the columns caught her eye. The column was halfway between her and the exit. Dani weighed her options and then bolted for the door.

She cried out when the hands seized her from behind, but her scream was cut short by the cord wrapped around her neck. While her heels flailed for traction against the gritty floor, Dani grabbed at the noose cutting into her throat. Her head and heart and lungs all felt as if they were about to burst, deprived of the oxygen they craved. She clawed at the nylon cord, desperately trying to loosen its murderous hold. The ill-lighted room was beginning to lose shape now, its shadowy corners ebbing and receding before her. She felt her legs giving out beneath her as bright spots exploded behind her eyes. When she pitched forward, she reached back, instinctively trying to catch hold of anything that would anchor her in the conscious world. Her hands snatched at a fuzzy mass and the cord loosened slightly.

Her windpipe ached from the sudden gulp of air, but it was enough to give her a second chance. Dani managed to get one hand beneath the cord while her other hand clung to the wiry orange wig. She wrestled around to kick at her assailant. One well-placed blow earned a muffled groan and yet another reprieve from the noose. This time, Dani managed to yank the cord loose enough to wrest herself free.

The now-bareheaded clown scrambled to recapture her. He grabbed at her shoulders and pulled her back. Dani jerked one fist free and landed a fairly solid blow against the garish white jaw. The slap that caught her across the mouth sent her falling back onto the floor. As he hovered over her, she scuffled back on her heels, just out of his reach.

"It's no use, Derek! I know all about what you did, how you defrauded Richardson and then killed him when you learned he was going to give his share of Bandeira Branca to me and you'd be found out. I've already told the police." It was a bluff that she hoped was convincing enough to throw him off guard, even if only for a few minutes.

The tattered clown paused and then shook its head. "If the police knew, Dani, they would be swarming this place. But only listen. Hear how quiet it is. No, I'm afraid no one knows but you and I. And soon it will be only I."

Dani crawled backward, trying to regain her footing. "You may fancy yourself a brilliant criminal, Derek, but you're going to get caught. Just how did you manage to trick poor Adele Whyte into pasting that note together and sending it to Richardson? How did you poison her mind?"

A low chuckle escaped the smeared red mouth. "That was the easy part. I didn't have to do anything! In fact, until you let the proverbial cat out of the bag just now, I was still guessing who sent that ridiculous note. You see, I had been wrestling with what had to be done, and Richardson unwittingly gave me the perfect cover when he showed me the extortion note he had received. The police would naturally link the note with Richardson's death—the perfect red herring, I might add."

Dani could see he was taking a perverse pride in talking about his scheme. How long the sinister fascination would last, she had no idea, but talking at least distracted him from trying to strangle her. "You did send me a note, didn't you?"

Derek's painted eyebrows rose slightly. "I wanted to discourage you, but unfortunately for you, my efforts have failed. You've been terribly tenacious, Dani, far more so than that pitiful excuse for a security man to whom you've gotten so attached. While he and the police were blundering around after the obvious—and useless—clues, you were thinking in more subtle terms. I was quite amazed when you showed up on the yacht that evening. You and I were on the same trail, you know, looking for things pinpointing the identity of Richardson's child. Of course, I knew what you only suspected, that he kept mementoes on the yacht. That's why I had to get rid of it."

Dani rocked back on her heels, balancing herself against the sandy floor with her splayed fingers. "And you got rid of the letters by sending Bea to collect them from Richardson's office. I suppose those papers she took from the safe involved Bendeira Branca."

Derek clucked softly. "You're not as clever as you think you are, Dani. I let Sapphira dispatch Bea to Richardson's office. The Whytes are so absorbed in saving face, they've never suspected something else might be afoot. Nor will they ever. In a couple of days, all vestiges of the Bandeira Branca Shipping Company will literally be up in smoke."

Dani tested her still unsteady knees. "Someone is going to find you out, Derek. You won't get away with this."

"They only say that in movies, Dani, and not very good ones at that."

Just as Derek stepped forward, Dani sprang out of her crouch. Her apron ripped as he grabbed her. She managed to dig an elbow into his midriff, but he was still quick enough to wield the cord. The rope burned her fingers as she struggled to pull it out of his hands. She lurched backward when Derek unexpectedly released his hold on the cord. His hands were on her neck now, his bony thumbs pressing the breath out of her. She squeezed his wiry wrists, trying to break their grip. Dani's eyes widened with terror, staring up into the face of a madman.

Suddenly, Derek's painted face gaped in surprise. His hands froze on her neck as Darth Vader and Rasputin charged through the door without warning. Derek stumbled, almost falling over the dummy redcoat. When he regained his balance, he studied his two adversaries and then made a break, trying to charge past the smaller of the two men. Rasputin caught him, sending Derek reeling back against the brick wall. While Darth Vader anchored handcuffs on Derek's wrists, Rasputin tugged impatiently at his mask. Still massaging her bruised throat, Dani blinked in disbelief as Ken's face emerged from behind the grotesque false face.

"What are you doing here?" she gasped.

"Looking out after you." The sleeve of the threadbare cassock ripped as he threw his arms around her, but Ken didn't seem to mind.

"I was about to lose my mind when I couldn't get in touch with you. And then when my stockbroker friend called tonight and told me about the worthless company that Richardson thought he had been investing in, I almost panicked. I couldn't reach you or Simpson." Now that she was out of danger, Dani was perilously near crying.

Darth Vader lifted his helmet as he guided Derek toward the door. "Thought I would suffocate in that thing," Joe Simpson complained, mopping his brow with his free hand.

"You?" Dani gaped at the police officer who now held her nemesis firmly in tow. She pulled back from Ken, frowning up at him. "How did you two find out about Derek's connection with Bandeira Branca?"

"We didn't," Ken explained. "After that row with Sapphira and Adele, I started asking myself who else could have known you were Richardson's daughter? Theo and Rebecca obviously did, but I had seen them on the piazza at the time of the murder. Then I remembered an inconsistency in Derek's conversation. He had told me that he knew nothing about Richardson's having a child, but you said that Sapphira claimed he knew all along. Derek was conveniently supposed to be helping cover the exterior of the house the night of the murder. He could even have made that mysterious phone call from his car phone."

"But why didn't you tell me you suspected him?" Dani demanded.

"It didn't gel in my mind until I was in Washington. By then, I figured I needed to get the hell back here before something bad happened to you. With my being out of town, I knew there was a good chance Derek would decide to act."

"You were right." Dani rubbed her neck again.

Ken smoothed her hair back from her brow, gently caressing the tumbled waves. "Do you forgive me for cutting out on you?"

Dani looked into the dark blue eyes that had suddenly grown earnest. "Yes, but only if you promise never to do it again."

Epilogue

As Dani had expected, a horde of photographers was lying in wait outside the courtroom. A murder trial was always big news, especially in a city where the ugly event was a rarity. Fortunately, one of Derek's attorneys had attracted the brunt of the press's attention today. While the lawyer offered the reporters a string of noncommittal remarks, Dani seized the chance to blend into the crowd exiting the courtroom. After the ordeal of taking the stand that morning, she was relieved to slip unnoticed past the photographers and reporters. She was halfway down the courthouse steps when she heard someone call to her. Dani wheeled to see Officer Joe Simpson climbing out of a patrol car parked at the curb.

"Miss Blake." The police officer tipped his cap to her.

"Good afternoon, Officer Simpson."

The policeman's dark eyes traveled to the door that had just opened on the flock of media people surrounding the attorney. "I'd like to talk with you, if you have a moment."

"Of course." Dani felt a great debt of gratitude to the policeman who had played such a critical role in apprehending Cannaday—and possibly saving her life.

Simpson nodded toward the street. "It might be a good idea to get away from this circus."

They walked along the car-lined street, stopping when they were a good half block from the boisterous crowd. "There's something I've been meaning to give you," the tall policeman began. He frowned as he dug in his pocket. Then he handed Dani a small plastic bag. "Just thought you might like to have that. We don't have any use for it anymore."

Dani held up the bag and recognized the tiny yacht pin that Richardson had given her. "Thank you, Officer Simpson," she whispered hoarsely.

"Thank *you,* Miss Blake." He stepped back, looking shy for all his proven physical prowess. "You take care."

Dani nodded, unable for the moment to budge any words from her tightening throat. She opened the bag, carefully removed the pin, and then cradled it in her palm. Just holding it made her feel oddly close to Richardson. *Close to my father.* The thought made her bite her lip, holding back the flood of bittersweet emotion. In the end, Richardson had done his best not to leave her alone in the world. Perhaps if you cared enough, you could overcome any obstacle. At that thought, a handsome, strong-boned face loomed in her mind. She couldn't afford to think about Ken right now, had to keep telling herself simply to take one day at a time.

She looked up in time to see Simpson climbing into his patrol car. The policeman threw up a hand, and Dani returned his wave. Her hand froze in the air and then fell to her side as she watched another man climb out of the passenger side of the cruiser. The police car pulled away, leaving Ken standing on the sidewalk.

Dani was so startled, she could only wait, immobile, as he walked to her. "I thought you were still in Washington," she managed to get out when he stopped short of her.

"That's the second time you've mistakenly thought that, if I remember correctly." A smile threatened to break the serious cast of Ken's face. "I knew you were going to testify today, so I hustled back on the first plane. I said I'd be down this weekend, but I didn't think you'd mind my showing up a few days early."

Dani was making a valiant attempt to recover her equilibrium. "Well, I certainly don't."

Ken glanced down the street at the throng still massed outside the courthouse. "I suppose some people are not particularly happy with the disclosures being made at this trial. Though it's all for the best, I'm sure it's nonetheless painful for the Whytes. How are they taking it?"

Dani paused and looked back at the courthouse. "The Whytes have been in Charleston since the late eighteenth century. The family has been through scandals before and emerged as solid as ever. This won't be any different."

"Even having such intimate family secrets made public?" Ken raised his eyebrows.

"No family likes being put on display. But you know, I can't help thinking that now, finally, Richardson can genuinely rest in peace. As bittersweet as the circumstances may be, he's finally able to share the secret he thought he never could—with me, with everyone. And for me to know him now that way and to know myself, I, too, am at peace. I'm glad it's over. But how about you? Did you get everything settled with Associated?"

Ken's slow nod had a suspicious air of finality to it. "Swift and clean."

Dani gave him a questioning sidelong glance. "What do you mean?"

"I quit, kiddo." Ken brushed his hands together. "Wham, bam, and it was over."

"Quit?" Dani wasn't sure she had heard correctly. Only the past week, Ken had seemed dead set on persuading his employer to find him an assignment near Charleston.

Ken looked adamant as he shook his head. "Derek was right about one thing, Dani. I'm a sorry excuse for a security specialist. Of course, I don't want Joe Simpson to ever hear me say that. He's promised to recommend me if I decide to open my own firm in this neck of the woods."

Dani made an effort to subdue her grin. "I didn't think you were all that bad."

"That's because I work well in a team," Ken countered. "We were a pretty damned good team, weren't we?"

"Uh-huh." Dani looked down at the cracked sidewalk. "Pretty damned good."

Ken cleared his throat, folding his hands behind his back as he glanced across the street. "It's too good to break up, Dani. That's what I was telling Joe on the way over here from the airport."

"Hold on now." Dani lifted both hands to caution him. "I know you're all set to launch a new career, but I'm not interested in any more detective work. One big case will hold me for a lifetime."

Ken's mouth twisted to one side. "That doesn't mean we can't be partners." He paused, waiting for her to take the cue and make it easy on him. When she didn't, he drew a deep breath. "I'm talking about marriage, Dani. You don't really think I came back to Charleston simply to make a career change, do you? I'm here because you are, darling. I want us to build a life together, the life I've always wanted and never thought I could have until I met you."

"You and me?" Dani knew her dimples were giving her away, but she did her best to look incredulous in spite of them.

Ken glanced down the street and then back at her. "I can't think of any other likely candidates. For either of us. Can you?"

Dani lifted her arms to encircle his neck. "No, I can't, partner. Not if I were to think for the rest of my life."

She felt his hands close around her waist, pulling her within range of his lips. Dani closed her eyes, meeting his mouth with a warm, lingering kiss of her own.

"Of course, I might want your advice if I ever get a sticky case." Ken's lips pecked her chin lightly.

Dani bestowed a quick kiss on the tip of his nose. "I'm sure we can work something out. Since I'll be turning the South Battery house into a bed-and-breakfast, I'll need some help. We could trade—my investigative consulting in return for your lending a hand at the inn."

"Sounds reasonable enough." Ken cuddled her against his chest, contentedly nuzzling her hair. "But on only one condition."

Dani's cheek brushed his tweed jacket as she looked up at him. "What's that?" She watched as the man she loved with all her heart broke into a big smile.

"Just promise me that you won't ever, *ever* ask me to tend bar."

H A R L E Q U I N

Season's Greetings

Christmas cards from relatives and friends
wishing you love and happiness. Twinkling lights
in the nighttime sky. Christmas—the time for
magic, dreams...and possibly destiny?

Harlequin American Romance brings you
SEASON'S GREETINGS. When a magical, red-
cheeked, white-haired postman delivers long-lost
letters, the lives of four unsuspecting couples will
change forever.

Don't miss the chance to experience the magic of
Christmas with these special books, coming to
you from American Romance in December.

#417 UNDER THE MISTLETOE
by Rebecca Flanders
#418 CHRISTMAS IN TOYLAND
by Julie Kistler
#419 AN ANGEL IN TIME
by Stella Cameron
#420 FOR AULD LANG SYNE
by Pamela Browning

Christmas—the season when wishes *do* come true....

HISTORICAL

CHRISTMAS

STORIES · 1991

Bring back heartwarming memories of Christmas past
with HISTORICAL CHRISTMAS STORIES 1991,
a collection of romantic stories
by three popular authors.
The perfect Christmas gift!

Don't miss these heartwarming stories,
available in November
wherever Harlequin books are sold:

CHRISTMAS YET TO COME
by Lynda Trent
A SEASON OF JOY
by Caryn Cameron
FORTUNE'S GIFT
by DeLoras Scott

**Best Wishes and Season's Greetings
from Harlequin!**

XM-91R

HARLEQUIN

Romance

A Christmas tradition...

Imagine spending Christmas in New
Orleans with a blind stranger and his aged
guide dog—when you're supposed to be
there on your honeymoon!
#3163 Every Kind of Heaven
by Bethany Campbell

Imagine spending Christmas with a man
you once "married"—in a mock ceremony
at the age of eight!
#3166 The Forgetful Bride
by Debbie Macomber

*Available in December 1991, wherever
Harlequin books are sold.*

RXM

HARLEQUIN

Romance®

**This December, travel to
Northport, Massachusetts,
with Harlequin Romance
FIRST CLASS title #3164,
A TOUCH OF FORGIVENESS
by Emma Goldrick**

Folks in Northport called Kitty the meanest woman in town,
but she couldn't forget how they had duped her brother and
exploited her family's land. It was hard to be mean, though,
when Joel Carmody was around—his calm, good humor
made Kitty feel like a new woman. Nevertheless, a Carmody
was a Carmody, and the name meant money and power to
the townspeople.... Could Kitty really trust Joel, or was he
like all the rest?